Chapter One

She left without waking him.

Reaching the office an hour later, Melanie pushed through the metal turnstiles and darted into an empty lift. On the fourth floor, she swiped her card at the double doors and stepped inside the trading floor.

Would she ever get used to this place, to this mass of men? The longest hundred feet in the world. But this was her first week at work and it was vital she didn't show her nerves. Melanie lowered her head to avoid all eye contact.

"Hey, baby." Probably the same man as yesterday, but it was better not to look. What a creep. Why couldn't he leave her alone?

From the same area, another one of the traders called out. "You're late today, sweetheart. What happened?"

Melanie blushed, but straightened her back and pretended not to hear.

"We like naughty girls," said another.

Melanie kept walking. Was it that obvious that she hadn't been home the night before? Perhaps the crumpled suit betrayed her. She cursed herself for being so irresponsible.

"She's playing hard to get." The first man again. "Don't worry, sweetheart. We don't bite."

"Speak for yourself." A different man. "She's just my type."

Melanie threw him a cutting glare. Such a low-life. What were these men doing in a place like this?

Twenty feet further and another whistle. Impossible not to notice the laughter when the first man shouted, "We'll be waiting for you later, baby."

She quickened her pace, desperate to get to the other side. Thank goodness she wouldn't have to work on that floor. It was a relief she had chosen a job in research instead of sales.

"Sorry I'm late." Melanie slid into her seat.

The tutor at the end of the table scowled. "This training programme is not an optional part of the job. In case you're wondering, I've already reported you to HR. Not a great start, young lady."

"I'm really sorry." Melanie gulped. "It won't happen again." If only she could think straight. How could she have messed up her career already, especially when she'd worked so hard to get the job? Her bloody brother. The night out had been his stupid idea. Why the hell had he left her alone with Max, anyway?

From her bag, the mobile vibrated loudly. Probably a text from Max. She'd have to respond later. Gorgeous though he was, it was the last thing she felt like dealing with.

Melanie glanced across the table at Jenny, who winked back. Immaculate, perfect Jenny. A stark contrast to her own clammy state.

That next hour passed in a blur of pounding nausea. When the break arrived, Melanie succumbed to the anaemic offerings from the coffee machine. Sipping reluctantly, she closed her eyes, praying for the pain to pass. It had been such a fun evening, but sangria had been an awful mistake.

"Good night?" Jenny sidled up to her.

"What do you mean?" Melanie took a step back. Not the time to start discussing her sex life.

Jenny grinned. "You're wearing the same clothes as yesterday, so I assume you had fun."

"Jesus," said Melanie. "I'm in deep shit, and you're making a joke of it."

"Relax." Jenny put a hand on her shoulder. "I told HR your brother was in hospital and it was an emergency. They totally swallowed it."

Melanie laughed for the first time that morning. She looked at her new friend with relief. "You're amazing. Thanks...but what about the tutor?"

Jenny raised her eyebrows. "That dumpy woman just now? She's irrelevant. A nobody in the back office. Trust me."

"Really? Are you sure?" How did Jenny know all this? It was only their fourth day in the office.

"But much more importantly, how was last night?" asked Jenny.

Melanie took another sip of coffee and frowned. "If you must know, I can't remember much. Just that my head hurts like hell."

"Hilarious," said Jenny. "What's his name?"

Melanie looked away, with fragments of the night jumping into her head. Flashes of the bar, the taxi, entering Max's apartment. But not much else. She'd never had a one-night stand before. At least, not one where she'd blacked out. "I never said there was a man involved."

"Isn't there always?" said Jenny.

"No, actually. My twin brother took me out to celebrate our birthday. Got carried away."

"Yeah, I forgot," said Jenny. "Happy birthday. Sounds like it was amusing anyway."

"Far too amusing." Melanie rubbed her head. "Won't be doing that again."

"Don't say that. I think it's fabulous." Jenny paused. "Would you like to hear about my night?"

"No. I mean, of course, but not right now." All she wanted was a decent coffee and an aspirin.

"Of course you do." Jenny waved at the man in the corridor. "Josh was amazing."

"What?" said Melanie. "Don't tell me you slept with him."

"Sure, why not? He was good. Really good."

"Are you mad?" Melanie stared at her friend in bewilderment.

"Why are you being so sanctimonious all of a sudden? You're the one that still stinks of alcohol." Jenny laughed.

Melanie took an instinctive step backwards. "That's not the point. Why are you mixing business with pleasure? It's the first basic rule of the workplace."

"Don't be ridiculous," said Jenny. "He's from the New York office. We won't see him once the training is over. Just a bit of fun."

*

When they returned to the room for the next class, Jenny grabbed her arm. "Wow. Look at that woman. I wonder who she is."

Melanie recognised her immediately. The one who had interviewed her six months previously. She'd thought about her often. Mostly in a cold sweat. "Victoria Something. She's a sales woman."

"How do you know that?" said Jenny, with her eyes still fixed on Victoria.

"I met her at my final interview. Complete cow." Understatement of the century; the bitchiest woman she'd ever met. It made her shudder to set eyes on her again.

"She can't have been that bad, if you got the job."

"Luckily she wasn't the only one there," said Melanie. "Her colleague must have liked me. I'd have been finished otherwise. Do you know what she said to me?"

But Jenny wasn't listening. "Check out her clothes. That's got to be Chanel. And love the shoes. Louboutin for sure. Maybe you can introduce me later."

"Yeah, maybe," said Melanie. Not a chance. She wanted nothing to do with the woman. They sat down in silence and waited for the class to begin.

A few minutes later, Victoria put down her BlackBerry and faced the ten graduates at the table.

"For those who don't know me, I'm Victoria Parker. Director in Equity Sales."

Jenny leaned forward to listen. She would be working in the sales team and, apart from the wardrobe tips, this would be an important presentation for her.

"Just like you, I joined as a trainee," said Victoria. "Seven years ago."

So she was around thirty. Already a director. How the hell had she managed that?

Victoria drew a circle on the whiteboard. "Stockbroking is very straightforward. Here in the middle is the fund manager. Our client. That is all that matters. Some of you will write research, some of you will sell those ideas to the fund manager and some of you will trade the stocks. But never forget that we are always working for the clients. They provide the commission that pays our bonuses."

Jenny called out, "Any tips on starting out?"

Melanie glanced over at her friend, willing her not to ask any more questions.

Victoria stared at Jenny. "Put your head down and work like hell."

"Can you be more specific?" asked Jenny.

"For starters, you'll have to be at your desk by six and when you make your morning call to the fund manager, you need to sound intelligent. They don't want to speak to a dumb blonde."

"I'm not a dumb blonde," said Jenny, clearly smarting from the unexpected abuse.

"I'm not suggesting that you are." But the woman's smirk indicated otherwise. She hadn't taken her eyes off Jenny. "Be aware that this job is demanding and the graduate drop-out rate is high. Especially among women."

Josh raised his hand. "Can you tell us about these clients, the investment managers? What do they look for, and how do you identify good stock ideas for them?"

Victoria turned to him with a perceptibly warmer tone. "Start slowly. All the fund managers are different, and they all need a distinct service. Figure out what type of investments they are looking for and, most importantly, which of our own research analysts are any good. Never promote crappy research. God knows we have plenty of that too." She paused and looked around. "A huge part of the job is to differentiate between our good analysts and those who are totally useless. Who's going into research?"

Melanie raised her hand reluctantly.

"Yes, I remember you." Victoria glared at her.

Melanie nodded her head in acknowledgement, but said nothing. Why was the woman still being so aggressive? Was she a complete psychopath?

"Let me give you a tip," said Victoria. "You know absolutely nothing right now. And you're not useful to anyone. Don't expect to be taken seriously by the sales team until you've shown you understand the companies you write about. We won't want your opinion for a very long time."

"Thanks," said Melanie. What a bitch. Nothing had changed since the interview.

Chapter Two

For the duration of the training programme, Melanie decided to stop partying altogether. They were all required to take a financial regulations exam at the end of the course and, given the firm's zero tolerance for failure, Melanie was determined to pass.

On the final Sunday before the exam, her twin brother David arrived unexpectedly, clutching a bag of croissants.

She was still in her dressing gown. David wrinkled his nose and gestured at the overflowing ashtrays. "What's the matter with you?"

"Nothing." Melanie pointed at her desk. "I've been studying." Her brother was such a drag sometimes. Couldn't he see that she didn't want company?

David dropped the paper bag on the coffee table. "You've turned into a tramp. Have some self-respect."

"I didn't ask you to come over, in case you forgot."

"I know," said David. "But you haven't called in weeks. And look at this place…"

"So?" Yes, she had ignored everyone for months. But didn't he understand the pressure she was under?

"You can't hide like this. We're worried about you."

"I'm fine. I need to get through the exams and I'll be back to normal. Only a few more days of studying." Why did he always start preaching? Just when she least felt like listening.

"Believe me, these exams are only the beginning. I still don't understand why you were so hell-bent on going into banking."

"What do you mean?" she said. "You know I've wanted this for years. I've worked like hell to get here." Going into banking had always been her dream and she was the only pupil from their school to have entered the financial markets.

"There's more to life than earning tons of money, you know."

"It's not about the money." Obviously it was about the money, but she wasn't willing to admit it. Especially to him. David was so amazingly unmaterialistic. He'd accepted a job offer in a Mayfair art gallery, which was hardly going to pay much. But money was the only way to avoid turning out like their mother.

"Then, why are you doing it?" he asked.

"For one thing, it's going to be really interesting." At least, that was the hope. The last three months had been mind-numbingly dull.

He inhaled. "Don't kid yourself. Didn't you read about the banker who died of a heart attack at his desk last week? Worked round the clock. He hadn't had a holiday for years."

"He was almost sixty, and probably going to drop dead regardless. Besides, I'm not afraid of hard work."

"If you ask me, it's not a job for a girl."

Melanie stared at her brother. "Don't be so bloody sexist. You, of all people."

"If you think I'm sexist, just wait and see how this pans out. They will treat you like dirt."

"You simply don't get it, do you?" she said.

"That's where you are so wrong. I only want the best for you."

"And what do you suppose that is?"

"To start with, I don't want you to turn out like that woman you keep talking about."

"Which woman?"

"The one who interviewed you. Veronica."

"Victoria."

"Whatever. The Bitch, as you call her."

"Hardly likely." Horrible thought.

He grabbed her by the wrist. "I'm telling you, it's not going to end well. Even if you do succeed, you might not like the person you become."

Melanie pulled away. "Is the lecture over?"

"Sorry, Mel." He put his arm round her shoulders. "We want you to have a life. That's all."

She brushed him off again. "We? You and your new girlfriend? My life is fine. Thank you anyway for all your concern."

"You've got to lighten up." He hadn't moved. "Listen. I have an idea. Remember my colleague Max?"

"What about him?" Melanie turned to face the kitchen, not wanting him to witness her blushing. She'd exchanged a few messages with Max and had considered calling him, but the whole experience had been incredibly awkward. Funny how it had affected her so much. She was hardly a virgin, but to sleep with a man and not remember? That made her a slut. Didn't it?

"He keeps asking about you," said David.

"Does he?" Melanie swivelled round. Despite having made a conscious effort to forget the whole episode, blurry images of that evening had kept resurfacing and it was pleasing that Max was also still thinking of her.

"Yes. All the time, in fact." David chuckled. "What am I supposed to say? My sister's turned into the most boring person in the world?"

Melanie shook her head. "Tell him whatever you like. You know why I'm reluctant. I'm so ashamed of what happened that night."

"Come on, Mel, he's a great guy. Give him a chance."

She sighed. "I'm sure you're right. The problem is that I haven't got time to think about Max, or any man, right now. He'd only get in the way and I can't risk my job at the moment."

Chapter Three

The desk job started in the first week of the new year.

Entering the building, Melanie smiled and took a minute to soak in the white marbled lobby and large green lettering on the wall. Silverton Brothers: "Integrity, Equality, Transparency".

She'd spent over three months on the training course, but today was different. Her first day with the team.

The research department was on the fifth floor. Her new home. Melanie walked out of the lift, down a short brown corridor and into a vast room, crudely divided into endless rows of desks. Seven o'clock and barely an empty seat. A sea of people, heads buried in computer screens. A delight compared to the traders only one floor below.

It must have been obvious that she was lost but, as she wandered, nobody looked up. Finally, the teenage post boy directed her to the correct area. The Industrials research team was at the far end of the room, hidden behind a wall of reports.

She'd met her new boss at her first interview and she approached him nervously.

Melanie coughed to attract his attention. Nothing.

Another slightly louder cough.

Tony Adams peered over a mountain of papers. "Yes?" He seemed irritated. Or maybe just busy.

"Hi. I'm Melanie." She smiled, hoping he'd be pleased to see her.

His small eyes narrowed. "Melanie?"

"The new graduate for your team." She bit her lip with concern. Why was he looking blank?

"Of course, of course." Tony rose to greet her. "How nice to see you again. We are so pleased to have you here."

At least he had the manners to look embarrassed. But that didn't change the fact that nobody seemed to be expecting her. Was she that unimportant?

"Thanks," she said. "I've been really looking forward to starting."

Tony scratched his grey hair. "Sorry, there is no desk yet. I don't think the IT department is ready for you. Always seems to happen. Um…excuse me a minute." He returned to his chair to make a call.

"Sure. No problem." Not the welcome she'd hoped for. But this wasn't the moment to show her frustration.

A large man leaned across the table, extending his fleshy pink hand. "Hi. I'm George. You can use this computer over here for now."

"Thanks." She shook his hand, grateful for his kindness.

"Have you passed your exams yet?" said George.

"Yes." Melanie grinned, pleased by the question. "The results came before Christmas." In fact, she'd sailed through, but everyone had passed, so possibly she had taken it too seriously. Just like all the exams she'd ever done. No wonder David always accused her of being a swot. Still, it was finished and now she was fully qualified to work in the financial markets.

"Terrific news," said George. "You're over the first hurdle. We'll take you out this week to celebrate."

"I'd love that," she said. This was much more encouraging. What a thoughtful man.

"Great idea," agreed Tony, clearly relieved that someone had rescued the situation. "Now, come meet the others."

"Wonderful," said Melanie, as Tony showed her around the desk.

"You've already met George but, actually, the most important member is Pamela. Team assistant. She's been here longer than anyone can remember."

Pamela raised her heavily powdered face and beamed. "Welcome."

Melanie smiled back, knowing instinctively that the woman would become a friend.

"And finally, this is Andrew. You'll be working with him at first." Tony paused. "Just a warning. He doesn't talk much."

Andrew grunted and chucked her a document. "Glad you're here. Don't know why they kept you on that stupid training for so long. Fill in the highlighted part."

George raised his eyebrows and chuckled. "Good luck."

And with that, the job began. For the next two days, that's all she worked on. With no guidance from Andrew. And when she handed her documents to him, he shoved them on to the pile next to his computer. To be completely ignored. It took him another day and a half to comment.

Late on Thursday, he marched over to her desk and threw the papers in front of her. "Was this the best you could manage?"

"Did I do something wrong?" Her work was scarred with red ink. Painful to look at it. Embarrassing that he'd hated it so much, particularly given the effort it had taken.

"It's complete shit."

She recoiled. "I wasn't sure what you were expecting."

"That you'd have learnt something on that course you took. Don't know why we waste the money."

"What do you mean?" She looked at him, confused by his venom.

"I mean, you're not a management consultant. No waffling. Get straight to the point."

Melanie glared at him as he collected his pinstripe jacket and left the room.

Pamela peered over her horn-rimmed glasses. "Don't worry about it. He's a rude bastard."

"Clearly." Melanie averted her head.

"No, I mean it," said Pamela. "My friend thinks he's autistic, but I reckon he's a plain son-of-a-bitch. He reduced last year's graduate to tears."

He'd managed the same with her too, but she didn't want Pamela to see. "What happened last year?" Melanie blinked furiously and pretended to focus on her computer. Nobody had mentioned a previous graduate.

"Nice boy. But let's say he wasn't cut out for this sort of job."

"Who is?" said Melanie.

"Don't stress, love," said Pamela. "You'll be fine. I've seen enough to know which ones make it. Just takes getting used to."

"Thanks." Melanie sat forward in her chair. Maybe David was right about this damned job. Apart from George and Pamela, it had hardly been a welcoming start. She hunched her shoulders and began to rewrite the document. While she was finishing the third draft, her mobile buzzed from behind the folders on the desk. She flinched, momentarily confused. An unknown number.

"Hello?"

"Hi, Mel. It's Max. Remember me?"

Her heart jumped. Of course she remembered. But this was the first time he'd called for months and she had assumed he'd given up. Not that she could have blamed him. "How are you, Max?" Melanie walked over to the corner office and closed the door.

"I'm great," he said. "Pleased to finally get hold of you."

Melanie rubbed her head. "Yeah, it's been a long time. And I'm truly sorry I've been so hopeless."

He laughed. "Don't worry. David told me to hold off. I know you've been wrapped up."

"That was kind of him."

A long pause before Max continued. "I was hoping that now you've settled in, you might have time for a drink."

"I'd love to. It's just that our last drink got me into real trouble at work."

"It doesn't have to be like that," he said. "I thought it would be fun to catch up."

"Yes." Melanie inhaled. "Truth is…apart from the whole work thing, I'm rather uncomfortable about seeing you again. It was a strange night."

She heard him sigh down the phone. "I know. And I'm sorry for how it all happened. I'd love to have a fresh start."

"That's very thoughtful, but—"

"Come on, Mel. I'll settle for a coffee. And I'll even venture into the City, so you have no excuses."

She could hardly pretend she was too busy for coffee. And despite all these ridiculous barriers she kept erecting, it was tempting. "OK. But this is my first week at the desk, so it will have to be a quick one."

"Great," he said. "I'm around all of next week."

Melanie clicked open her diary, horrified by the number of meetings that had been slammed in. "Gosh, next week is a nightmare."

"It's only a coffee," he said. "I promise you'll be fine."

"Of course you're right." She scrolled through the calendar. The end of the week was much calmer. "What about next Friday morning, around eleven o'clock. Does that work?"

"Super," he said. "Really look forward to it."

"Me too, Max." She hung up and took a deep breath. What had taken her so long to see him again? He was damned hot. Most girls would be salivating at the chance, as David never ceased to remind her.

The next day, after work, her team took her to the pub on the corner. She passed it every morning but, in her haste to get to the office, had never paid it much attention. Her heart sank when they entered. A complete shit hole. Why hadn't they chosen one of those places she'd read about in the magazines? Still, a free drink was always worth having.

Andrew bought the first round but didn't stay long, muttering something about his wife. Once their colleague had disappeared through the narrow wooden doorway, George leaned over to her. "Since you're part of the team now, I'll tell you a secret."

"What's that?" Melanie looked up at him.

"He's not going home to his wife."

"So?" Andrew was a stuck-up toff. Hard to care where he was going.

George chuckled. "He's shagging one of the girls in the back office."

Melanie sat up straight. "Seriously? Andrew? I don't believe it."

"Yeah. You'd never guess it looking at him. Not exactly a Lothario, is he?"

"No." Andrew the Lover was not an image that sat comfortably. Disgusting thought.

"But I can't blame him," said George. "His wife's a complete hag. For some reason, he refuses to leave her. Probably can't face the alimony."

"Excuse me?"

"You know. Usual stuff. No prenup. Not that it makes much difference anyway. They've got two kids and he'd have to cough up a fortune." George laughed.

"What's so funny?" she said. "That's a horrible story. Poor wife."

"Oh, it's understandable enough," he said. "Bloke's worked like a dog for twenty years. He can't face giving the old trout half his money. Not to mention the house in Chelsea."

"How do you know all this?" said Melanie.

"I know just about everything there is to know." George smirked and finished his glass. "Stick around, I'll tell you the rest too."

After a couple of drinks, the others made their excuses and left, but George ordered another bottle of wine. "You'll share this with me?"

"Sure, love to." Melanie edged her stool closer to his. What other gossip did he have? It promised to be an interesting night.

"Fantastic," said George. "We'll turn you into an alcoholic like the rest of us in no time."

"Actually, I've cut back recently." Since that blackout with Max, she hadn't had many nights out.

"Good for you," said George. "Otherwise, you'll look like me soon enough."

She laughed, unsure how to respond. He did indeed look much older than his thirty-two years. Perhaps it was his previous job as an accountant that had aged him, or maybe it was his thinning hair. Those morning bacon sandwiches weren't doing him any favours either.

He topped up her wine. "I've been meaning to ask you about your friend."

"What friend?" she said. Of course she knew who he was talking about.

"The new sales girl. Jenny."

"What about her?"

He licked his lips. "She's hot."

"Guess so," said Melanie. It was annoying how all the men focused on Jenny.

"Does she have a boyfriend?" he asked.

Melanie sighed. "Everyone asks me the same question. I don't know."

"Don't be coy. I see you two together every day."

"Honestly, I don't know." Truth was that Jenny had tons of men after her. It wasn't clear which one was the official boyfriend. If any at all.

"You're useless," he said. "Still, let me give you some advice."

"What...?"

"How many good-looking girls work in the research department?"

Strange question. "I haven't thought about it. Alice in Oil and Gas?"

"Alice? Seriously? Have you seen the size of her backside?"

"I think she's pretty." Bloody hypocrite. What was it about men? He was no oil painting himself.

"Whatever," said George. "Apart from a few of the desk assistants, there are no pretty girls on our floor. Well, none until you arrived. All the hot ones go to sales, like your sexy friend Jen who everyone's talking about. But you're different. Very rare in fact – pretty and intelligent. It's such an advantage; you'd be stupid not to use it."

Melanie wrinkled her nose. "I'm not sure I understand where you're going with this."

"Shush. Listen to me, I'm serious." He banged his hand on the bar. "It's very obvious from where I sit. How many of our clients have recently hired young male juniors, just starting their careers?"

"How could I possibly know the answer to that?"

"I'll tell you." George waved his arms in a circle. "All of them."

"So?" Melanie drained her glass.

"Stop interrupting, woman." His face inched closer. She tried not to focus on the nasal hair. "Do you think those young men would prefer to speak to some boring spotty male counterpart, or to a beautiful young woman like yourself?"

"It's not about how I look," she said. "Not in this day and age."

"Don't be naïve. We're not officially supposed to say these things, but human nature never changes. You've got a major asset. Don't waste it." George reached for the bottle to refill her glass. She was too stunned to refuse.

"Darling, you need to get cracking with the juniors. They know nothing anyway, so it's hardly going to be difficult."

"How am I supposed to do that? They don't know me."

"I am sure you have a little initiative. You can't have got this job by being useless."

"It's not the same thing as being pimped out."

"Just listen, will you?" said George. "Call them up. Take them out for lunch, drinks, coffee. Whatever you like. Since it's client entertainment, the company pays. You'll see, they'll be flattered and they'll vote for you. Tony will be pleased, and you'll get a pay rise. It's simple."

He sat back, visibly satisfied with his lecture. But an instant later, he swivelled round. "I almost forgot the most important thing."

"What?" Melanie glanced at her watch. George was drunk and now he was becoming tiresome.

"Never, ever sleep with a client. It might be fun for a week, month, possibly a year, but eventually it will fuck your career. They will toss you aside and you'll lose all credibility. Just like those stupid sales girls."

She sat up. "Which sales girls?" Was Jenny in trouble already?

"Too many to count. That bitch Victoria is a classic."

"Victoria?" she said. "She's so successful. What are you talking about?"

"Victoria, successful?" George chortled and almost fell from his stool. "That woman is such a joke. Have you heard her come up with a single original idea of her own?"

Melanie shook her head and waited for George to continue his drunken rant. "She's slept with half the trading floor, not to mention one or two of the management team. Would have been sacked a long time ago, apart from the fact that she's currently having an affair with the head of Brendon Capital."

"Sorry. What's Brendon Capital?"

"Get with the programme. Jesus. Only one of the largest hedge funds in the City. Gives us millions of pounds worth of commission."

"My God."

"As long as she's got that man's attention, she thinks she's untouchable, that we can't afford to lose her. She may be sexy, but she's a total nightmare. Just wait. It always ends the same way. Always has, always will. Never seen it work out. He'll get bored and then she'll be finished. Not that anyone will care."

"That's true enough." Something deeply satisfying about The Bitch getting her comeuppance.

George didn't bother to conceal a wide yawn. "Time to go. What do you think?"

"Sure," she said, still thinking of Victoria.

They walked outside and he hailed a taxi. "Hop in," he said. "I'll get this one."

Melanie nestled into the back seat and watched the taxi wind its way through the slow London traffic, passing the bright lights of Knightsbridge and further into the darker, smaller roads of Fulham.

The car jolted to a halt outside George's flat and she smiled sleepily at her colleague, waiting for him to get out.

Instead, he pulled her close. "Come upstairs. I quite fancy another drink."

Melanie froze. What the hell was he doing? She stared blankly at him, before mumbling a feeble excuse. "Oh, um, George, I'm a little tired. Maybe another time."

He laughed. "You're great. Was just testing. You're going to get a lot more of those types of propositions. Admittedly they might be rather more attractive than me." He patted down his stomach. "Not that I would mind shagging you, of course."

She moved deeper into the taxi. "You shouldn't say things like that. You're my colleague."

"Don't act so shocked. I'm not that stupid. Take care, kiddo."

Melanie watched him twist the key unsuccessfully into his front door and asked the taxi driver to keep going. What was going on? She wanted to be taken seriously and sex was not going to be part of the equation.

Chapter Four

George never mentioned his proposition again, but he didn't drop the subject about the clients.

After the morning meeting on Monday, he walked over and placed a sheet of paper in front of her. "Do you know what this is?" he asked.

"Think so." Of course she knew. It was a list of all the bank's top clients.

"Look carefully," he said. "I spent the last ten minutes making it."

"And?" What was George concocting this time?

"And it's brilliant. All the new male fund managers. Tony, Andrew and I speak to the bosses. You take care of the rest. Start with Simon. He's a decent bloke."

"Who's Simon?"

"Right here." He pointed at the name at the top. "Happens to work at the biggest commission generator for our team. Started at the same time as you."

"What the fuck, George. What am I supposed to say?"

"Introduce yourself. But stop swearing so much. Not very lady-like."

"Sorry." It was true. Her language had deteriorated over the past few months.

"It's very simple. Do it today. He'll be friendly, I guarantee it." He tapped her on the shoulder and returned to his desk. She sat there, staring at the paper. Apart from all those HR departments, she had never cold-called anyone in her life. How humiliating. She waited, knowing that George was watching. Finally, when he left for a meeting, she picked up the phone. Hearing the ringtone, she prayed for it to go to voicemail.

"Hello, this is Simon."

Shit. "Hi, Simon. How are you?"

"Sorry, who is this?"

She straightened her back and continued. "Simon, hi, my name is Melanie Collins. My colleague George Wright suggested I call you."

"Oh, yeah, I met him last week. He was very complimentary about you and said you'd be calling. How can I help?"

That was easy. Melanie pushed her chair forward in excitement. "Well, since we're both new at the job, I figured it would be nice to meet up. I'm sure we'll be working together a lot in the future."

"Sounds great," said Simon. "What about later this week for a coffee?"

"Perfect," she said. "When are you free?"

"Let me check." There was a long pause. "Friday morning would be good. Maybe around ten. Does that suit?"

Melanie opened her calendar, remembering her prior engagement with Max. There would be just enough time to see him afterwards. "Fantastic. That works for me."

She hung up the phone triumphantly. Her very first client! And such an important one, too.

The rest of that week passed quickly, ensconced in meetings, writing up reports and reading about the sector. She wanted to be as prepared as possible for her new client.

On Friday morning, George frowned when she gathered the PowerPoint presentation for Simon.

"Don't bother with all that," he said. "Just go and have a coffee with the bloke."

"I have to take him something. He's a client, not my friend."

"You see, you're missing the point. Again. He will get boring brokers showing him presentations every day of the week. He might not realise it himself, but what he subconsciously desires is to befriend a hot chick."

"Shut up. I'm taking the presentation and that's the end of it."

George stood up and pointed a chubby finger at her. "Remember to wear a skirt next time. You'll thank me for it later."

She would never admit it, but George was right. Simon wasn't interested in the presentation, happy to have a break from the office. Although she'd had no idea what to expect, it was a pleasant surprise. A gentle, affable man. They laughed as they exchanged stories of their respective first interviews and jobs. Simon was keen to meet again and for her to call regularly with the team's best ideas. Nothing too tricky there.

Walking out the door, she felt a profound sense of relief. It didn't need to be about sex. She had won her first client, with no agenda.

Having lost track of time, Melanie glanced at her watch and froze with horror. She raced two blocks to another small coffee shop and elbowed through the glass door.

Max was reading a newspaper in the corner. He smiled as the door crashed open, startling an old lady by the window.

"Better late than never," he said.

"I'm so sorry," she said. "You must be furious."

"Frustrated, rather than furious. You're a hard woman to pin down."

Melanie took a deep breath and sank into the red sofa next to him. "Life is manic, I guess." But she beamed at him. What a good-looking man. Even better than she had remembered. Not that she remembered much from that evening.

"Can I get you something?" he asked.

Melanie shook her head. "I'm fine, thanks." She paused. "It's good to see you, Max."

He leaned sideways to look at her. "I know we're doing this the wrong way round, but I'd love to get to know you better. At whatever pace you're comfortable with."

Her eyes hadn't moved from his face. "Do you mean that? I know I've been useless these past few months."

Max put down his mug. "Don't worry about it. I haven't had much time myself. Just got back from Vienna, actually, looking at some private art collections."

"That sounds fun." Melanie blinked in confusion. She'd assumed he hadn't called due to her reticence, not because he'd been too busy himself.

He must have read her thoughts. "But that's not the reason I've been out of touch. David told me I needed to tread carefully."

She stiffened and stared at the floor. "What?" Bloody David interfering again.

"I just mean, he says your work is all-consuming right now." Max took a sip of water. "It's the only thing that gave me hope. It's not easy to be ignored."

"And I'm really sorry about that." She gave a wry smile. "David is right, of course. The trouble is that I've just started at the bank and I want to do well. The hours are demanding and there doesn't seem to be time for much else."

He reached out and took her hand. "I think you've got the wrong impression. I didn't come here to stress you out. Funnily enough, it suits me."

She gave him a quizzical look. "So why are you here?"

"Not sure. You're far more serious than I'm used to." He grinned. "But I can't deny how utterly gorgeous you are."

She blushed, happy with the compliment, but unsure how to respond.

Max continued. "No, seriously, let's take it easy. I've recently ended a long-term relationship and if your job forces us to go slowly, that's fine by me."

She leaned into him and he placed his arms round her. Other customers came and went, but they stayed there talking. After half an hour, he lifted her head with his left hand and kissed her on the mouth.

He grabbed his coat. "Darling, I'm so sorry but I've got a lunch meeting and I better make a move."

"Me too. My boss will be wondering where I am." Melanie twisted her arm to look at her watch. "But I'm pleased we did this."

"I absolutely loved it," he said. "Perhaps we can meet again for a drink?"

She nodded. "Sure, give me a call."

Chapter Five

Perhaps he just wanted company, but George took her everywhere with him. Corporate events, PR meetings, financial results, even meetings with top executives. It was the beginning of her list of contacts throughout the City. The goal was to build on it every week.

After the third month, she even received a compliment from Andrew. He had made no changes to her research and had incorporated it into his report on the latest sector trends. She'd been published! Career launched. Her name was on a research report. She sent a copy to David. Destined for the bin, no doubt, but the point had been made. She took a copy home and placed it on her bookshelf. The beginning of a new library.

The morning routine became mechanical: rising with the alarm clock, into the shower and robotically to the Tube station. The coffee bar at the other end was the first mission of major importance; the hot drink sufficiently cooled for a quick sip in the lift to the fifth floor. Since starting at the desk, she had begun to arrive earlier, enjoying that first half hour in the office when the darkness of the night was still tangible and she had the place to herself. Being the junior on the team, she also had all the spreadsheets to update before the stock market opened. The days passed quickly, filled with new knowledge and challenges. It was a thrilling environment and despite the early starts, she was almost always the last to leave.

Her newfound energy was a stark contrast to the unemployed slothfulness of the year before. How far she had travelled. From sleeping half the day, and spending the rest in a smoke-drenched dressing gown, she now barely saw her apartment and slept an average of four hours per night. It was a hard pace of life, but she found herself enjoying it immensely. Her body somehow survived until that heavenly moment every Friday night, when she plunged into bed, ready for twelve hours of blissful oblivion.

Apart from grabbing a sandwich for lunch, her only other break in the day was her morning cappuccino with Jenny. They always met inside the dark Italian coffee shop down the lane, where surprisingly they never saw anyone else from the office. It was their haven and Melanie loved the fifteen minutes of gossip and fun. Jenny always had so many men chasing her and the stories were hilarious.

Studying her friend, Melanie knew that she should make more of an effort on her own appearance. It must be wonderful to have all that male attention. Max often crossed her mind. They'd met for drinks one evening but, despite enormous temptation, an early start the next morning had prevented her from going to his flat. Since then, she'd called him a few times but their schedules rarely overlapped and, disappointingly, he hadn't pursued it further. Most likely he'd come to the conclusion that she was indeed far too earnest.

Over the months, her former friends drifted out of her life and Jenny became her main point of contact on weekends. Saturday evenings invariably started in a bar in the West End. It was on one of those nights that she found Jenny quietly crying in the corner. A strange sight; she had never seen this side of her normally boisterous companion.

"Jenny?" She bent down to look at her friend.

There was no response. Jenny stayed in that position, holding her head in both hands. Putting an arm round her, Melanie waited for a few minutes. They were in a dark corner and it was a good place to sit for a while. This early in the evening, other customers were only just starting to arrive and nobody had noticed them yet.

Finally, Jenny raised her head and began to talk. "I've been an idiot. Completely messed up this time."

"What's happened?" asked Melanie.

Jenny looked up with uncharacteristically swollen eyes. "Have you met Zack? He's one of the head traders on my floor."

"Of course I've met him. Sits sort of in the middle. Quite old. That one?"

Jenny nodded and blew her nose.

"What about him?" asked Melanie.

"He and I…"

"You slept with him?" Melanie sat back. "How did he force you to do that?"

"He didn't force me. It's been going on for a few weeks."

"But he must be at least forty-five. That's disgusting."

"I know, I know. That's why I didn't tell you. Knew you'd disapprove. You are unbelievably straight." Jenny gave an unhappy chuckle.

"I'm not that straight."

"Believe me, you are. Can't even pluck up the courage to call your brother's friend. Talk about pathetic."

"This isn't about Max." Melanie peered at her friend. "Don't tell me he's married."

"No, don't worry. He's not married. Far worse than that."

"I'm not understanding," said Melanie.

"He's been a complete bastard. Told the whole trading floor. Hasn't spared a single detail. So graphic. I'm a total laughing stock."

"That's horrible." How could Jenny have allowed that to happen? With a trader, of all people. What had she been thinking?

"I know. How can I stay there?" Jenny turned away. "I have to resign, there's nothing for it."

"Don't be dramatic." Melanie pulled her friend back. "OK, you've been careless. But you yourself told me that the traders are always talking about sex. You're the latest topic, but they will move on to the next one soon enough."

"But I will always be remembered by those stories." Jenny wiped her eyes. "I can't face going in again."

"What rot," said Melanie. "I thought you were tougher than that. If you resign, you give in to the git."

"What choice do I have?" said Jenny.

"Come on. Everyone loves you. It's all I ever hear about. Tell them he's only making it up because he couldn't get it up."

Jenny laughed. "That sounds pretty funny coming from you."

"Shut up. I might not be as bad as you, but I'm not perfect, believe me. Besides, there are enough men in the world without having to mess around in the office. I don't know why you keep doing that."

"He was the first in the London office," said Jenny.

"Well, make him the last. Otherwise you'll end up like Victoria."

Jenny frowned. "You're right, of course. She's an idiot."

"Complete slut, as we all know. And to think we were scared of her. Do you remember?"

"Yeah, funny isn't it?" Jenny shook her head. But a moment later, she was focusing on a man in the far corner of the bar. "Hey, that guy is looking at us."

"He's after you, darling." As usual. Not that it mattered. Tonight Jenny needed to be cheered up.

"Don't know," said Jenny. "Not sure if I'm in the mood."

"Come on," said Melanie. "Let's get drunk and forget about the whole damned thing."

She poured Jenny another glass and motioned for the man to join them. He was German, tall and reasonably attractive. Although not the most intelligent of companions, he was passable entertainment for the evening and could be counted on for a couple of rounds. Jenny introduced herself first. This time she became a hairdresser for the evening. She rarely used her own identity. Perhaps she didn't want them to get too close or perhaps she felt they would be intimidated by her relative success. It was a harmless game they had repeated many times before, but tonight Jenny needed the distraction more than ever. Anything to take her mind off the week's events.

They amused themselves with the flirtation and giving him wrong phone numbers. Zack was soon forgotten as they teased the hapless stranger and waved him off with meaningless promises to meet again.

Parting with her friend later that evening, Melanie strolled from the Tube station towards her flat and reflected on the recent events that were beginning to create a picture of City life. It was becoming depressingly predictable, all in such a short period of time. First Victoria, now Jenny. Was sex an inevitable part of this career?

Chapter Six

That first year at the desk passed in a blur of work, caffeine and pounding treadmills. A brutal schedule, and Melanie's limbs ached with fatigue.

She'd never have known it was possible to function like this. From the minute she arrived at six o'clock, there was always so much to do; reading the breaking news, responding to endless emails and writing up reports for the sales team before the market opened at eight.

After that very first week, she never overslept. Sometimes she was able to leave by 6pm, but when there was a corporate deal involved the additional work meant that she often stayed longer into the evening.

But it was all worth it. Thrilling to be writing research, earning her own money and making a mark on the world. In January, she'd been promoted to associate and the Christmas £20,000 bonus had been accompanied by a £15,000 salary increase.

No longer a newcomer, she had settled into the office routine. The work was fascinating and her colleagues were mostly friendly. Still not much progress with Andrew, but he had stopped being egregiously rude. Presumably on account of his improving sex life. At least, that's what George kept saying. Dear fat George, who never seemed to have a life of his own.

As the job increasingly consumed her time, her old friends continued to slide into the background. David was growing tired of her repeatedly cancelling dinner and, as the year passed, he became more distant. She scarcely noticed. Her life was full and, for the first time, her brother didn't form a significant part of it. And no more news from Max.

*

One late-February morning, Melanie stepped out of the office for her usual cappuccino. Jenny was away travelling, so she was hoping to find a seat in the coffee shop and get hold of her brother. He had left her a message a couple of days previously, but she'd been too busy to return his call. As she was collecting her coffee, her mobile rang loudly from her bag. Juggling the cup and her wallet, she grabbed the phone. Her heart sank when she realised it was her boss. That didn't bode well for a quiet coffee break.

"Hello, Tony. How can I help?"

"Where are you, Melanie? I need you right now."

Melanie groaned to herself. "Just popped out for a quick coffee. Will be right over."

"Make it quick."

Damn. Terrible timing. Her head was particularly heavy today and she had been relishing the prospect of her coffee all morning. She'd pulled an all-night stint at the office the day before, and needed the caffeine. Melanie poured the contents into a takeaway cup and ran.

Tony was waiting at his desk and wearily stood up to greet her. The bags under his eyes seemed more pronounced than usual. He had been noticeably irritable over the past week. Was it because of the redundancies? They hadn't seemed too widespread and she hadn't given it much thought until now. Was Tony about to sack her? Totally inconceivable, surely? Her year-end review had been stellar. She obviously wasn't one of the main analysts, but the clients seemed to like her. Simon had continued to be a huge support and many of the other junior clients had voted for her personally. She was working round the clock, for a comparatively cheap price compared to some of the older analysts. Tony wouldn't let her go. Or would he? The investment banking industry was notorious for its punitive and often indiscriminate redundancy rounds.

Tony summoned her to the meeting room. "Close the door," he said.

It was an ominous sign. Apart from conference calls and personal phone conversations, nobody ever closed that door. She looked down at the blue carpet with its two large coffee stains. Unable to meet his eyes. Those few seconds felt like an eternity. "Sit down, Melanie. We need to chat."

"Sure." She positioned herself opposite him. What was she going to do if she lost her job now? Just when she was getting used to all this money. No other career could possibly compare.

He pulled out a package of papers. "George and Andrew have resigned. I tried my best to persuade them to stay, but Grays was offering too much and management is refusing to match it."

"Oh. Gosh." Not what she had expected. George hadn't mentioned anything. Dark horse. How could he have kept that a secret from her? He told her just about everything else.

Tony inhaled. "Bloody terrible timing. Without them, it's going to be practically impossible to finish our deal. Corporate finance is having a fit and they want me to get some backup. But there is no way we can find anyone in time."

"What are you going to do?" she said.

Tony's small eyes bored into her. "It's about what you're going to do."

"What does that mean?" Melanie looked sharply across the table at him. Her immediate sense of relief was morphing rapidly into apprehension.

"It means you're going to have to market this deal with me."

"But…" she said.

"I know you've only been doing this job for a year, but we're going to make it work. It's not going to be easy but I have faith in you. Obviously none of us wanted this to happen so suddenly, but you have my total support."

Her heart sank. "Are you sure, Tony? I am still such a junior." Not to mention that she knew very little about corporate finance. It was completely different from stockbroking.

"Melanie, you are only as junior as you allow yourself to be. This place will eat you alive unless you inject a little backbone."

"OK." She stared at him, wide-eyed. How odd to hear him speak like that.

But he was not being unkind. "I mean it. You've had a year to learn the ropes. It might not be ideal, but you're the brightest recruit we've had in years. So in your case, it's enough."

Melanie sat up, surprised by the unexpected compliment. "The thing is, I've never worked directly with the investment bankers before." They were different creatures, those slick men on the eighth floor.

"I know. But it's not that difficult. I have every confidence you can do it and, besides, I'll be here to help."

"Thanks," she said. Obviously it was an amazing opportunity, but it was also way over her head. She was familiar with the deal, but mostly just through helping George with the PowerPoint. Quite a leap from creating pretty graphs to running the whole damned presentation. She had no idea about the numbers and hadn't even met the corporate client. All she knew was that the fees were good and it would be one of the more lucrative deals of the year. As usual, all the bankers in corporate finance were desperate for results. If the deal was pulled off, the bonus round would be bumper. She eyed him, aware that his gaze had not shifted.

"Well?" said Tony.

Melanie pinched her fingers beneath the table. Important not to show weakness. "That's certainly quite a challenge. But I'm up for it. Where do we start?"

"Good." Tony pulled out the presentation and opened it. "You've been helping to work on this already, and now you need to familiarise yourself with the details."

"What details in particular?"

"All of them." His thin lips parted in a wry smile. "The numbers, the valuations, you name it. And you'll need to study the IPO prospectus."

Her mouth fell open. "The whole thing?"

"Yep." He pushed over the 200-page document and put it on top of the presentation. "You're going to be speaking to our clients in New York, and believe me they can be tough. There is no substitute for preparation."

"New York?" Even George hadn't been scheduled to talk to the New York clients.

"You're going on Sunday night. Instead of Andrew. Pamela's already swapped the tickets."

"Seriously?" She gulped. New York! She'd never been to New York. "I've heard the investors are extremely aggressive there. Won't they tear me to pieces?"

"Like I said, prepare yourself. You'll be fine."

"It's a lot to do before Sunday. But OK." Melanie picked up the prospectus and fingered the pages. It was terrifying.

"You can inspect it later," said Tony. "We need to go upstairs now."

"Where to?"

Tony stood up and motioned for her to follow. "Banking."

They took the lift to the eighth floor, to find the investment banking team. Tony showed her into a corner office and called over one of the bankers. She recognised him from a presentation he'd given at the training programme. Mitch Cooper. American. Another one that Jenny had been infatuated with. He was as groomed as ever. Blue tailored suit and crisp white shirt, set against a flawless tan. Straight out of a Brooks Brothers catalogue.

"Hi," said Mitch. "How can I help?" Bright white teeth sparkled as he fixed his cold green eyes on her.

"Have you met Melanie?" Tony asked.

"Sure, the new graduate?" said Mitch.

"Not that new," said Tony. "I've asked Melanie to take the New York leg of the roadshow."

The man's smile twisted into a mean curl. Not so smooth after all. "Forget it. Who's going to take her seriously? She's only been here for about five minutes."

"She has been here for over a year and she is extremely capable." Tony's face flushed with indignation.

"It's an embarrassment. I simply won't allow it." Mitch stepped closer to her boss.

"We don't have a choice," said Tony. "I am going to be tied up in London and Europe and there is nobody left in the team. We need to see those clients and Melanie is the best person for the job. I have full confidence in her ability and that's the end of the matter."

"You're kidding. Do you realise how important this deal is?"

"Yes. And that's why it has to be Melanie."

"Look at her." Mitch glared at Melanie, who had moved backwards towards the wall. "She's a child. They will eat her alive. Not to mention discredit the firm."

"She'll be fine," said Tony.

"Over my dead body." Mitch stormed out of the room, slamming the door behind him.

Melanie tried not to look upset as they made their way back to their desks. Did her year at work count for nothing? Was she really as insignificant as that man thought?

Tony spent the next two hours locked in the corner office, his eyes glinting furiously as he spoke into the receiver. It was clear that he was discussing her with Mitch, and she was determined not to be a disappointment. If nothing else, her pride was too great to let that American get the better of her. Fuck him.

The next few days were exhausting; they toiled through the nights and into the weekend. Tony arranged a conference call with the finance director to ask a few more questions and spent hours going through the financials with her. The company was a niche Manchester-based engineering firm, trying to list its shares on the London stock market. Melanie had helped on a few IPOs before, but only as the junior analyst. Nothing like this.

Taking the Tube home on Saturday afternoon, she had her first anxiety attack. New York was so sophisticated. What on earth was she going to wear? There was no time to go shopping and, even if there were, she wouldn't know where to begin. Somehow her tattered blue suit from Zara didn't quite look the part. She only had one friend who might be able to help… She switched her route and headed to Notting Hill.

"Great timing," said Jenny, opening the door. "The wine is just cold enough."

"I didn't come to get pissed, for a change," said Melanie. "I need your help."

"There is nothing that can't be helped along with a glass or two."

Jenny threw Melanie's coat onto the sofa, reached for the open bottle on the coffee table and poured out the wine. "Here, take one."

Melanie grinned and accepted the drink. "Look, I've sort of been promoted. Well, I don't know if it's a promotion, but I'm going to New York tomorrow."

"Congratulations. See, I told you a drink was important," said Jenny. "And cool news about New York. Great bar scene."

"I'm not going for the bars." Typical of Jenny to focus on the nightlife.

"You can always make the time. Why don't you call our American friend? Remember Josh from the training programme? He's such fun."

"You mean, *your* American friend?" Melanie laughed. "He's not remotely interested in me."

"He's a great guy," said Jenny. "I'm sure he'd love to show you around."

"I doubt I'll get the chance. The thing is, I haven't got anything to wear. For work, I mean."

"Now you're talking. Come with me." Jenny led her to the spare bedroom, and opened the cupboard. "Help yourself."

Melanie stared at the endless racks of designer clothes. "Jesus. How do you afford all these?"

"Oh, you know… Presents, mostly."

"From who?" What kind of men was Jenny dating?

"Daddy, mostly. It's guilt money. Thinks it makes up for the fact that he's a complete arsehole."

"That's so lucky." No wonder Jenny always looked so hot. Hard not to with all that money.

"Do you think that's lucky? To be paid off rather than loved? By your own father, who's too busy swanning around the world on his yacht?"

"You're one up on me. My father buggered off entirely when we were nine. With a complete bimbo of a secretary. Left my mother with a small house and that's basically it. Haven't heard from him since." Melanie pointed at herself. "No wardrobe allowance here."

"You never told me," said Jenny, pouring more wine.

"I don't like to talk about it. Hate wasting the time thinking about him. Especially now Mum is dead."

"You poor thing. That's ghastly." Jenny put her arm round her.

Melanie shrugged and took a sip of wine. "Yeah, but let's get back to the clothes. Much more interesting."

Jenny laughed. "Which one do you want? Have anything."

Melanie pulled out a black trouser suit from Joseph. "This one looks about the right size."

"Sensible choice. Not overly attractive though." Jenny's free hand was clutching another option.

"Not that one," said Melanie. "I'm not trying to be sexy."

"Yeah, I keep forgetting, the serious girl."

"Shut up. I am in research, you know. I need to look the part."

"But at least take these shoes." Jenny pulled out a pair of Gucci stilettos.

"You're joking. I can't wear those."

"Of course you can. It's New York we're talking about. I'm not having you walk around in some boring old flats."

"My shoes aren't flat."

"Might as well be." Jenny dismissively eyed Melanie's feet.

"OK, let me try them." Melanie sat down and squeezed her feet into the shoes. "They're too tight."

"They're perfect!" said Jenny. "Now you're sorted, let's finish that bottle and get stuck in to proper group therapy. There's certainly enough material in both our lives that would keep Freud happy."

Chapter Seven

Her phone rang as the Heathrow Express pulled out of Paddington station on Sunday afternoon.

She fumbled through her handbag. "Hello, this is Melanie."

"Melanie, how are you?"

She felt a flicker of irritation. Why did men never introduce themselves? Even more frustrating was the fact that she knew immediately who it was. "How can I help you, Mitch?"

"I wanted to wish you the best of luck."

This was an unexpected surprise. "Thank you."

"And Melanie…"

"Yes?"

"Don't screw it up. Your career depends on it." The phone went dead. She stared at the blank screen. What a creep. Not the pep talk she would have hoped for. What was wrong with these people? But she had to focus on catching her plane, and pushed thoughts of the American temporarily to one side.

Finally on the aeroplane, she sank into the comfort of her business class seat and was already sipping her first glass of champagne when a tall man moved up the aisle. He removed his blue overcoat, loosened his tie and took the chair next to her. "Hello, Melanie, I thought I'd join you. I hope you don't mind."

She looked across at him, puzzled by the stranger. His accent was unmistakably French and his face was incredibly familiar. It took her a few seconds to place him. The senior partner from Paris who had interviewed her at the very beginning. At the same time as The Bitch. He'd been the friendly one. She'd stressed so much about Victoria that he had somehow been forgotten.

"Pierre, how are you? How nice to see you."

"Great to see you too." He smiled at her. "I am so glad you accepted our job offer. I have been following your progress."

"Thanks." Melanie sat up in her seat. "What a coincidence you're here."

"It's no coincidence." Pierre reached for a glass from the passing stewardess. "They wanted someone to accompany you to America, and I jumped at the idea. I was overdue a visit to the US anyway."

"Who's they?" she asked. "Not Mitch?" Such a bastard.

"Among others. The investment bankers obviously can't come to your meetings, so here I am."

"Oh. That's great." How patronising. They were treating her like a child, but at least Pierre seemed kind. He was the one who had got her the job in the first place. It could have been worse.

She observed her companion. Unlike at the interview, she now had the time and presence of mind to look at him carefully. Thick features, put together in an oddly attractive way. Inquisitive brown eyes. Her gaze dropped to his hands, noticing a slight yellow staining on his fingers. A fellow smoker. That was quite rare these days. No wedding ring. Also quite rare. After the plane took off, he turned to order another glass of champagne and she used the opportunity to pull the thin blue blanket over her shoulders. She dozed off, sensing that he was watching her, but her mind was on the presentation. She prayed it would go well.

The Manhattan skyline shone brightly as the taxi wound its way in from JFK airport and Melanie was captivated by Pierre's stories of the various landmark buildings. He had spent a few years working in New York and knew the city well. Entering Midtown, the streets were vibrant and loud. Music poured from cars and people of all nationalities filled the pavements. The snow on the ground was grey and melting. A gritty, filthy place with rubbish strewn across various street corners. But the atmosphere was electric and alive.

Happy to be an observer of the night, Melanie was almost disappointed to reach their destination.

After checking in, she held out her hand to wish her colleague a good night.

Pierre chuckled. "You English girls need to be a bit softer." He kissed her on the cheek and walked her to the lift, before escorting her to her room. "Good night, *chérie*."

The room was a surprise. For such an expensive hotel, it was tiny. Minute, actually. The bed was scarcely larger than a single and there wasn't much space to even open her case. Somehow she had expected more comfort; but probably she'd been given the cheapest room. Not that it mattered. She took a hot shower, stepped over her bag into the bed and plunged into a fitful sleep.

It was going to be a gruelling roadshow, with no gaps in the timetable for the entire two days. Lunch and dinner would be fully dedicated to work. The list of people she was scheduled to meet meant nothing to her. Tony had gone through the clients with her before she had left, but she still had no real understanding of who they were. Maybe it was easier that way.

Given the jet lag, she woke up early the next morning, desperate for caffeine. The transparent liquid in the downstairs restaurant was barely a comfort, but there was no other option.

At quarter to eight, Pierre was waiting in the lobby with Chris, their local sales man, and they walked three blocks to their first client meeting in Midtown. The biting wind caught her by surprise and her unfamiliar heels slipped on the icy pavement. Chris glared at her. "Didn't you know it was cold here in February?"

"Sorry." She blushed, knowing she was slowing them down.

"Don't worry," said Pierre. "There's plenty of time." He took her arm until she steadied herself.

"Thanks." She smiled gratefully back. She hadn't dressed appropriately and it was comforting to have him there. It wasn't the longest walk but, given the weather, it was a relief to arrive at the office. She gazed around the cavernous white lobby as they made their way to reception.

"ID, please," said the receptionist.

"ID?" she said.

"Yes. Driver's licence or passport." Half-dead eyes stared back at her.

"I left my passport at the hotel," she said.

Chris didn't bother to conceal his exasperation. "What kind of a fucking idiot are you?"

"Please don't speak to me like that," she said.

"But seriously, how the hell are we going to have a meeting if you can't get into the building?"

"I'm sorry, but nobody mentioned I needed ID. We don't require that sort of thing in London, you know."

"This is New York, not some fucking outpost."

Melanie took a step back. She was used to tough talk, but this was worse than usual.

Pierre put his hand on her shoulder. "It's not a problem. Melanie, give me your room key, and I'll get the passport. It will be quicker that way. Chris, start signing us in and I'll be back in no time."

Again he had come to her rescue. She handed him the room and safe keys and took a seat on a black leather chair on the other side of the lobby. Her nerves were already torn to shreds. It hadn't been a good start.

When Pierre returned, they took the lift to the twenty-second floor and turned right into the second meeting room down the corridor. Pierre was showing her the view from the oversized window when an old bald man shuffled in.

Chris stepped forward to greet him. "Howard. Good to see you."

The man grunted. "You're late."

"I'm sorry. Some logistical issues." Chris looked pointedly at Melanie.

"Not very impressive," said the old man. "What have you got for me today?"

Chris cleared his throat. "As we discussed the other day, we've got a new issue coming out in London. Small UK engineering company. Our analyst is over to go through the presentation. Let me introduce you to Pierre and Melanie."

Howard's red fleshy face turned to Pierre. "Sit down."

Pierre pushed his business card across the table. "Thank you for your time today. As Chris has probably mentioned to you already, we are very excited about this IPO. The management has taken the decision to float the business, and the valuation range looks very attractive. I'm co-head of Continental research, so am going to hand over to my colleague, who is the sector specialist."

Melanie smiled and pulled out her paperwork. "Um, here's our presentation. We are bringing a small components manufacturer to the market." She was uncomfortably aware of Howard's small hard eyes flashing at her.

"Another piece of engineering crap," said Howard. "We had one of those last week. They are all the same."

"This one is particularly interesting," she said. "Profits are growing nicely. The order book is solid and—"

"Don't tell me, private equity selling out?"

"Yes, they invested five years ago and—"

Howard banged his right hand down on the table. "Always the same old story. And I'm supposed to be the idiot to swallow it."

Melanie blinked. "It's not like that."

"Tell me, young lady. What is it like? You don't look like you've seen a market cycle and can I ask you –" his face came in closer and she tried not to choke at the staleness of his breath "– have you ever met this private equity team that's selling their stake?"

Pierre intervened. "As a matter of fact, we have done a number of deals with this particular team. All of which have been a success in the market. You might be encouraged to know that the management team is not selling at all. In fact, they are locked in for at least three years. On top of which is the fact that there is a hurdle rate for them to be able to sell at all in the future."

"I still don't see why it's of interest to me. There won't be much liquidity."

Melanie studied them both. It was odd how these New Yorkers felt the need to be so aggressive. But with her colleagues watching, she couldn't afford to look weak.

Despite her nerves, she leaned forward to catch Howard's

attention. "Our team has a lot of experience, and I'd like the opportunity to explain the deal. Particularly since we've taken the trouble to fly over to see you. I'm not sure why you agreed to the meeting if you aren't prepared to listen."

Howard chuckled, visibly amused at her answer, and she could sense Pierre's approval.

The next client was much younger and incredibly charming. Good-looking, blond and with an energy that reminded her of her fellow trainee, Josh. He offered them a coffee, which she accepted gratefully. Finally, something that would allow her mind to function normally.

"Thank you for coming today," he said. "I've been reading about this one and we are quite interested in finding out more."

"Wonderful news," said Melanie. What a relief.

"I don't mean to be impolite, but I'm a little short on time today," he said. "Do you mind if we plough straight into the details? I've got some very specific questions to ask."

"Certainly." This was an improvement after cantankerous old Howard.

Melanie glanced at Pierre, who was smiling quietly in his seat. The young man put on his glasses to inspect Melanie's papers and began asking very detailed questions about the profit margins. She could tell he was impressed by her knowledge. Finally, she seemed to be gaining some traction. What she lacked in stature, she made up for by hard work. She had studied the numbers and wouldn't be easily tripped up.

Her first presentation after lunch was at their Midtown office. She spotted Josh in the corridor and waved excitedly at him. He rushed to greet her with a warm embrace. "How's my second-favourite English girl?"

"I feel totally beaten up, if you want the truth," she said.

"Nonsense. I heard your meetings are going fantastically well. Anyway, and much more importantly, any news from Jenny?"

Melanie laughed. Josh hadn't changed. "Jenny misses you terribly. We are all so lost without you."

"She's a crazy chick. Never returns my calls," said Josh.

"Funny, that's what she told me about you," said Melanie.

"I guess that's true. But she wouldn't return them if I did. So why bother? I'd love to see her again though. Those were such fun days."

"They really were." That's not how she remembered the training programme, but it was good to see him again. In a sea of strangers, it was a relief to find a friend. It was exactly the encouragement she needed. If only she'd had more time to spend with him.

She was exhausted after her first day and was heading towards the lift after their dinner meeting when Pierre took her by the arm. "*Chérie*, you can't go to bed yet. I chose the hotel because of the bar. You're going to love it. Come see."

"OK. What the hell." It would be a crime to miss a night out in New York. She allowed herself to be led across the lobby and through the black door on the right.

"What do you think?" Pierre held the door open for her. "Not bad, right?"

"Wow. It truly is cool here." Unlike any bar she'd been to in London.

"You see, not feeling tired anymore?" said Pierre.

She shook her head. "How come everyone is good-looking in this city?"

"They aren't. Look carefully. They are all very self-important and spend a lot of money. It's their aura that makes them appear good-looking. Great fun, but a bunch of fakes."

"It looks pretty amazing to me." Melanie noticed a couple of leggy girls at the bar. With their immaculate blow-dried hair. Why was it that everyone else was always so much more glamorous than she was?

"Let me get you a drink," he said.

"Thanks." She stood there watching the crowd. He was right; it was some kind of self-assurance that radiated from their pores. Funny. Maybe it was a New York thing.

Pierre produced a Cosmopolitan and patted the sofa, indicating that she should take a seat next to him. "Cheers, *chérie*."

"Cheers. Why do you keep calling me *chérie*?"

"You are funny. I'm French. You're a beautiful girl. What else am I supposed to call you?"

She blushed, not sure why he was calling her beautiful, especially given the extraordinary range of women in that room. "My name would do."

"Don't be ridiculous. Silly girl. Drink up and I'll order another one."

That first cocktail had an immediate effect and Melanie barely managed a few sips of the second before fatigue began to crush her. The jet lag and stress had taken their toll and the alcohol was the final straw. She turned to Pierre and kissed him on the cheek.

"I'm dead," she said. "Just can't keep my eyes open. Time for bed."

"Of course." He stood up and escorted her to the lift. "There will be other opportunities. Goodnight."

Entering the room, she kicked off her shoes gratefully. The full assault on her throbbing feet was only noticeable now that she was able to completely relax. She vaguely wondered how she would cope with another day, but the immediate task of getting to bed was far more pressing. Her head hit the pillow and she succumbed instantly to slumber.

Again, she woke up early. The city was still asleep while she checked her emails and called Tony from her room. He was having coffee with colleagues in Paris, but seemed eager to speak to her.

"Melanie. You're up early. I've been dying to talk to you. How's it going?" He sounded happy.

"Not bad, I think. The first meeting with Howard was tough."

"Howard never changes. I'm not a fan either. But we have to see him every time. Don't worry about that. The feedback from the rest has been fantastic."

"Really?" she said.

"You're a funny girl. Can't you tell it's gone well?"

"To be honest, it's hard to make these Americans out. They are damned smart, but unbelievably rude sometimes."

"It's a cultural thing, my dear. They just like getting straight to the point. Still, Pierre emailed me last night. Told me one of the clients seems interested."

Melanie laughed. "I got an order?"

"It's a little early to get orders, my dear. That's not quite how it works. But there is interest," said Tony. "Fabulous news."

Melanie bit her bottom lip with excitement. It must have been from her second meeting. She knew that one had gone well, but she hadn't expected any results so quickly.

"Keep this up and you'll be putting me out of a job."

Tony was clearly delighted and she sighed with relief, tangibly feeling the stress lifting from her shoulders. Just the tonic she needed.

With an hour to kill before her meetings, she went downstairs to the gym and began her workout. She found herself thinking about her presentation and with every pounding of the StairMaster, she felt herself growing in confidence. Thank God Mitch would have nothing to complain about. The exercise boosted her adrenaline and her newfound self-assurance must have been apparent to Pierre when, later that morning, she rushed up to him and kissed him on the cheek.

After their last meeting on Tuesday, Pierre grasped her arm and led her down the street. "You have been marvellous. Come, I want to treat you to something special."

"Where are we going?" She eased out of his grip. "It's rather early for a cocktail."

"I'm not taking you to a bar." He laughed.

"So?" she said.

"You mentioned that the suit wasn't yours, and you deserve a decent one that will keep for years. This won't be your last business trip."

"Don't be ridiculous," she said. "You're not taking me shopping."

"Shush, you'll love it."

Curiosity took her to Fifth Avenue. Not only was it the first time she had entered a designer shop, it was the first time she'd entered a store with a doorman. The place was enormous. A well-groomed assistant bounced over and showed them a selection of clothes.

Pierre settled into a large white chair. "Get one with a skirt," he said from across the room. "You shouldn't hide your beautiful legs. It's a waste."

The assistant handed her an appropriate suit. Melanie spotted the price tag. "I can't accept this."

"Go try it on," said Pierre.

Melanie hesitated.

"Now," he said.

She relented, moved to the changing room and locked the door. Looking in the mirror, she gasped; the suit was incredible. She took a deep breath and stepped outside to show him.

Pierre whistled. "That's the one for you."

Melanie blushed and hurried back to change into her own clothes. She handed the suit to the assistant and Pierre whisked out his American Express.

When the woman presented her with a beautiful black bag, Melanie looked at Pierre. "I don't know what to say. Nobody has ever bought me something like this."

"That is the only crime. You deserve to be spoiled."

Melanie coughed nervously. "It's all rather awkward."

Pierre laughed. "Don't be ridiculous. It is my pleasure."

"But how can I ever thank you?"

"Relax, *chérie*. The only thing I want in return is that you allow me to take you to lunch next week in London."

"That would be wonderful. But definitely on me."

"Let's not worry about that right now," he said. "I shall look forward to it."

They crossed the street and she hailed a taxi for the airport. Pierre gave her a single kiss on the cheek. "*Chérie*, I'm staying for a few more days, but I'll be in touch once I get back."

Chapter Eight

The flight arrived into Heathrow at seven thirty. No time to go home. Tony had left a message for her to come straight to the office. She'd have to shower in the downstairs locker room, like all those eager sweaty cyclists. By the time she reached her desk it was already half past ten and the office was at full throttle. Seventeen voicemail messages and thousands of emails to wade through. On top of her normal research job, there was still a lot of work to do on the deal and she needed to start calling clients.

Adrenaline powered her through the day until finally she dived into bed that night at eight o'clock. The rest of the week blazed by in a blur of meetings and presentations, but she had had her first glimpse of power. What a difference a short week had made. Now, her phone rang constantly and when she ventured onto the trading floor, everyone knew her name. Tony asked her to present internally to the sales team; it meant more work, but it felt exhilarating. She was no longer a junior nobody, confined to the fifth floor; she was apparently being taken quite seriously.

Crossing the trading floor on Friday, she heard the wolf whistle. She knew it was meant for her but she didn't turn around. Not because she was scared, but because it felt wrong to gratify the idiot with a response.

"Hey, sexy." Melanie kept walking, but the man shouted louder. "You can't ignore me forever, babe."

Curiosity got the better of her. She turned and saw Zack. Revolting creature. She glared at him.

"I love that skirt." He was clearly delighted that she had stopped.

"Such great legs. You got a man in your life right now?"

"Piss off, Zack," she said. The fat man next to him smirked.

"Fighting talk," said Zack. "I love a feisty chick."

"You can love what you like, but it won't be funny when you get done for harassment. You won't think you're such a hotshot then."

Zack shrugged his shoulders. Not much fazed the traders. Melanie kept going, pleased nonetheless that she had given him her best riposte.

Back at her desk, she answered a call from Jenny.

"Heard about Zack." Jenny laughed. "Well done. Oh, Jonathan wants to speak to you. I'll pass the phone over."

Jonathan was one of the senior UK sales men and it was the first time he had ever spoken to her directly. "Hi, Mel. How are you?"

"Fine, thanks. How can I help?"

"We were talking about you earlier. Think it's about time you joined us for one of our desk outings. Are you free tonight?"

"Actually, I was planning on having an early night." She instantly regretted her words.

"It's settled then. You haven't got any other plans. See you later." He hung up.

It was the last thing she felt like, given her exhaustion, but she was flattered by the invitation and knew she had to keep networking. The sales force was incredibly important for gaining exposure to the investment managers, who were ultimately her clients. With their support, her career could blossom.

The penthouse bar facing the Bank of England was throbbing with young professionals, happy to be greeting a weekend. Many had been there since lunch and the noise was overwhelming. It was so unlike New York; the people here were crude and loud. She laughed at her own snobbishness. All from one silly trip abroad.

Jenny was already at the bar and waved. "Hi. You've got some catching up to do. I've just ordered a G&T. Want one?"

"Sure, what the hell." Melanie wearily accepted the glass and took a sip. The pick-up was almost instant.

"Everyone's outside, under the heaters," said Jenny. "Come on."

"Good idea. I could do with a cigarette." She hadn't been able to have one since her lunch break and it would keep her going for an extra half hour. Relishing the nicotine, she didn't notice Victoria step onto the terrace.

"Got a spare one?" Victoria asked.

"Yeah, sure." Melanie held the packet open, allowing the woman's manicured hand to deftly collect a cigarette.

"You're making quite a name for yourself, you know," said Victoria.

"Thanks." It was hard to forget their first encounter at interview stage and Melanie was taken aback by the sudden warmth.

"You've made some good calls recently. Just today a client of mine was telling me that he likes your research."

"Gosh, that's good to hear," Melanie said. Why was the woman being friendly to her?

"It's a virtuous circle here. I think I told you that before."

"Sort of."

"You see, if the clients like you, it makes us look good and then we push your work harder. You're doing a great job."

"That's very kind of you." Melanie eyed the woman with suspicion. Was this some kind of joke?

"No, seriously. It's not easy to crack the clients. Keep it up. Thanks for the cigarette too. Really needed it today."

She watched Victoria walk back to the bar. What was that all about? Perhaps she should take it at face value. Maybe the woman wasn't such a bitch after all, and she had to admit the conversation had been incredibly gratifying. To be acknowledged as a colleague. Praised even. And by such a glamorous woman. She couldn't understand why someone like that would compromise herself with a married man.

Melanie finished her cigarette and considered lighting another. But it was way too cold, even for an addict like herself. Time to go inside. She pushed open the large panelled door. Jonathan called her over.

"Hi," he said. "I'm glad you made it."

"So pleased to be invited." The attention tonight by the senior sales team was incredible. First Victoria, now Jonathan.

"Good," he said. "I was hoping to get to know you a little better. You've been the hot topic on the desk."

Melanie blushed, at a loss for words. She hoped he wouldn't notice. But of course he must have.

"You're an unusual analyst," he said. "Normally the girls are pretty square. You know, the cardigan-sporting type."

"Not sure I know what you mean," she said.

"Don't be bashful. We all know you're one of our best junior analysts, but you're also damned hot."

"Oh, thank you, I suppose." Why couldn't she be cool like Jenny?

"Seriously, where have you been hiding all this time?" he said. "Can't believe you're only coming out with us now."

Not knowing where to look, she drained the rest of her glass. Jonathan inched closer and whispered into her ear, "And I love the fact that you can handle a drink or two."

His fingers rested on her shoulder and she smelled his subtle cologne. None of her boyfriends had ever worn cologne, but she found herself drawn to it. She shivered involuntarily. Her first drink had given her some energy and she was beginning to enjoy this. How odd that she'd never realised how attractive he was before. His desk was next to Jenny's, so she must have passed him a thousand times. But this was the first time he had paid her attention and his intensity was strangely compelling. She hadn't kissed a man for almost a year and she felt an unexpected urge to end her dry spell.

Jonathan took her empty glass. "Let me get you another. What are you drinking?"

"That's very kind. G&T please." She watched him stroll across the room towards the bar, her eyes lingering on his lean torso.

In that instant and from nowhere, Jenny appeared, startling her.

Melanie laughed guiltily.

Jenny shattered her illusions. "Careful of that one. He may not be the best-looking guy around, but he is a complete womaniser. He always manages to leave the party with the hottest girl."

"What?" said Melanie.

"He hasn't stopped talking about you all week. Sorry, I meant to tell you earlier."

Melanie's face reddened. Had it been that obvious? "I don't know what you're talking about. I wasn't remotely thinking of it."

"It's me you're talking to. I know you quite well, remember?" said Jenny. "But believe me, don't go there. He's got a torrid reputation and you'll be dumped the instant he gets into your pants."

"How do you know that?" Melanie said.

"I work next to him, remember? It's quite a formula. Seen it a few times. The way he treated Katie in HR was abysmal. Not to mention that poor girl in IT. She resigned over the whole thing. He's very smooth. Makes Zack look like an amateur."

"You're wide of the mark with this," said Melanie. But she was startled. The alcohol had made her soft. She had to remember her vow to stay away from men at work. She moved to another group and, despite Jonathan's repeated attempts to corner her, managed to steer herself away from him for the rest of the evening.

She noticed Victoria in the corner, whispering into her phone and collecting her bag to leave.

One of the women sniggered. "We all know where she's off to."

"Such a tart," said another.

Melanie watched Victoria leave the room, elegantly dressed in a tightly fitted skirt that flattered her sculpted figure. She felt a surge of sympathy and compassion; surprised to find herself caring about the woman. The humiliation had to be unbearable. Prada handbags were a scant consolation for that type of sacrifice.

After a few more drinks, she left with Jenny to catch the Tube. While the girls waited for the lift, Jonathan rushed towards them and took her arm. She winced at his tight grip.

"Come," he said. "I've ordered a bottle of champagne. Share it with us."

"I'd love to," Melanie said. "But my boyfriend is waiting for me at home."

"He won't mind a few more minutes." Jonathan tugged her arm again.

She wriggled free. "No, seriously. But it was lovely to get to know you. See you on Monday."

The girls laughed all the way to the Tube station. It had been a fun night and they had both drunk too much. Thankfully, rush hour was over and they managed to find a seat immediately; a pleasant change from the usual squash.

Jenny was visibly delighted for her friend. "That went well."

"Apart from almost snogging your colleague."

"Ha, you admit it." Jenny giggled, startling the passenger sitting next to her.

"You're so annoying. I'm just tired and a bit drunk. Not a good combination."

"Basically, you need to get laid," said Jenny. "But not with him. We'll go hunting this weekend."

"Stop it. I don't need your help," said Melanie.

"You're damned strange. How long has it been?"

"I don't want to talk about it," said Melanie. "Especially not here." Broadcasting her sex life on public transport wasn't exactly classy.

"I find it hard to manage a week with no sex. You're a bloody nun."

"Better than being the source of office gossip."

The teenage girl across the carriage sniggered.

"That's unkind," said Jenny.

"I didn't mean you. Sorry. Came out all wrong." Despite being envious of Jenny's obvious appeal to the opposite sex, she had had no intention of upsetting her.

"Don't worry. I'm not easily offended, as you know. But don't you miss it at all?"

Melanie lowered her voice. "I don't know. I guess it will happen again at some point. But thanks for saving me from Jonathan. What a nightmare that would have been."

"What are friends for? Anyway, now you know the boundaries, you should hang out with us more often."

Chapter Nine

The magnum was waiting on her desk a week later, when she arrived from a breakfast meeting in the West End. Pamela was grinning and, as Melanie approached, Tony jumped up to greet her.

"Congratulations, Melanie. You are the youngest Vice President at the firm."

"Oh my God." She was stunned. "Are you serious?"

"Completely. It's so deserved and I couldn't be prouder."

"But I was already made an associate in January. I didn't know it was possible to get another promotion so quickly."

Tony laughed at her confusion. "To tell you the truth, I was rather surprised myself. Management called me yesterday for my opinion. With Andrew and George gone, it was either a promotion for you or I'd have to hire someone more senior. What was I supposed to do?"

"I'm speechless." She beamed at her boss.

"It's wonderful news and I'm as pleased as you are."

"Oh, Tony!" Melanie moved forward to hug him. He had been incredibly supportive. The promotion was highly unusual and it would mean a massive pay rise. £100,000 per year plus bonus. If only her mother were alive to witness this.

Tony extracted himself from her embrace. "Now, let's get to work. We need to hire a junior analyst for the team. They are holding the interview rounds this month and we need to put forward our case."

"A junior? That would be amazing."

"Melanie." Tony frowned. "You're already working round the clock. And we both know you're far too talented to spend your life on spreadsheets. If you're going to assist me on pitches and marketing, I've got to find someone to help you."

"Fantastic! Thank you so much." She'd never imagined being someone else's boss.

"And good news. Mitch called about another deal and he wants you involved."

"I thought Mitch didn't like me." And it was certainly mutual.

"Mitch only cares about his year-end bonus," Tony said. "You proved to him that you're good for his bottom line, so he's happy. It's not complicated."

"I'll take that as a compliment."

"You should. Anyway, he received the mandate a few days ago and wants to discuss it."

"What is it?" Melanie had enjoyed the last experience and didn't mind the prospect of another corporate client, even if it meant dealing with Mitch.

"It's made for you. A German one this time. Based in Frankfurt. Quite small with a decent management team. Mitch said the family is selling a large stake."

Tony wandered away to collect some papers and she returned to her desk. Her phone was ringing and she picked it up, not recognising the internal number.

"Good morning, Melanie," came the now-familiar East Coast drawl.

"Hi, Mitch," she said. "How are you?"

"Extremely well. You did great on the roadshow. We always knew you were the girl for the job."

"Thank you," she said quietly.

"And good news about the promotion. Makes it much easier to put you forward to my clients now you're a VP."

"I'm sure." His gain from her success instantly soured her previously celebratory mood. Still, she should focus on the money. Not much point in taking it personally.

"As a matter of fact, I have found another project for you."

"Tony told me."

"It's a slow burn, but I look forward to working with you on it."

"Thank you, Mitch. I can't wait." She hung up the phone with as much grace as she could muster. What a two-faced son-of-a-bitch.

Pamela was peering at her. "You seem to have quite a fan club."

"Excuse me?" said Melanie in confusion.

"That's the third time he's called today, asking for you."

"He's a wanker," said Melanie. "Only being nice to me because we are pulling off his deal and he'll get a big payout. He doesn't give a damn about me. No doubt he would have arranged for me to be sacked if it hadn't gone well."

"Such nonsense. Don't put yourself down," said Pamela. "He's definitely got a crush on you."

"What a revolting thought," said Melanie.

"Oh, I don't know. He's rather handsome, don't you think? Gemma was talking about him the other day. Apparently he's just split up with his girlfriend. You'd be in with a chance."

"You can't be serious," said Melanie. "I haven't got time for this sort of rot." How disgusting. She could think of nothing worse than Mitch Cooper and wanted to get him out of her head as soon as possible.

She watched her black computer screen. IT had rebooted the systems overnight and it was taking an age to start. Her mind began to wander. How had she come so far in just over a year? It was truly amazing. The hours were hellish, but she loved her boss, loved her work and, with a few notable exceptions, most of the people were friendly.

As she started daydreaming, she noticed Pierre approaching. It was the first time she'd seen him at this end of the room.

He walked over to Tony and she heard them discussing her success in New York.

Tony beamed and Pierre's eyes wandered over to her. "Lovely suit." He was subtle, but she could tell he was examining her legs.

Melanie blushed and tucked her chair under the desk. Hopefully Tony hadn't noticed the innuendo.

Pierre turned to Tony. "I hope you don't mind, but I promised Melanie a lunch to celebrate her triumph in America."

"That's a fantastic idea," said Tony. "And I can't thank you enough for recommending her for promotion. From what I heard, you convinced management. They barely wanted my view."

Pierre smiled. "Not at all. She certainly deserves it." As Melanie's mouth gaped open, Pierre looked at her. "Where would you like to go for lunch?"

Melanie blinked a few times. "Anywhere suits me," she said. "It will be a treat to go out. I don't mind."

"In that case, meet me downstairs at half past twelve. I know a lovely spot."

"Great. See you later." She turned back to her computer and tried to breathe normally. What a crazy, marvellous couple of weeks.

Pierre was waiting in the red chair by reception, reading the *FT*. Standing up, he gave her a single kiss on the cheek and pushed the revolving door for her to pass through. The cold air came biting on the other side and Melanie tugged her coat round her neck. She declined his instinctive offer of his scarf. They walked down the main road and turned into the little cobbled lane, past the coffee shop and pharmacy, and entered a small door to an old Italian restaurant.

They were among the first to arrive, but it was fortunate he'd reserved a table, because it filled up quickly. She wondered why her team didn't go out more often. It seemed everyone else did.

Unlike the stories she'd heard from some of the older brokers, it was no longer conventional to drink at lunchtime. Even with his best clients, Tony would always turn down a glass of wine. But Pierre had pre-ordered a bottle of champagne and it was on ice, waiting.

He poured her a glass. "This is to your blossoming career."

"Thanks." She blushed.

"You are a fascinating woman." He took her hand.

She pulled away. "Please…please don't do that."

"Don't be silly, *chérie*. You are being far too English. Come, let's celebrate your promotion." He pushed the glass towards her.

She eyed him, uncomfortable with his familiarity. But she needed to be more grateful for his help. "I can't thank you enough for that."

"Don't mention it," he said. "I always strive to support talent.

Much better to promote you internally than have someone else headhunt you away."

Pierre called for the menu, giving her time to compose herself. In disbelief, she spotted Mitch enter the room. The man seemed to be stalking her. She wrinkled her nose in distaste. Had he followed her? Surely not possible? He was deep in conversation with another man and was clearly there on business. Pierre laughed softly.

"Do you know Mitch?" she asked.

"Of course. Who doesn't?" said Pierre. "He's a complete prick, if you ask me."

Melanie's laughter was spontaneous, endangering her mouthful of champagne. She wiped her lips. What a relief that someone else felt the same as her.

"But let's not waste our time talking about him," he said.

"I couldn't agree more." She studied her companion. An interesting man. He must be around forty. Not conventionally good-looking, although he did have a certain charm. Maybe because he was French. She hadn't met too many Frenchmen before, apart from the occasional boy at university. The man's dress sense was immaculate; his suit was clearly tailored. Engraved gold cufflinks. PMD. She vaguely wondered what the M stood for. She was no expert on watches, but he clearly had a passion for them. He had been wearing a Rolex in New York and was now sporting a Patek Philippe. When he wasn't looking, she unfastened her plastic Swatch and shoved it into her handbag.

"Tell me, did you enjoy New York?" he said.

"To be honest I was terrified at the beginning. But it was amazing. I can't thank you enough for your help. Especially with that first meeting."

"And the shoes," said Pierre. "Which are very sexy, by the way."

"How can I forget the shoes?" she said. "I won't make that mistake again."

"*Au contraire.* It's very important to be yourself. A beautiful feminine woman. Who happens to be extraordinarily intelligent."

"Please…" Melanie blushed again and took a sip of the champagne. She wasn't sure how to handle the compliment. But the bubbles felt good on her tongue and she began to relax. Maybe the French always talked like this. What was the harm? Anyway, he was clearly a powerful ally. And good for her new networking initiative. Jenny kept telling her she needed to make more contacts. It was hard to meet many people, with her desk hidden away on the fifth floor.

Lunch lasted for over two hours. A rare diversion from her usual sandwich break at Pret A Manger. A delicious midday decadence, made all the better by the fact that her boss had signed off on it. It was business after all. At least, that's what she told herself. They spoke about many things, and she was careful to remain professional. She started when Pierre reached across the table and touched her neck, but he was looking at the love knot on her necklace.

"It's beautiful," he said. "Did someone special give you that?"

"It was my mother's. She's dead now." She stopped there; this was not the time to discuss her private life.

"I'm sorry for your loss." He held the necklace a few seconds longer than she would have liked, withdrawing his hand slowly and deliberately.

After they finished the bottle, Pierre looked at his watch. "Unfortunately, I have to go soon. A boring meeting in Canary Wharf. So dreary. I'd much rather spend the afternoon with you."

"Please don't apologise," Melanie said. "It's been such a treat." She began to gather her handbag.

"Not quite so quick, *chérie*." He gripped her hand. Perhaps it was the champagne, but this time she didn't feel the need to pull away. "There is always time for an espresso. It is moments like this that I wish I could smoke in here."

He couldn't have been more gracious, that charming Frenchman with impeccable manners. Lunch had been an unusual luxury and she smiled up at him as they left the restaurant together.

He kissed her on both cheeks and crossed the road to wave down a taxi.

Melanie needed to clear her mind before getting back to the office. A few yards away, she found a small wooden bench facing St Paul's Cathedral. She lit her first cigarette of the afternoon and sucked hard, observing the office workers hustling past on their daily business.

Her head was spinning; it wasn't a good idea to drink at lunchtime.

While she sat there, absorbing the cold, she gazed around. The grandeur of these buildings never ceased to amaze her. The eternal splendour of the cathedral blended perfectly with the pulse of the daily movement below. It was beautiful here. And she was fortunate to be a part of it. The wind was biting and light snowflakes were beginning to float in front of her, but it felt good to be outside.

Tony looked up in surprise when she returned to the office. "You took a rather long time."

"Sorry," she said. "Unbelievably slow service."

"Hope it was fun." He shrugged and turned his attention back to his screens.

Melanie sank into her chair, hoping nothing further would be said. Pamela hurled a packet of mints at her.

"Thanks," said Melanie. How embarrassing.

When Tony left the room a few minutes later, Pamela winked at her. "Who did you go out with?"

"One of the management team. Wanted to congratulate me on my promotion."

"Who?" said Pamela.

"You probably don't know him. Pierre, from the Paris office."

"Yeah, I know. Not bad looking."

"Not that rubbish again."

"I'm glad to see you're having fun at last," said Pamela.

"It was work, you know."

"Trouble with you is that you're too serious. Life's not all about work."

"I know, I know." The constant reminders were getting boring. "But if it makes you feel any better, I'm totally smashed, so I won't be doing much more today."

Fortunately, there was nothing pressing to do that day and she was able to spend the rest of the afternoon staring blankly at the screens. The numbers bounced in front of her and she was unable to focus. But it didn't matter. As long as there weren't any deadlines, nobody ever troubled her. That was one of the many good things about this job.

As she was preparing to go home that evening, her phone pinged with a message. Shit, she had completely forgotten drinks with her brother's girlfriend. Of all days. All she wanted was to curl up. But cancelling was out of the question. She'd already done that far too many times. And David was insistent she become friendly with this girl, dull though she was.

The lunchtime alcohol had taken its toll and Melanie yawned as she entered the pub. She spotted Samantha sitting alone at the bar.

"Hi, Samantha," she said with no enthusiasm.

"You look terrible," said Samantha.

"Thanks. Any more pep talk?" Not a great start to what was likely to be a tedious evening.

"I mean, you look amazing as always," said Samantha. "Just terribly tired."

"Busy day." Melanie sighed. The last thing she wanted was to be here, with this tiresome woman. "Shall we get a drink? I'll get you another glass." She waved at the bartender. Best not to order a bottle. She didn't want to be stuck here all night.

"Thanks," said Samantha.

"How's David?" asked Melanie.

"Fine."

"Good." Melanie reached for a packet of nuts.

"But actually, if you want the truth, he's upset with you," said Samantha.

"Why?"

"Says you're always cancelling on him."

This was becoming even more irritating than she had expected. But there was no point in arguing. "I know. I need to make more of an effort."

"How's work, apart from being busy?" said Samantha.

"It's cool. I get to travel a lot and, actually, I was promoted today."

"Congratulations." Samantha raised her glass. "Any nice men at work?"

Jesus. Here we go again. "Best not to mix, don't you think? And not much time outside. So, no. Not right now."

"That's a shame," said Samantha.

"Yeah. Whatever." Melanie rummaged at the bottom of the packet for the last cashew. Not that she was remotely hungry.

Another pause. "What about Max?" said Samantha.

Melanie sat up. "Max? What about him?"

Samantha smiled at her reaction. "He still asks after you."

"Does he?" She hadn't heard from him in such a long time.

"Yes. Quite often, in fact. Why don't you give him a call?"

Melanie frowned. "For the record, I did call him a couple of times. He hasn't been in touch either."

"He told David he was waiting for your work to calm down. Didn't want to harass you apparently."

"Well, I still don't see why I should make the first move."

Samantha clearly had no intention of dropping the subject. "He's cute. By far the best of David's friends and I don't understand why he hasn't been snapped up. Such an interesting man."

"I know he is," said Melanie. "And I'm not saying he's not a great guy. I just don't have the time to think about it."

It was bad enough for Jenny to make these comments, but David's bloody girlfriend? If Samantha thought she was going to become her best friend by talking about men, she was barking up the wrong tree.

Melanie reached for her glass, but it was already finished. Trying to catch the bartender's eye, she was caught off guard when Samantha brought up the subject of her long-term first boyfriend.

"David spoke to Robert the other day." Samantha's fake casualness instantly revealed the purpose of the meeting.

Melanie curled her lip. Why the hell was she bringing this up? "What's that got to do with me? I haven't seen Robert for years."

Samantha continued her obviously pre-prepared speech. "He's getting married, you know. Nice girl. The date's been set for June, in Devon. David and I are going."

"So? We broke up ages ago. I haven't spoken to him since."

"I thought you should know."

"Fine. Now I know. Are you happy?" God, she needed that second drink. What was it about Samantha that made her want to get smashed the whole time? Blot the woman out.

"Don't be like that," said Samantha. The hurt on the stupid woman's face made her even more infuriating.

"Don't be like what?" she snapped. "Is this why you brought me here? To give me a sermon on how to lead my life?"

"I'm not telling you how to lead your life."

"It sure sounds that way. Did David put you up to this?"

"No. Well, we discussed it. I was happy to come along."

Melanie thumped the bar. "To hell with David too."

Samantha didn't flinch. "He loves you. We're worried, that's all."

Melanie glared at her. "There's no need."

"It's not normal, this life of yours. You haven't had a boyfriend in ages and you're half killing yourself."

"OK, I'm knackered. So what? I also happen to be very happy. Tell me your job gives you the same satisfaction."

"It doesn't pay that well, but I have a life," said Samantha.

"Your life is different from mine. Why is it strange that I don't want the same thing as you right now? I don't need a man to make me happy. Since you were so sweet as to mention it, yes, I'm exhausted and want to go to bed. Let's call it a night."

Melanie threw down some money and hurried out of the pub. Fuck David and fuck Samantha. What right did they have? Still, she thought about Robert the whole way home. That was definitely a door she had slammed shut. Marriage was something she and Robert used to talk about a lot. At least, he had talked about it. She had never been keen. And definitely not now.

Of course she was happy for him, but the news still made her queasy. How grating that it should affect her at all, particularly when she hadn't thought about him for such a long time. He had been a sweet boyfriend. Too sweet for her.

She turned the key in her door, threw her coat down and flicked the light switch in vain. The bulb had blown a few days ago. She had been planning on asking David to bring a ladder over on the weekend, but not anymore. Using the light from the corridor, she made it to the kitchen and opened the fridge door. A lonely half pint of milk sat on the middle shelf. Cornflakes for dinner, again. She wasn't that hungry anyway and certainly had no energy to go to the shops.

That night, she lay in bed, but sleep didn't come to her. She listened to a couple's muffled voices on the street below and heard the distant sound of sirens. She stared into the darkness of the room and shuddered as her mother's image seemed to jump out in front of her. Her mother had always adored Robert and would have loved grandchildren. It would have broken her heart to see him marry someone else.

But her mother had never understood her.

Chapter Ten

Oblivion. It was one of life's most basic pleasures.

Drugged with fatigue, Melanie craved her bed most nights and often crawled back to her flat, took the briefest of showers and jumped straight under that soft white duvet. She had had a particularly hard day and was fast asleep when the phone rang at ten o'clock, puncturing her dreams and forcing her rudely into reality. She cursed herself for not turning it off. She didn't recognise the number, but answered it anyway.

"*Cherie*, it's me, Pierre. I need to see you."

"I'm sleeping," she said.

"Sorry to disturb you. I just wanted to speak to you."

"Not now." She switched off the phone and flung it across the room. At that moment, she didn't care if it broke. Pierre was starting to annoy her. Over the past month he had become increasingly insistent, calling her every day. This was the first time he had disturbed her in the evening.

At one level, admittedly, it was flattering, but his presence was becoming intrusive. If only she hadn't accepted that damned suit. Or the lunch. Not to mention the promotion. But he was very senior and she couldn't afford to offend him. She cursed him one more time and rolled back to sleep. She would deal with the consequences in the morning.

Arriving back from a lunch meeting the next day, she found her desk covered in flowers with a small note. "One dinner, please?" There was no name, but of course she knew who had sent them.

The taunting bouquet filled her with anger. He had no right to encroach on her like this. It was bad enough that he kept calling her, but now he had crossed the line, bringing it into the office for everyone to see.

Pamela peered over the desk. "Who's the admirer?" This new development clearly amused her.

"It doesn't have a note," said Melanie.

"A secret admirer. How exciting." Pamela lifted her glasses to inspect the flowers. "He's got good taste. Expensive too."

"He's not my sort," said Melanie.

"Ah, you do know who it is." Pamela chuckled with delight at this minor revelation.

"You can get as excited as you like, but I'm not remotely interested. He's become a bit of a stalker."

"Is it Mitch, by any chance?" Pamela whispered conspiratorially. "He keeps asking after you."

"What?" Mitch was the farthest thing from her mind.

"Yes," said Pamela. "He came just yesterday, when you were out. Specifically wanted to know where you were."

Melanie widened her eyes in horror. "Him? You must be joking."

"I don't know, he's so handsome. And charming too."

"Mitch, handsome?" said Melanie. "He's a self-satisfied wanker, if you ask me."

"That's rather harsh, don't you think?" When Melanie proffered no response, Pamela continued. "Whoever it is, you should give him a chance."

"Fuck off, Pamela."

"Language, my dear! You are starting to sound like the traders."

"Sorry, Pam. I'm infuriated by the whole thing. The man is not as bad as Mr PermaTan, I grant you, but still not my form at all."

"Please, for your own sake, stop being so serious and have some fun. You're far too much of a workaholic for your own good. He's just asking for dinner. No harm in that. Give me his number, I'll call him myself."

Clearly, that wasn't an option, so Melanie reluctantly agreed to write the text herself. Under Pamela's gaze, she wrote. "OK. I'm free next Wednesday. You choose the venue." Wednesday was far enough into the future; she wouldn't have to think about it until then. She would fabricate an excuse closer to the time.

Melanie pushed the bouquet across the desk. "You have the flowers if you like them so much. But get them out of my sight."

The days passed and Melanie didn't give the date much thought. But when Pamela arrived in the office on Wednesday morning, she came directly to Melanie's desk. "Where are you going on your hot date?"

"Not so loud." Melanie turned round to check that nobody else had heard.

"OK." Pamela lowered her voice. "Where is he taking you?"

"Nowhere," said Melanie. "I'm going to cancel."

"You can't do that."

"Of course I can. I'm always rescheduling because of work. I'll pretend I've got a report to finish or something."

Pamela slammed her bag down. "You are too young to be acting so staid. Life is more than work, you know. Give the guy a chance. What's the worst that's going to happen?"

"He hasn't called all week. Maybe he's forgotten all about it." Funny how she couldn't be sure whether she was pleased by his recent lack of communication, or disappointed.

"He won't forget." Pamela laughed. "You can't get out of it that easily."

"Please don't torment me any further. It's exasperating enough as it is." At that moment, her mobile rang and Melanie froze.

"Is it him?" Pamela had such a grating smile sometimes.

Melanie stared at the screen and refused to answer, willing it to stop. But it didn't stop; or perhaps he called a second time. Pamela lunged for the phone and Melanie was forced into action.

"Hello." She blushed, aware that Pamela was watching. "OK. Pick me up at eight thirty."

Looking at her watch, she cursed. She really did have a report to write that day and now she had a deadline. Worse, the words weren't flowing. She wrote the first paragraph three times before deleting it. It was no use. She was suddenly anxious about the evening. She hadn't had any intention of going on this ridiculous date. How could she have put herself in this awkward situation? It was exactly the wrong thing to do.

Entering her flat that night, she panicked. What was she going to wear? It couldn't be too sexy. There was no question of being provocative. That would be a terrible mistake. Obviously she needed to be presentable, but it mustn't look as if she had made any effort. A simple shift dress with basic jewellery. Thick black tights. No lipstick. She was determined to keep it professional. At least there was no need to shave. No way was she going to sleep with the man.

When she was ready, she poured herself the end of the previous night's bottle and lit a cigarette to calm her nerves. Finishing them all too quickly, she began to pace her flat, listening for the bell. He arrived promptly and waited in the hallway. With one last glance in the mirror, Melanie gathered her coat and went downstairs. He was standing at a respectable distance. Maybe it wouldn't be that bad after all.

He broke her train of thought. "*Chérie*, you are so beautiful." He moved forward and kissed her on one cheek.

She stiffened. "Pierre, please…"

He laughed and took a step backwards. "Come, my car is over here."

She followed him with a heavy heart, hating herself for being in this situation. Damned Pamela, it was all her fault.

Pierre commented on the weather and some other forgettable news as he drove through the residential roads towards South Kensington. He parked neatly in a narrow tree-lined street. It dawned on her that he wasn't taking her to a restaurant, as she had stupidly assumed.

He opened her car door and took her arm. "I'm not a terribly good cook, but I want to try a new recipe on you. I hope you don't mind."

"Is this your place?" She didn't know why she asked this most obvious of questions.

"Yes, I hope you like it."

"I'm not sure this is such a great idea." She was angry to be trapped in this way, infuriated to have been so easily conned.

"Relax," he said. "I don't bite. It's just dinner, I promise."

"Just dinner. OK." She inhaled, not believing him. But at least he was being gracious. Melanie followed him up the pale stone steps to the first floor.

Pierre turned the key, pushed the door open and motioned for her to enter before him. The flat was obviously new and had been freshly painted. White, empty walls. Sparse furniture, with a couple of oversized sofas and a large television. A few scattered books, but generally very bare and corporate. He closed the door behind him and slipped her coat from her shoulders. "Sorry about the flat."

"It's lovely." She glanced around, not particularly caring.

"I bought it last year and haven't had the time to make it a home yet. Perhaps you can help me."

Melanie shook her head in disbelief. "I'm not much of an interior decorator, I'm afraid…"

Pierre poured two glasses of wine and clicked on the music. Jazz. Couldn't fault him for effort, at least. "Thank you for agreeing to come," he said. "So pleased you're here."

She raised her glass, thankful for his good manners. "OK. But you definitely tricked me. I hope you do understand this is just dinner."

He tilted his head. "You know I hate it when you behave strangely. I want to get to know you better, that's all. Hard to do that in the office."

Melanie tensed her fists and perched on the edge of the sofa. "We could have gone to a restaurant."

"Relax." He patted her leg. "This is much more pleasant. And, besides, I almost never have the chance to enjoy my flat in the company of such a beauty."

"Stop it… You and your peculiar sense of humour."

"It's not funny. You are beautiful. I am honoured to have you here."

Melanie stood up. The conversation made her uneasy. She needed more wine.

Pierre jumped up and grabbed the bottle. "I'm glad you like the wine. From my friend's vineyard." He poured her a generous glass. "And while you enjoy your drink, I shall prepare dinner."

With a sideways glance, he wandered off to the kitchen and returned a while later with two small salads. Pierre pulled out a chair and motioned for her to join him at the table.

He was not a natural chef. After the next course of over-cooked pasta, he lit a cigarette from the pillar candle and offered it to her. She didn't refuse. At least he wasn't one of these boring clean-living health freaks. The nicotine certainly helped and thankfully the wine continued to flow.

Pierre stood up to find another bottle and she lit a second cigarette from her butt, flicking the ashes onto her empty plate. For such basic fare, it was turning out to be the longest meal in the world and she was exhausted. When he returned, Melanie looked pointedly at her watch, but he pretended not to notice her anxiety. Or maybe he was oblivious. She knew Tony was expecting her early the next day. She cursed the secretary. This would be the last time she was taking Pam's advice.

Pierre took a long sip of his drink and stared at her. The brown eyes had become more intense. "Tell me again, why don't you have a boyfriend?"

Melanie shuffled in her chair. "Who said I don't have a boyfriend?"

"You told me. Remember? I've been wondering about it for a while."

"Actually, I'm back with my ex."

"Since when?"

She gulped. "Last week."

"That's a great pity. For me, anyway." He looked down at the table.

It was definitely time to wrap things up. "That was a delicious supper. But I'm tired—" she began.

"*Chérie*, I've got some delicious ice cream."

"No thanks. I've had masses."

"An espresso then. I know you like coffee." His tone had definitely changed.

"I have to get home. Early start tomorrow."

"Just a few more minutes."

"You've been very kind," she said, trying to remain calm.

She stood up to pass his chair, somehow expecting him to move. A flicker of disappointment crossed his face.

"Don't leave now. You only just arrived." He grabbed her wrist.

"Please stop." This was getting more uncomfortable by the second.

Finally he let go. "I understand. It was such a pleasure to see you." Pierre moved away from the table and let her walk to the door.

She reached for her coat, hanging on a metal hook.

He leapt forward and wrapped his arms round her. "Please don't leave."

She stiffened in fear. "Pierre…this is not going to happen. It's not appropriate. I told you already."

But his hands didn't move. She raised her voice. "I'm not going to sleep with you. Why haven't you understood that?"

"I understand." His mouth moved towards her and he kissed her forcibly.

Melanie pulled back. "What are you doing?" But he started again. Perhaps it was the wine, perhaps it was the months of abstinence, but despite her previous intentions, she couldn't deny it felt good. It was only a kiss… No harm in that.

She closed her eyes and parted her lips. It was the sign he'd been waiting for and she allowed herself to be led to the sofa. His hands moved deftly, loosening her clothes, pushing her against the armrest, so that she was unable to move. She didn't resist. Too late for that now. Her body had taken over.

The music in the background, the brackish scent of his skin, his mouth, his touch…he was everywhere. And then it happened. Almost unbearable and she couldn't breathe for the explosion. All concerns evaporated; he filled her every pore. The pain, the yearning, melting incoherently into one. He was a beast, bruising her inside and out, and her body was no longer hers. It responded enthusiastically. Her fingers scraped his back unknowingly, in a desperate attempt to have more. The ecstasy was complete and she could think of nothing else. It seemed to last forever, but at the same time it was over too soon.

"You are my great passion," he murmured afterwards. "I can't live without you. I will want you until the end of my days."

She lay in a stupor, the burning still coursing through her veins. "You tricked me." But this time, there was no anxiety in her voice.

He clasped his right arm round her back. "It wasn't meant to be a trick. But I am so glad you stayed."

She studied her lover, inspecting the sweat on his brow, seeing him for the first time. "You gave me no choice."

"There is no choice. This is meant to be." With his free hand, he stroked her hair, his breath still heavy from exertion.

Leaning into his warmth, her head was spinning in confusion. This was the last thing she had expected. How had he known it would end this way? Why had she received the rough treatment so willingly? She hadn't had many lovers in her life, but knew this was different. He filled her entire being, but it wasn't love. This wasn't what she had read about as a young girl. Her thoughts drifted into unconsciousness and she fell asleep, still pinned in his arms.

Extricating herself from his grasp an hour later, she looked at him and pondered her sudden change of heart. He had picked her from the crowd and had stalked her until she relented. She couldn't begin to understand it, but in that moment she knew she didn't need to. He had been sent to her.

She left him lying on that large green sofa, needing to run away from the power that had engulfed her. Dizzy with emotion, she collected her coat and left. That night she strolled home, desperate for the moist, cool air to provide answers. It had been a bolt from the blue; completely and utterly unexpected. Her body, awakened after a long year of neglect, was scorched from the sensation. She had never been involved with an older man before, and it was unlike everything before.

Her heart was still pounding when, an hour later, she turned the lock in her blue door. It would be a sleepless night and with no reason to go to bed, she smoked quietly on her terrace, watching the darkness beneath her. A young couple passed by, unaware of their silent observer, and an old man hobbled round the corner. She watched them with ambivalence, not caring about their lives, not caring about anything except him.

Before the sun rose that morning, she reluctantly took a shower, having preserved him for the night. She closed her eyes as she washed, remembering his hands and the bewildering lust he had inexplicably inspired.

Naked in the bathroom, she inspected herself in the full-length mirror. Her face glowed with the aftermath of passion. Glancing down, she saw herself as if for the first time. She had never considered herself beautiful, but her legs were long and her breasts were full, still blessed with youth. She was surprised for liking the image, aroused by the concept that this being had provided such pleasure to another.

Back in the office, she convinced herself that she was exactly the same person as the woman who had left the day before.

But Pamela's glance showed her that she had registered everything. "Good night, then?"

Melanie tried to conceal her embarrassment. "He was a total bore. Such a waste of time, just like I told you he would be."

"I know you're lying," said Pamela. "I can see it in your eyes. It's obvious. I was young too, you know."

"Please, Pamela, I don't want to talk about it." God, she could be irritating.

Pamela laughed. "I knew it! Who was it? Perhaps that lovely boy on the sales force. Jonathan, I think. He calls up here a lot."

Melanie shook her head, not bothering to respond, so Pamela continued. "Don't worry, my sweet. Your secret is safe with me. Good for you. Aren't you glad you took my advice? Once you're married, you can't do these things anymore."

"I'm not in the mood for this."

But Pamela was warming to her theme. "Take full advantage of your youth, sweetheart. That's the one thing that you can't have back. Even if I weren't married, I can tell you, no man would send me flowers like that. Whoever he is, you're damned lucky."

While Pamela droned on about the state of her marriage,

Melanie's thoughts remained on the previous evening. The memories of the night lay heavy on her mind. She could still feel his insistent breath on her neck and bruising grip on her wrists. Nothing made sense and she couldn't begin to verbalise her emotions.

Pamela must have sensed that she had lost Melanie's attention and changed the subject. "Did you hear about Victoria?"

Melanie swivelled round. "What about her?"

"She's left the firm. Didn't you hear?" said Pamela.

"No, I didn't. I'm not a gossip like the rest of you." Melanie turned away, feigning indifference.

"You are slow off the mark. Probably the last one to know."

"What? I suppose you're going to tell me anyway," said Melanie impatiently. It was typical of Pamela to keep her in suspense.

"She's been a complete idiot," said Pamela. "Totally had it coming."

"Just tell me. You and your silly games," said Melanie.

Pamela chuckled. "Apparently her lover's wife caught them in flagrante and there was hell to pay."

"Jesus," said Melanie.

Pamela began discussing the details of Victoria's undoing and Melanie shook her head in wonder. Poor Victoria. She was so glamorous and had such style. Why on earth had she ruined everything by sleeping with a married man? She could have had anyone. There was way too much gossip in this firm. To a lesser degree, Jenny had also suffered. A fortuitous and timely warning. She vowed to keep her new relationship entirely private. It was nobody else's business and she didn't want anyone making unprofessional comments.

Her phone was ringing from inside her bag and she turned to pick it up. She smiled with delight when she saw his name and, under Pamela's watchful eye, she entered the glass office, closed the door and took the call.

"*Chérie*, you are a naughty girl."

"What are you talking about?" she said. Despite thinking of him all morning, she hadn't been prepared for this conversation.

"Why did you leave me so early?" he said.

"I had to get to work, Pierre."

"At midnight?" He laughed, with that deep-throated sound that she was beginning to love. "You know I am not going to let you go so easily next time. I am back next Tuesday and I very much hope you're free for dinner."

"That would be lovely."

"Don't be so English," he said. "Remember, I know you better than that."

"How can I forget? Goodbye, Pierre."

She sat down on the chair, not trusting her legs, now weakened by a furious trembling. The impact was undeniable and she was breathless. Before she had gathered enough strength to stand up, her phone rang again.

"Hello, Pierre," she said. This time it was funny and she laughed at his childish behaviour.

"I am not joking. You are my passion and I will not let you go. I will call you later." He hung up and she stared at the phone, knowing something momentous had happened. She had never felt so desired and the effect was intoxicating.

From that moment, he came alive in every aspect of her life. Wherever she looked, there he was. In emails, in casual conversations with her colleagues. How had she not noticed before?

If the days were long, the nights were unbearable. Alone with only her imagination, she could hardly bear the intensity of this new infatuation. Every inch of her body ached desperately for him. What had he done to her? She had never known such an excruciating craving.

It would be a long wait until Tuesday.

Chapter Eleven

Although Pierre was based in the Paris office, he came weekly to London, spending a night or two in town. That first encounter turned out to have been typical of the ones to follow, except that now she entered his flat willingly. And they made love before dinner. Often, in fact, dinner was entirely forgotten. She relished giving in to his forceful demands, and handing her body over to him.

When in London he regularly organised client meetings, in order to take her to a nearby hotel in the City afterwards. There was never any choice and she happily obliged. In the office, he would simply ambush her in a meeting room or stairwell.

At times, he would pass her desk, pretending to look for someone else. In the half second that his gaze lingered, she knew he desired her intensely. Melanie began to take more pride in her appearance and increased her visits to the gym. Apart from the need to pound out her sexual energy on the treadmill, she wanted her figure to be flawless and she glowed with her newfound confidence.

He called insistently, several times a day and always at night. Some of their calls lasted for hours and some just for seconds. It was always a challenge to disguise her delight when her mobile vibrated from inside her bag. She would ring him back from the stairwell, whispering down the phone. Pamela must have guessed but, for a change, was remarkably discreet. Tony, amazingly, seemed oblivious.

At work, Pierre continued to advance her career, assisting her with reports and recommending her to his contacts. And outside the office, he would always bring a gift: flowers, books, jewellery – and sometimes he would buy clothes. The size was always perfect. His penchant for lingerie was strange, given that he never spent time admiring it.

Although discretion remained a priority, she decided eventually to discuss her bewildering affair with Jenny. The girls were at their usual Saturday-night bar when Melanie broached the subject.

She shunted her stool closer to her friend. "I need to talk to you about something."

"Oh?" Jenny took an absent-minded sip of her wine, still focusing on the man at the end of the room.

"I've started seeing someone." Melanie blushed, unsure how to continue.

"What?" Jenny twisted round and stared at her friend. "Do I know him?"

"I'm sure you do. He works at the bank. Please keep it to yourself."

"You're a dark horse." Jenny grinned. "Who?"

Melanie inhaled. "Pierre from the Paris office."

Jenny choked on her drink and began to laugh.

"What's so funny?" said Melanie.

"You're such a hypocrite...Pierre?" said Jenny.

"What do you mean?" Maybe this wasn't such a good idea. Jenny was as much of a gossip as everyone else at the firm.

"You know what I mean. There you are telling me not to sleep with the traders and you're fucking one of the management team."

"He's not my manager."

"But he arranged your promotion, didn't he?"

"Sort of… But—"

"And he's introduced you to countless new clients. I can't believe I didn't spot it earlier."

"It's not like that…"

Jenny laughed again. "You be careful."

"Honestly, he doesn't have much to do with my day-to-day work life."

"Whatever you say." Jenny took another sip.

Already regretting her confession, Melanie grabbed her friend by the wrist. "Just promise you won't tell anyone."

"Don't worry, darling. I know how sensitive you are."

"Seriously. It would be awful if others found out."

"OK. OK. But tell me. How, when?"

Melanie began detailing her affair, but stopped when Jenny giggled.

"Why are you laughing?" asked Melanie.

"Well, apart from the whole management issue, the relationship itself is pretty bizarre, especially coming from you…"

"What's that supposed to mean?"

"Come on. It sounds completely masochistic. You go from being a nun to this sort of thing. Normally there is a gentle path in the middle."

Melanie rubbed her head. "I know and actually, that's why I wanted to talk to you about it."

Jenny stopped smiling. "What are you worried about exactly?"

"I'm not sure. He totally dominates me. I mean sexually. It feels immoral somehow… Not what love is supposed to be."

"Love can come in many forms. Nothing wrong with it, as long as you like it."

"Do you think so?" said Melanie.

"I'm no shrink, but what I think is that you need an outlet from being Miss Serious all the time."

"I'm not that serious."

"Give me a break. You work like hell, everyone loves you, you never seem to put a foot wrong. All that shit takes its toll and until now you've bottled it up. What you need is to lose control sometimes. Let someone else take the reins for a change."

Melanie nodded, grateful her thoughts were being articulated. "You don't think it's weird that he's aggressive sometimes?"

Jenny inched closer. "I only have one question for you. And it's the only one that matters."

"What?"

"Are you having fun?"

Melanie sipped her drink and gave her friend a shy look. "I do quite enjoy it."

"That's your answer then." Jenny's tone became stern. "But you have to keep an eye on it. The minute his sadism strays beyond the bedroom, it's time for you to walk."

"What do you mean by that?"

Jenny narrowed her eyes. "This type of man is not easy to handle. He's used to being the boss at work, and specifically he is your senior. Just be careful that he doesn't confuse your submission in bed for anything else. If he starts abusing the relationship, you have to dump him."

"I'm certainly not planning on dumping him. And besides, splitting up is hardly going to be easy, given the work issues," said Melanie.

Jenny put an arm round her. "Then, let's hope it never comes to that."

Chapter Twelve

Pierre called one morning while Melanie was on her way to work. "I'm on the Eurostar. I need you to be my whore tonight."

Melanie swivelled round, irrationally worried that somebody had overheard. "I'm yours already. You know that."

"No, I mean it. I'll see you later." He hung up the phone and she tried to regain her composure before passing through the revolving doors at the bottom of the office building.

The security man laughed when she produced the wrong card to get through the barrier. "Bad night, darling?"

"No," she said. But she was worried.

The day dragged by, as she wondered what would happen later. In her distraction, she chewed through another pen and, while she was wiping her blue lips in the bathroom mirror, she eyed herself critically. The man had turned her into a nervous wreck. A mind of jelly. A miracle she was managing her job at all. The next few meetings passed in a blur; she could focus on nothing but him.

"Hot date tonight?" Pamela asked when she came back from her lunch break with a fresh blow-dry. Melanie couldn't suppress a smile and Pamela howled with laughter.

With no particular deadlines that day, Melanie left work early, passed the gym and took the Tube to Knightsbridge, directly to the Harvey Nichols lingerie department.

Later, at home, she lit candles in the sitting room and fiddled nervously with her new black suspenders. They'd been a nightmare to put on, but Jenny had assured her they were worth it. God knows how women used to manage before hold-ups.

The doorbell rang at eight o'clock and she listened anxiously to his footsteps on the stairs.

He knocked loudly and she rose to open the door. Her eyes widened at the sight of the young man behind him.

"This is my friend Carlo," said Pierre. "I'm going to watch."

"Pierre…?" What the hell was he doing?

"Don't worry, you will love it." Pierre summoned the boy into the apartment.

"I don't know about that," she said.

But it was too late. Carlo had already started stripping her and binding her mouth. She screamed, but the sound was muffled. The man was hurting her and she struggled violently against his tight grip. What was going on? She didn't want anyone else. Why was Pierre doing this? She shifted her head and grimaced in discomfort, but Pierre lit a cigarette and settled into the leather chair. At that moment she hated him absolutely. She couldn't move, couldn't scream, with her back bruised against the hard wooden floor. Utterly powerless. Why was Pierre enjoying this excruciating humiliation?

Her body grew numb with the pain, and she attempted to distance herself from the scene, as if it were happening to someone else; anyone else but her. She glared at the boy. Beads of perspiration were gathering on his knotted forehead. Empty dark eyes bored into her. Except they weren't looking at anything. No expression at all. She didn't know whether he was enjoying it; he had clearly been paid to violate her. There was no pleasure for her either. She stared at the ceiling, willing it to end. She focused on the cornicing and the small damp patch in the corner. Anything to take her mind off this hell. It seemed to go on forever. Pierre kept smiling down at her.

At last, Pierre jumped up and pulled the man off her. "You're mine. This boy doesn't know how to please you."

He climbed on top and she clung on to his neck. He pummelled her body, ramming her head behind the sofa.

For a long time afterwards, nobody spoke. The young man in the corner was entirely forgotten as Pierre gazed into her eyes.

Finally he whispered in her ear, "You were fantastic."

Melanie wiped a tear from her eye. "There was nothing fantastic about that. It was rape."

"Darling. There is nothing wrong with pushing boundaries. If you let me show you, you'll see it can be liberating."

"You're a psychopath." She turned her head away and stared at the table.

But he didn't respond. The excitement had exhausted him. He rolled over onto the wooden floor and was asleep a few minutes later.

Melanie watched Carlo collect his clothes and head discreetly out of the flat. She didn't move until the man had gone. She had no idea where he had come from, but didn't care. Hard to focus on the fact that she had just been raped by a complete stranger. She waited until the door clicked shut, stood up and stepped over her lover. Her hands were shaking and she needed a cigarette.

She poured a shot of whisky, sank into her armchair and drank deeply. The soothing impact of the alcohol was instant and she put down the glass to light a cigarette. Curling her tongue, she blew three angry smoke rings into the air. The boy had left large bruises on her arm, but her back hurt the most. Tenderly, she placed her thumb on a large area of raw skin. She tried to remember where she had been thrown, and how she had lain. What had that been about? None of it made any sense.

Melanie lit another cigarette with the stub of the first and contemplated Pierre. It felt strange to watch him deep in slumber; he was normally so vital, oozing with energy. Looking at his masculine, rough face, she noticed for the first time that his hair was beginning to thin at the crown and she smiled to herself. He would hate that. The man had an intense power over her and it was satisfying to find an imperfection.

He woke up thirty minutes later and pulled her close. She stiffened in his embrace and averted her head, unsure how to act. Finally, he stood up and walked to the kitchen to pour a glass of water.

She followed him, with hands on her hips. "What the hell was that about?"

"Didn't you enjoy it, *chérie*? I thought you might like it."

"No, not at all. And don't you care that another man was raping me?"

Pierre laughed. "It wasn't rape. He was following my orders and you were mine entirely. It's not about penetration. That's not the point."

"What is the point? I'm confused. And very angry."

"Don't you see? I'm not jealous about sex. It's all in the mind. You can fuck a thousand men, but nobody will dominate you the way I do. You belong to me."

Melanie raised her voice. "I am not your possession and you can't treat me like that."

"*Chérie*." He took her arm. "You inspire the passion in me."

She shrugged him off. "Stop it. I'm not going to let you get away with that."

He laughed but she spat at him with anger. "I'm fucking furious."

"But *chérie*. You liked it, didn't you?"

"No, I most certainly did not." Melanie gulped. "And it makes me worry that you did."

Pierre reached out to hold her hand. "OK, my darling. I'm sorry. I won't do it again, I promise. The important thing is that we are made for each other."

She sighed, wanting to believe, hoping she would be strong enough to handle him. It was a strange relationship.

Chapter Thirteen

There was a question that had been bothering Melanie for months and one night she needed an answer. She waited until the end of the evening, knowing he would be calm then.

Passing him a cigarette, she perched on the bed next to him. "Pierre, when did you decide to pursue me?"

He kissed her. "How can a man not want to pursue you? I have always been attracted to you."

"Since when? New York or my interview?" The timing was key.

He sucked down his cigarette. "I know what you're asking. Is this why I made sure you got the job?"

"Is it?" It was a possibility that she had rejected a thousand times. But always, it came back, that small lingering doubt that she hadn't deserved the job; that he had bought her. In the end, she was no better than the rest.

"Don't look upset. The truth is that Victoria wasn't sure about you, so I did arrange the job."

"I knew it." Melanie looked away.

"Will you listen?" He pulled her close with his free hand. "Victoria made a point of never hiring other pretty girls. She hated the competition."

"But she thought I wasn't good enough. It's as simple as that."

"Now you're being ridiculous. I could sense something special in you. It was the easiest decision I have made."

It was true. Damn it. She had been chosen for sex. Did her intelligence count for nothing in this world? She huddled into herself.

"You are a funny creature," said Pierre. He put out his cigarette and wrapped his arms round her. "I didn't pick you for this reason, although I wouldn't have hesitated if I had known at the time."

"Why did you pick me then?" she said.

"*Chérie*, I hate that you doubt yourself. Why are you asking these questions? You are a remarkable woman. Unbelievably restrained on one level, but incredibly sensual on another. Your mind enchants me and I know I haven't discovered half of it yet. I love you intensely."

"Do you mean that?"

"Of course. Silly. Anyway, you've been a huge success at the firm. Your client reviews are incredible. The sales team loves you. I'm proud of my instincts and happy to take full credit for a wonderful decision."

"Yes, but in fact, I couldn't have done any of it without you." Melanie hung her head in despair. "My promotion for example. Without you, I'd still be a junior."

"Nonsense. For starters, Tony is one of your biggest fans."

"You still haven't answered my original question."

His face was close to hers, but he didn't kiss her. "If you want the truth, I was obviously attracted to you from the start, but I didn't give it much thought until our trip to New York. That lovely tight trouser suit of yours…"

His hand slid under her dressing gown and he covered her mouth with his. End of conversation.

Perhaps it didn't matter anyway. Perhaps he was right. She had proved her worth in the office and, although he had helped her so much, Pierre had very little to do with her daily work life. In any event, it was all worth it. She loved this man and didn't care how it had transpired.

A company trip to Amsterdam provided a new opportunity for an unexpected visit. She had mentioned her plans to Pierre, but was horrified when he appeared unannounced at her hotel, carrying an expensive-looking red shopping bag.

"Hello, *chérie*," he said. "I was hoping you were free for dinner tonight."

"No, Pierre. I have a lot of work. I can't go out." She glanced across at the mound of unread papers on her bed.

"We don't need to take too long. You'll be back here in plenty of time. Anyway, don't you want to see the present I bought you?"

Despite her irritation, she was curious and reached for the bag. "What?"

"Wait, wait." He put his hand inside to slowly reveal its contents. Chanel lipstick, a leather miniskirt, fishnet stockings and red lingerie.

"I don't know about this, Pierre." This was pushing things too far. Again.

"That is unkind. I've come all the way from Paris to see you. Let me dress you for dinner at least. This has been my fantasy for a very long time. Don't you want to please me?"

She nodded. There was no argument to make and he knelt down, his brow taut with concentration as he fingered the cheap stockings and applied her make-up. It was strangely erotic to stand motionless before him while he clinically transformed her into his whore.

Melanie saw her reflection in the windowpane. "I'm not going out looking like that."

"What do you care? Nobody knows you here."

"They'll recognise me at reception." How could she possibly walk through the lobby like this?

"Believe me, they've seen a lot worse here." He chuckled.

Visibly pleased with his results, Pierre led her out of the hotel and into the night.

He'd booked a restaurant down a side alley flanked by rows of twisted narrow houses, two blocks from the Grand Canal. Melanie stumbled on her high heels down the cobbled pathway and blushed when a couple of elderly American tourists pointed and stared at her in disapproval. The short skirt revealed the tops of her stockings. She was dressed like a hooker, and that was what he had intended. Despite her earlier complaints, it felt good to please him. It was becoming a strange obsession, but she loved belonging to him. They entered the restaurant and she was relieved to find that their table was in a shadowy corner. They were barely noticed.

After dinner, they strolled through the small hidden streets behind the canal until Pierre found the place he'd been searching for. He threw her into a dark corner and slapped her on the face. She kept her balance and laughed at him. But he had clearly not intended for her to be amused. His next swipe was more forceful, bruising her right cheekbone. She gasped with pain and he shoved her against the wall, forcing himself on her. He pulled her hair, tugging her head backwards. She wasn't laughing anymore; he had overwhelmed her.

The next morning, she was woken by a clatter of footsteps outside her room. Her face was throbbing with pain and her head was groggy with confusion. As she absorbed the small blue room, scattered clothes and sleeping lover by her side, she sat up sharply.

Panic set in when she realised the time. Her alarm hadn't gone off, or perhaps she had slept through it. In any event, she was dreadfully late for her first meeting.

Fumbling through her unpacked suitcase, she found her suit and dressed, then stared with horror into the mirror. A dark blue welt had formed on her right cheekbone and the swelling could not be concealed with foundation. But she was late and there was no time to waste.

She rushed to her car downstairs and told her driver to hurry. The man shrugged with indifference, barely looking at her, navigating the roads at a glacial speed.

He parked with agonising precision outside an office block by the edge of the Grand Canal. Melanie jumped out of the car before the engine was off, and raced into the glass-fronted office. She'd been there a few times before and knew where to go.

A white-haired lady at reception peered over her steel-framed spectacles, her eyes filled with suspicion. "How can I help?"

Melanie caught her breath. "Good morning. I have a nine o'clock with Hans Johansson."

"You're rather late." Fine lines popped out of the woman's lips as she sucked her mouth in disapproval. Melanie tapped her fingers on the desk, waiting while the woman called upstairs. "Fifth floor." The woman pointed at the lift and gave her a pass.

"Thanks." Melanie crossed the hall, feeling the cold eyes boring into her from behind.

The finance director of the small industrial company glanced at his watch when she came through the door. He curled his top lip. "You're extremely late."

She could sense his condemnation, knowing he was inspecting her swollen face and bloodshot eyes. "I'm sorry, Hans," she said. "I had an incident."

"I can see that." Completely monotone. No mercy then.

She pulled out her papers and tried to continue with as much dignity as she could muster. She was unprepared for the meeting and he was clearly unimpressed.

After twenty minutes of questions, he stood up abruptly. "Melanie, if you want to take up my time, please prepare yourself better. I'm a busy man."

"I'm sorry," she said again.

"Save your apologies for someone else." He stormed out of the room. The door slammed loudly and she hung her head in shame.

Her driver was waiting outside the building, but she had half an hour to kill, so she entered a small café on the corner. Her head-ache began to ease with the first sip of coffee.

She wondered what she should do about Pierre. On the one hand, he was incredibly supportive but, on the other, he didn't seem to care about interfering with her work. Melanie sighed. This was what Jenny had warned her about. The man was getting out of con-trol and she would have to address it.

In the meantime, she had to get through the day. Fortified by a couple of strong espressos and an apple pie, Melanie climbed into the back of the black Mercedes and closed her eyes. Blissfully, the drive to the next meeting would take twenty minutes, giving her time to rest. The remainder of the day was only marginally better than the beginning, but she managed to struggle through, although she was dreadfully underprepared.

Melanie took an evening flight home and arrived into her flat at ten o'clock. Despite her exhaustion, she had a sleepless night, worried about the consequences of her disastrous day. The next morning, Tony was waiting for her in the office. It was unusual to see him in so early and she could tell by his face that he was furious.

"Melanie. We need to talk," he said.

"Is it about yesterday?" She knew the answer already. "I'm afraid I messed up."

"What the hell were you doing? What were you thinking?" He was shouting now. Of course she deserved the wrath, but it was not something she'd ever heard before. Certainly not directed at her.

She shifted her position, unable to find an adequate response.

"Do you have any idea what this means?" he said.

"I'm sorry," she said, meeting his eyes. "I won't do it again."

"You just don't get it, do you? Investment banking is closing in on a deal with Hans. He called Mitch to say they are reconsidering their choice of advisors. Because of you."

"I didn't know that," she said.

"Of course you didn't, but it doesn't change the facts. Mitch is furious."

She squirmed beneath his gaze. "Tony, I wasn't myself. It won't happen again."

Tony turned away, breathing deeply. She sat in silence, waiting for him to calm down. "It's completely out of character, Melanie. What happened? Are you OK?"

"I'm fine now. It's hard to explain. I'm sorry. Let me go grovel to Mitch." The last thing in the world she desired, but it had to be done.

"Go now. He came in early and is waiting for you."

Mitch was upstairs in the office. He glowered as she approached.

"You look like shit," he said.

"I know. I came to apologise."

"You'll need to do a lot more than that. Fuck, I'm pissed off with you."

"I know. I'm sorry." This was gruelling. God, she hated sucking up to him.

"You do realise that if I'm going to keep this deal, you are no longer able to cover the stock. Hans made that very clear. Doesn't want to hear your name again."

"Was that his idea?"

"Mine, actually. But he accepted it." Mitch sneered. "You're not quite the hotshot you thought, are you?"

"I never thought that."

"Of course you do. Everyone's noticed it. You're becoming very arrogant. Watch your step, missy. One more incident like this and I'll get you fired."

She twisted her hands with anxiety. "Seriously, Mitch. It was an accident. It won't happen again. How many times do I need to apologise?"

"I'll be keeping an eye on you," he said.

She shuddered and turned to leave.

"Oh, Melanie, what the hell happened to your face? It looks like an interesting story." His laughter was tinged with cruelty.

"I don't want to talk about it."

"You don't have a choice."

Melanie hesitated. "If you must know, I think my drink was spiked at the bar, because my friend said I passed out after only one vodka. Fell on the floor and…" She pointed at her face. "It wasn't my fault."

"Don't go out drinking next time. You should be taking your job more seriously. Goodbye, Melanie."

She reached for the door and left.

She found it impossible to focus for the rest of the day. She needed to get her life back on track, needed to speak to Pierre. But although she kept calling him, he didn't answer until hours later. When he finally picked up, she moved into the office and closed the door.

"I've been trying to reach you all day," she said.

"Sorry," he said. "It's been a crazy day."

"For me too. But I wanted to talk to you about Amsterdam."

"What a wonderful evening, didn't…"

She interrupted him. "How can you call that wonderful? I'm so pissed off."

"I'm sorry for hurting you. It was not my intention to bruise you."

"It's not only about the bruise, which is appalling. Especially given that I look like shit for the world to see. I'm furious about that. But I need to talk to you about us in general."

94

"Tell me, *chérie*. You seemed to be having fun."

"You have to stop doing this." She was yelling now. "It's fucking up my life."

"Calm down." He paused. "There's no need to be dramatic. We are perfect together."

"No, Pierre. This isn't perfect and I can't keep seeing you if you interfere with my job. I've had enough of it."

"*Chérie*," he said. "I promise not to bruise you again. But not seeing me is impossible. You know that."

"Pierre…"

"This is not a good conversation to have on the phone."

"Will you please just talk to me?"

"We can discuss it further when I'm next in London. But, right now, I'm stepping into a meeting. I will call you later."

Conversation over. Nothing resolved. How did he always do that? But what had she expected anyway? For him to agree to her demands? He wasn't that kind of man.

Conscious of the need to prove herself again, her determination to succeed brought her a renewed vigour at work. Her reputation was at stake and it was vital that the Amsterdam incident was widely perceived as a one-off.

While she had no intention of ending her relationship, Pierre could not be allowed to wreck her career. It would not be an easy task, but the time had come for her to rein in her man. Unable to confront him directly, she began to subtly alter the dynamic.

From that day, Melanie was careful not to tell Pierre of her more important travel plans. And although she would never know when he might appear at her door in London, she would often let the doorbell ring unanswered.

Over the months she continued to stand her ground and, as time passed, he slowly seemed to recognise her need for space. Her only sadness was that she began to see him less frequently, but that was a small price to pay for containing his erratic moods.

Chapter Fourteen

Someone coughed next to her. Melanie kept working. Another stilted cough. She looked up, annoyed at being disturbed mid-sentence; it was always challenging to get the momentum back.

A young man was hovering a few feet away. "Good morning," he said. "I hope I'm not disturbing you."

"Hi. How can I help?" Melanie wrinkled her nose in confusion. The boy must have been in his early twenties, and was clearly anxious. He shuffled his feet and fingered what appeared to be an old school tie.

"Um. Hi. I'm Alex. The new graduate," said the man.

"Yes, of course. We met earlier this year, at the interview round." Melanie rose to shake his hand. Poor kid. "How are you? It's good to see you again."

"Thanks." He gave her a shy smile.

"Do you know something funny?" she said. "Same thing happened to me a couple of years ago." Hard to imagine where the time had gone. "They've sent you to the wrong place."

"Where am I supposed to go?" he asked. "Reception told me research was on this floor."

"It is. But you won't be working here for a few months, I'm afraid." Melanie grabbed her bag. "I was just going for a coffee anyway, so I'll take you out to HR. It's sort of on the way. I am sure they are expecting you there."

"OK, thanks," he said.

"You're on the training programme, right?"

He nodded.

"Let me tell you a secret. It's going to be spectacularly dull. The training, that is. But don't worry. It gets much better once you're at the desk."

"You know," he said, "I've been worried about all the news recently."

"What do you mean?" she said.

"The stock market crashing over the past few months… I thought they might call off the graduate programme this year."

"Don't worry about all that. Stock market crashes happen with alarming regularity." She gave a wry chuckle. "Not your problem."

"Won't it affect us?"

"Not too much I hope. There might be a few lay-offs, but it certainly won't impact you. We need cheap labour."

The boy smiled. Melanie introduced him to Pamela and then led him to HR on the fourth floor. Her own beginnings seemed an eternity ago and she remembered the angst that he also must be experiencing.

Three weeks later, management summoned her to make a presentation to the young trainees, in order to discuss her own experience at the bank. Walking down the corridor to the training centre, she caught a glimpse of herself in the reflective glass and paused to admire the tall elegant figure. Like Victoria without the terrible temper. Incredibly satisfying to have achieved so much in a relatively short space of time.

Speaking to the young crowd, she pondered on her success. There was no doubt that her work was going well, but there was something more, something intangible that had propelled her forward. She had gained a confidence over the past few months, a confidence that Pierre had breathed into her. He was a handful, but she was managing him well and their relationship had taught her so much. Because of him, she had become stronger. Powerful men and big presentations no longer frightened her.

She knew her work was highly regarded and people seemed to respect her quiet confidence. These young kids with their shining, naïve eyes were light-years away from her, and her authority over them amused her.

Her career had accelerated so unexpectedly and it was at moments like this when she realised how proud she was of her achievements.

In the new year, the team celebrated Alex's exam results in that same dingy pub George had taken her to all that time ago. Melanie hadn't been back since, but it was the appropriate rite of passage.

After Tony and Pamela had left, she poured the remainder of the wine into her glass and looked at Alex. "It's been a long week. Shall we order another bottle?"

"Sure," he said. "That would be great."

Melanie waved to the barman and, while leaning across, her long legs accidentally brushed against his.

"Oh, sorry," he said.

She laughed. "Not your fault." What an endearing boy.

Melanie topped up his glass and watched as he visibly relaxed with the effects of the alcohol. "So, how's it all going? Still enjoying the work?"

"Loving it, especially this first week at the desk," he said.

"I told you the training programme was nothing compared to the real thing."

"Yeah." Alex fingered his wine glass. "I particularly like working with you."

She smiled. "It's a fun job if you don't mind working hard."

He peered at her. "Can I ask you a question?"

"Fire away."

"How did you manage to get to VP so quickly? I mean you're not that much older than me, are you?"

"Not much older, I guess. I'm twenty-six. What about you?"

"Almost twenty-four," he said. "In a few months."

"Wow. Only two years' difference." It was amazing; he looked like a child.

"So?" he continued. "How did you do it?"

Melanie paused. Pierre had played a massive role in her promotion, but she was unable to admit it. "I guess it's mostly about hard work. And a lot of luck. The trick is for the person above you to resign, or get fired. Then you have your big chance. To fill their shoes, that is."

"But I'd hate it if you left."

"Then you'll be pleased to know I've got no plans to go anywhere." Melanie glanced across at him. It occurred to her that he was flirting. But Alex was no threat. He might have been her type at school, but now she had moved on. How life had changed.

Alex's first months were hard work, and she trained him intensively, passing most of her mundane jobs to him. She was demanding and the work had to be faultless, but he proved to be both intelligent and hard-working. She began to delegate more freely and, with Alex at the desk in the morning, Melanie allowed herself an extra fifteen minutes in bed each day. It felt luxurious to have a lie-in, although she knew she was still waking up hours before most of the city.

Melanie began to take Alex to meetings, introducing him to her clients and pushing the juniors towards him. It was harder for him than it had ever been for her, but he was charming and slowly he began to make good contacts.

Alex's progress reminded her of George. Dear old George. He'd had such an important role in her first year and had vanished just as quickly. They'd met for a drink shortly after he'd resigned, but she hadn't heard from him since. Not that she had made any effort to call him either. Her life had moved on seamlessly without him and presumably he'd forgotten about her also.

She would never forget the meeting in late February with Tony's client, a disgruntled man whose stocks had underperformed – he'd wanted to discuss them in detail. Tony was travelling and had asked her to attend in his absence. At the last minute she decided to take Alex with her.

Jeremy Baites was well into his fifties. A small man with thinning hair and hyperactive eyes. Looking at them both, he snapped, "Where's Tony?"

"Apologies," said Melanie. "I thought Tony mentioned I was coming in his place."

"He didn't. Bloody rude of him."

"Gosh, that's not like Tony. Maybe the message didn't get through." Belligerent bastard.

Jeremy sucked his teeth. "Well, since you're here, please can you get me a coffee."

Melanie raised her eyebrows. But Jeremy continued. "Young man. Sit here. I assume you are able to discuss the sector with me. Won't be as good as Tony, I'm sure, but you might as well stay for a few minutes."

Alex shifted in his chair and glanced at Melanie, who had begun to pour the coffee. Despite the rudeness, the situation was amusing. She gave Jeremy his coffee. "Milk?"

"Yes. One sugar." The man barely glanced up.

"Jeremy, I think there has been some misunderstanding," said Melanie. "Alex has recently joined us. I am the lead analyst on quite a few of the stocks. Perhaps I can be of some assistance?"

"What?" Jeremy shunted his seat backwards. "Oh, well then, come sit down, my dear."

He patted the chair next to him and scratched his head, noticeably grimacing at his mistake. Melanie took the milk back to the sideboard and pulled the presentation from her bag.

"Where would you like to start?" she said. "I've brought the full sector report or would you prefer to concentrate on the individual stocks in your portfolio?"

"Only the ones I own. Let's start with the UK mid-caps. I'm not sure whether or not to bite the bullet and get rid of the bloody things."

"Why don't we start with Abacus? Last week's results weren't helpful, were they?"

"Understatement of the century. Why have you still got a BUY on the stock? Bloody useless."

"Quite the contrary," she said. "I think the market has been overly focusing on this quarter's revenues. A complete irrelevance."

"What are you talking about?" He was still being aggressive, but she could tell she had his attention.

"Take a look at this." Melanie pointed to some figures in her report. "It's far more important. Look at the recurring revenue stream and the massive project that kicks in next quarter. I'd be adding to your position now. Take advantage of the dip in the share price."

"None of the other brokers are saying that. I saw one yesterday."

"Therein lies the opportunity, don't you think?" she said.

The man was in a fluster. "Perhaps."

"But honestly, if you want to talk about dogs in your portfolio, this one here is a disaster waiting to happen." She pointed to a name on his list. "Useless management, in my opinion."

"Funnily enough, I haven't met the new CEO yet."

"Do. You'll see what I mean and you'll sell right away. The man's a moron. Who thinks he's clever."

"Worst kind of combination." Jeremy chuckled into his mug. "Can I offer you another coffee?"

"Lovely," she said. When he had turned his back, Melanie winked at her junior. It was clearly going to be a long meeting, but the man had been successfully turned around.

Afterwards, they laughed their way out of the building. "You were fantastic," said Alex. "And the look on his face at the beginning. Total classic."

"Not much point getting upset about it. He's a fossil – been around far too long to be politically correct."

"Sure, but he was impressed. You could tell."

"I hope so. It's a step in the right direction, I guess. But it will take a while before attitudes change completely."

"How can they not, with women like you?"

"You are sweet." Melanie smiled across at him.

They walked back to the office and she looked at her watch. Five thirty. "Hey, I think I'm going to leave early today. Want to go to the gym."

"God, you're disciplined."

"No, not really. The truth is I am way too lazy to get to the gym before work."

"Still," he said. "Where do you find the time?"

"I make the time. Better to pound away at the treadmill than yell at stupid clients. I don't see an alternative."

Alex laughed. What she didn't tell him was that she wanted to pound away the frustration of not seeing her man often enough. Her recent focus on work had meant fewer evenings with Pierre and she missed him.

Chapter Fifteen

The yearly March conference in New York was the major highlight of the calendar. She'd never been invited before, since there had always been someone more senior from her team going. But this time, Tony's wife was heavily pregnant with their third child and he had asked her to take his place. The bank was preparing a conference for their investors and her role was to introduce some of the companies.

Melanie arrived on Tuesday evening and went directly to her hotel, off West Broadway, where she had arranged to meet Josh, her old friend from the training programme. The hotel was eclectic but stylish, and the club room was throbbing with young men and impossibly glamorous women. Josh was already at the bar, talking to the waitress. He had changed since her last visit. Older and better looking. He carried his maturity handsomely, with the inner confidence of success. He had also been promoted and was clearly enjoying life on Wall Street.

Accepting a drink, Melanie sat down next to him. "So tell me your news. Have you moved on from Jenny yet?"

He grinned. "Jenny broke my heart, as we all know."

"Bullshit." Melanie smiled into her drink. "So who's the new girlfriend?"

Josh chuckled. "Nobody has a serious girlfriend in this town, Mel. There are too many hot women here. It would be impossible to choose. Not to mention a total waste."

Melanie shook her head. "No wonder you and Jenny get on so well. You are her male equivalent."

"Jenny's a total babe. I do miss her. But what about you? You've never talked much about your sex life."

"Not much to talk about."

"I don't believe that crap for a minute. You are pretty sexy. I am sure you know that."

"Oh, I don't know…"

"The thing is, you get hotter every time I see you. You were totally timid on the training course. Something must be going right in your life."

Melanie blushed. "Yeah, I guess so."

"Hopefully that means you're dating a lot then?"

"I'm a one-man girl."

Josh inched closer and winked. "Am I going to be that man tonight?"

Melanie pushed him away and giggled. "Sorry, darling. I don't share with my friends. Anyway, you're not my type."

"To hell with it. You're not my type either," he said. "Let's get pissed. Isn't that how you say it?" Josh waved at the barman and ordered another bottle of champagne.

It was amusing to see him again and, over the course of the next two hours, she enjoyed the banter. Josh never took anything too seriously. Such a shame he didn't live in London. She needed more friends like him.

There was no trace of hangover the next morning, with the jet lag working wonderfully in her favour. Plenty of time for coffee and a long hot shower.

The conference centre in Midtown was too far to walk, and Melanie waved down a taxi outside the hotel.

From the window, she watched the masses rush to work. Everyone in a hurry, earnestly speaking a little too loudly into their phones, in that self-important manner that seemed unique to the Americans. Or perhaps it was just New Yorkers. Those men in slick suits and elegant women with their incongruous white trainers. Americans were just different.

They arrived at the side entrance of the hotel and she paid the driver, who yelled at her after she closed the door. He clearly wasn't impressed by her European tip. She'd have to remember that for the next time.

With plenty of time to spare, Melanie made a diversion to the bathrooms and took a few minutes in front of the mirror to compose herself. Checking her hair and make-up, she burned with pride. She had come so far and was now about to present to hundreds of complete strangers.

Adrenaline buzzing, she bounded upstairs and made her way to the podium. She had arrived early and, with the exception of two young analysts at the back, the room was still empty. The two men paid her no attention, presumably still making notes from a previous presentation.

It was an odd thought that, in a few minutes, this huge room would be brimming with people and she would be addressing them all. At least it wouldn't be that difficult; she was only there to make an introduction and ask a few questions. But it would be the largest audience she had ever seen and, for a short while, they would all be listening to her.

Once the auditorium was full and it was her turn to stand on the stage, the projectors came on and the light temporarily blinded her. She blinked a few times, but the words tumbled out. All pre-rehearsed and terribly easy. It was over in a flash and she handed the podium to the Scottish CEO on her left.

With her job finished, she relaxed and began to look into the audience. A sea of men in blue suits, with an occasional dash of colour. It was odd that there were so few women in the crowd. She had always assumed that American women were more aggressively career-oriented and had expected to see more.

After the presentation, she walked out of the auditorium to stretch her legs.

"That was very impressive." A dark-haired man was standing inches away.

"Excuse me?" She was aware of herself staring at him, instantly compelled by an extraordinary magnetism.

"How rude of me. I'm Lorenzo and I am very pleased to meet

you, Melanie." Honeyed eyes bored deep and for those few moments, the crowd disappeared and time was suspended. She stood still, mouth agape.

"Lorenzo." She could barely whisper his name, speechless by the power he exuded. Who was this man?

"Melanie. Melanie!" She was abruptly brought back to reality by her sales man. "I've been looking for you. You're on again in five minutes."

"Oh. OK. Thanks." But she was still looking at the Italian. Saying nothing further, she handed him her business card, then reluctantly turned away from him, back into the darkened room. She knew that something powerful had happened and that he would be watching her still. She stiffened her back self-consciously and vainly tried to focus on the task ahead.

Later, she would not be able to recall the speech she gave on that stage or who she had been presenting to. Her mind was clogged. Lorenzo? Who was he? How had he known her name?

Instead of concentrating on the presentation, she was trying to remember what had been written on his label. Impossible; she could only think of his face, those eyes. The rest had happened too quickly.

Was he a fund manager, perhaps a client of hers? She had never heard of him, but anything was possible. Perhaps he was a company director. What was he doing here? She had to find out more.

When the session ended she rushed back to the lobby, but he had gone, disappearing from her life as suddenly as he had arrived. And he didn't return for the remainder of the day. Confused by the surge of emotion, she packed her bag after her final presentation and stepped outside.

The sheer mass of people streaming out into the cold annoyed her intensely. Difficult to cross the street without being jostled by a stranger; everyone was in a hurry. And, without exception, they all seemed to be in a bad mood. But she had nowhere to go for a few hours and she meandered through the crowds. Finally, she took a taxi, her feet fatigued by the pain of wearing stilettos for a full day.

*

Lorenzo was still on her mind when she returned to her hotel room and kicked off her shoes. The attraction had been instant and powerful. For the first time she found herself thinking of a man other than Pierre.

Perhaps she had imagined it, but his smile had suggested he was interested.

With every inch of her body, she willed him to call. And willed him to call soon.

Rubbing herself dry after a hot shower, she heard the phone ring and raced to answer. A New York number. Was it him?

He didn't disappoint. "Melanie. How are you?" No need for an introduction. What an incredible voice he had.

"How lovely to hear from you. I just got back to my room," she said.

"Where are you staying?"

"In SoHo."

"I love SoHo. Great choice. Listen, are you free tonight? My business dinner has been cancelled and I would very much like to take you out instead."

No need for games. "That sounds tremendous. I have no plans tonight."

"Wonderful. I will pick you up at seven thirty."

Melanie called Josh to cancel their prior plans, feigning a headache. Her mind was set and she prepared herself for the evening. An inexorable path, which she was incapable of resisting.

Time dragged. She filled the hour, applying make-up and blow-drying her hair. There wasn't much choice of wardrobe, but she'd thankfully packed a decent bra.

Entering the lift, she glanced at herself in the mirror and checked her hair, pleased with what she saw. Her infidelity to Pierre had already happened in her conscience and she cast aside all feelings of guilt. Pierre was not the possessive sort and, in any event, she didn't plan to tell him. Tonight, there was no place for being rational.

The lift stopped and she took a deep breath before entering the marbled lobby. He was waiting for her. She looked straight into his eyes. Desire coursed through her veins. How improbable and how unexpected. She had never felt such attraction at first sight. He clasped her waist and kissed her on the cheek, his mouth tantalisingly close to hers. She almost begged for more, almost begged him to come straight to her room, but the evening would be long enough for everything.

They went to a restaurant on West Broadway, only a block away from the hotel. There was no doubt where the night would end and they flirted, deep in the knowledge that they would be back in the hotel shortly. Perhaps they spoke about their lives but she would never remember the details. Their identities made no difference.

He took her fingers across the table and kissed them slowly, looking up at her, seeking confirmation in her eyes. She moved closer to him and he placed his mouth on hers. This man exuded sex and her whole being burned for him.

Wordlessly, he took her back to her room. Every pore demanded him and he was flawless. Her skin seared as he unbuttoned the back of her dress and slid his hand underneath. He gasped at her lack of underwear. His fingers probed deeper.

Gripping the pillow, she arched her back and pushed herself towards him. The warmth spread and she shuddered with the revelation; until this man, she had never been able to enjoy the art of receiving. Breathing heavily, she pulled him upwards, enjoying his taste, his smell, his very essence. She had become entirely his and, feeling him against her body, she wanted him desperately. She was ravenous for him; this stranger who had come from nowhere and was now everything she craved.

She kissed him again, cried out with pleasure and let go entirely. She would never remember how many times, or perhaps the entire experience was too intense to differentiate one from the next.

They lay together for a long while after, his head on her stomach. She stroked his sweat-streaked hair.

Finally he spoke. "I have never met anyone like you."

Perhaps it was a lie, but it was a sweet lie and she leaned forward to kiss him. There were no words for what had happened. No need to talk.

She lay convulsed, in a trance. No shame, no guilt. Gazing at her new lover, she wondered at the authority of her body. It had dictated that this happen. A culmination of all her desires and fantasies; there could have been no other option tonight. He was unlike any other lover she had had. Pierre was totally different, so much rougher. It was impossible to compare the two. Certainly, Pierre had begun to mould her, but now she was moving forward on her own, learning how to express her needs more fully.

They made love again that night and he left before daybreak. He kissed her and promised to call. She closed her eyes, desperate to keep the moment fresh. Knowing that she would see him again.

Chapter Sixteen

But he didn't call and, despite the initial disappointment, a few evenings with Pierre helped to shove Lorenzo firmly into the past. When she thought of that night in New York, it might almost have happened to someone else. A dream that had no place in her life. At least that was what she managed to convince herself – until the day he found a reason to contact her.

She was at her desk as usual at seven o'clock. One of Tony's favourite companies had just unexpectedly produced their results. Tony's phone was ringing.

Melanie picked up the line. "Hello."

"Hi, is Tony there?" It was Jenny's colleague, Jonathan.

"No, it's Melanie. How can I help?"

"Have you seen Samaris's figures? Market seems to be saying they're OK. Got a client wanting to know his thoughts."

"He's travelling. Marketing in Asia somewhere. God knows where. I've already tried calling him but he's not answering."

"Shit," said Jonathan. "Makes us look incompetent."

"It's not his fault. They didn't tell us the numbers were coming out today."

"Still, that's not great," said Jonathan. "What can we do?"

"Don't worry. I'll keep trying him. We're also going through it and will have something for you soon."

The truth was that although everything seemed fine on the surface, something about the numbers didn't make sense to her. She opened Tony's spreadsheet and spent a few minutes poring over the numbers, comparing Tony's forecasts with the company's results.

She turned to her colleague. "Jesus, Alex. I'm going to have to downgrade. Look at this." She pointed to some of the figures that were out of sync.

"Are you sure? Tony's going to kill you," said Alex.

"I know. But that's part of the job, I guess. Try calling him."

"I have." Alex paused. "You don't have to do it, you know. He can always downgrade when he gets back. It's only a matter of a few days."

"But then I wouldn't be a good analyst if I ignored my instincts."

Melanie took a deep breath and returned to her computer to compile a quick report. Once it was finished, she pressed the send button, phoned compliance and raced downstairs to the trading floor. It was too late for the morning meeting, but there was still time before the market opened at eight. She spoke to the head trader and took the microphone.

"Good morning. This is Melanie Collins from the Industrials team and today we are downgrading our recommendation on Samaris from BUY to SELL. Although the numbers are superficially in line with market expectations, we have grave concerns about the earnings quality and believe that margin progression has deteriorated substantially in their key steels sector. The note should be on your emails and we will be publishing a detailed report later today."

Jonathan ran up to her. "Are you sure about this?"

"Yeah, I'm sure." She was terrified, but it was never a good idea to show weakness. Especially on the trading floor.

"You better be right," said Jonathan. "Not a single other investment bank has made that call."

"I know," she said.

"Does Tony know about this?"

"Not yet. Wish me luck." She laughed with a confidence she didn't feel and moved off around the floor to deal with further questions.

Back at her desk, she held her breath. When the stock market opened at eight, she watched in trepidation as the stock price ticked steadily upwards.

Had she made a terrible mistake? Pierre was always telling her to be more controversial, to stick her neck out. To be different from the rest. He would have approved of this, but maybe she'd pushed it too far. On Tony's stock. What had she been thinking?

By the time the conference call with the company's management team began at half past eight, she was a wreck. Desperate for a cigarette, but with no time to go outside.

After the finance director gave his presentation on the call, Melanie asked him a question about the company's underlying profitability and the man's answer was fumbled and weak. The silence that followed spoke volumes. She had been right all along. Within minutes, her screen showed the price slide sharply and, within an hour, the stock had dropped fifteen per cent. Alex was watching too. He grinned.

Her phone rang all morning and by midday, she was tired of her own voice, of repeating the same answers again and again. She was unprepared, though, for the call that came at two o'clock.

"Hello, Melanie." The Italian accent was unmistakable and she lurched backwards in the chair. Despite herself, she bit her lip with excitement.

"Lorenzo, how are you?" The morning's exhilaration evaporated. He had her entire attention. The fact that he hadn't called before didn't matter now.

"I am short of that stock; you are doing me a real favour."

She laughed. "I'm happy someone is pleased."

"I'm more pleased to be speaking to you," he said.

"Me too."

"I need to come to London in the next month or two. I wondered if I could see you. I could come earlier if that suited you."

She froze. Every inch of her body remembered that night of pure sex, remembering his mouth, his touch and the yearning she had carried with her for weeks. She hadn't stopped thinking about him. But it wasn't fair on Pierre. He wasn't the most conventional boyfriend, but he'd been more respectful recently and this didn't feel right.

"Lorenzo," she said. "I'd love to see you. It would give me such pleasure, as I am sure you know. But I have a boyfriend and I can't do this."

He laughed. "Of course you do. It's impossible that someone like you can be without a man. You are too special. But let's meet for a coffee. Nothing more, I swear. I need to see you."

"I'd love that," she said. "Call me when you make your plans."

She put the phone down and kept writing her report. Not that it was easy to concentrate. She wanted that man so badly. She forced herself to focus. It had to be finished that day, and she didn't particularly want to be up all night.

Tony called a few hours later to congratulate her. "Sorry it's taken me so long to get back."

"That's OK, Tony. Panic over."

"But seriously, well done. Can't believe I was hoodwinked by them. I met the CFO last month and he assured me everything was fine."

"I think that's what he told everyone," she said.

"Congratulations. It was a good call. Ballsy too. I'm proud of you."

"Thanks, Tony. Do you want to see my report? I'm almost done."

"Sure, send it through. I'm picking up emails now and will go through it right away."

Melanie hung up the phone. What an extraordinarily gracious man. Somehow he lacked the ego that was prevalent in so many of her colleagues.

Chapter Seventeen

Life neatly divided into four. Easier to handle when she thought of it that way. Work, play, gym and sleep. The only areas of overlap were drinks with clients. She could have lunch with the least interesting ones, but often she would take her better clients for a drink after work. Her favourite remained Simon, who had continued to support her progress. Since their first coffee, they had spoken on a weekly basis and his backing had boosted her reputation within the investment community, as well as on her own trading floor.

A month after changing Tony's stock recommendation, she met Simon at a bar near his office. He was grinning. "Hey, I have great news."

"What's that?" she said.

"My senior fund manager is retiring next month. Which means…"

"That you'll be in charge from now on." She leaned over to kiss him on the cheek. "What fabulous news. Let me buy you a drink."

"That's not a celebration." Simon rolled his eyes. "You always buy anyway, remember? You're the broker, I'm the client."

"Yes. But I'll buy it this time. Me. Not my company. Just to show you how much I care." She beamed at him.

"You know what this means?" he said.

"What?" Of course she knew, but it was polite to pretend.

"My vote counts for more and you'll get my vote every time."

She hugged him. "You are such an amazing friend to me. How can I ever thank you?" It was thrilling news. There was a direct correlation between the votes and the commission her firm received.

And she would gain a great deal of the credit, not to mention a bigger bonus. Definitely worth buying him a drink, not that she wouldn't have anyway.

As she was drinking her final glass of wine, her phone rang loudly from her bag. It was Jenny.

Melanie excused herself and took the call.

"Mel. Hello. Mel?!"

"Yes, hi, Jenny."

"I'm at JB's. Met a great guy. Come and join." Melanie held the phone away from her ear. The background music in Jenny's bar meant that her friend was yelling.

"Not now. Just here with Simon."

"Bring him along," said Jenny. "Haven't seen him in ages. It's Thursday. Come on."

"Not sure. Let's see later. Got to go now." Melanie shoved the phone back into her handbag.

Simon smirked. "That friend of yours is a bit mad, you know that?"

"Yeah, but she's great."

"She must be doing something right," said Simon. "My colleagues never stop talking about her."

"She is really pretty." Melanie swirled her glass. She had yet to meet a man who didn't find Jenny attractive.

"Sure. But she's also unbelievably clever. Apparently she's one of the best sales people in the City right now. They love taking her calls."

"Seriously? I mean, doesn't surprise me, but that's great." Finally a compliment that wasn't based on Jenny's looks. So refreshing.

"What did she want anyway?" said Simon.

"She invited us to a bar. Want to come?" said Melanie.

Simon laughed. "I think my girlfriend is pretty understanding for not minding me having a drink with you…but you and Jenny? Forget it!"

"I thought you weren't judging her by her looks," said Melanie.

"I'm not, but my girlfriend might think differently."

"You're saying I'm not pretty enough to upset Fiona?"

"Shut up. That's not what I'm saying." He blushed furiously.

"Don't worry. I'm teasing," she said. But actually it was annoying. Of course she never wanted to flirt with Simon, but somehow it still hurt.

"Darling, speaking of my girlfriend, I should get going. I'm supposed to go to hers for dinner tonight. She's cooking for a change."

"Sure, of course. Lovely to see you."

"You too." He kissed her on the cheek and left.

Melanie watched him depart. Such a good man. Why couldn't she have ever fancied a stable man like that? So much easier than Pierre. Not to mention Lorenzo.

Her phone rang. Jenny again.

She answered. "Fine, I'm coming!"

The prospect of going home to her empty flat didn't appeal, particularly after a few glasses of wine. Melanie crossed the street and stopped at the corner, near the traffic lights. A taxi appeared two minutes later; she curled into the back and gazed outside. They drove up the Strand, past the bright lights and down an unpromising alleyway.

She paid the driver and meandered down the street until she found the neat black entrance, complete with a green neon light.

Stepping inside, she smiled. Typical of Jenny to have found it first. Cool and slick, with a beautiful young clientele.

The darkness of the room made it difficult to locate her friend and Melanie inched self-consciously around the bar. Finally she found her, sitting on a bench in the corner. Jenny was laughing. Obviously drunk, with one leg draped over a man's lap.

Jenny waved her over. "Hey, you made it. You've got a lot of catching up to do."

"Uh, hi," said Melanie. "Are you sure I'm not interrupting?"

"Don't be silly. This is Oli." Jenny pointed at the man. "We met for lunch and have carried on until now."

"We've been waiting for you," said Oli. Not handsome, but with the self-assurance of a wealthy man.

"Sorry I'm late," said Melanie, sitting down. "Client drinks. You know."

"Oli," Jenny said, "Melanie loves champagne."

"Of course she does," said Oli with a wry look. "Just like you apparently. At least you're both cute, I guess. I'll get another bottle."

Melanie watched him walk to the bar. "Where did you pick up this one?"

"He's my new big client. We've been emailing for weeks. Finally met him today."

"Why are you flirting with your client, for God's sake?" said Melanie. "Not as if you're desperate."

"Don't be boring. He's so much fun." Jenny giggled. "Anyway, what do you think?"

"OK, I guess," said Melanie. "Not crazy about the slicked-back hair though. Bit sleazy-looking."

"He's hot property," said Jenny. "Been running his own hedge fund for five years. He's only thirty-two. Made a killing apparently."

"Why are you so impressed by money? You've got enough of your own."

"It's not the money, idiot. Just love successful men. They're much sexier. Don't you agree?"

"Whatever," said Melanie. "He's not my type and I'm not in the market anyway."

"Suit yourself," said Jenny. "Apart from the dodgy brown shoes, he's perfect."

"You're such a snob." Melanie glanced down at Oli's pointed toes when he returned, clutching another bottle.

He poured the glasses. "Here you go." He passed one to Melanie. "We have a lot to celebrate."

"What are we celebrating?" said Melanie.

"Launch of my new fund," he said. "Fucking fantastic news."

Melanie raised her eyebrows. Maybe he was drunk, but the man hadn't taken long to irritate her.

"That's amazing news." Jenny flicked her hair; a guaranteed sign of her interest. "How much have you got under management?"

"For the new fund, only fifty million for now. But that's on top of our existing two billion."

"Wow," said Jenny. "Not bad. I mean, it's not easy raising funds right now."

"Not for most people. But for us, the money is rolling in. I tell you, we've been shorting the shit out of the market. Made a fortune this year. Clients love it. Not to mention my bank manager." He chuckled to himself.

Melanie looked away. Another arrogant hedge fund manager. They could be such wankers sometimes. Was she supposed to be impressed by this self-promoting tycoon of the investment industry? Just because he'd happened to have hit the jackpot? She had yet to spot any redeeming features apart from his obvious newfound wealth.

A few glasses later, she leaned over to her friend. "We should get out of here. I need to eat something."

Jenny reached over to the other side of the table for a bowl, without taking her eyes off the man. "You'll be fine. Here, have some nuts."

"That's hardly going to help." But Melanie took the cashews, knowing that her sense of judgement was diminishing by the second.

When they'd finished a third bottle, Oli called for the bill. "Let's get out of here. There's more at my flat."

"Fantastic idea," said Jenny.

Melanie put on her coat. "I think I'll call it a night. Got some results tomorrow. Best to get some sleep tonight."

"You can't leave. It's still early." Jenny grabbed her hand. "Just a quick drink. I need you. Please come."

Melanie nodded her head wearily. "OK. I'm not hanging around though."

They climbed into his black Audi and, despite the alcohol, Oli drove them smoothly back to his flat in Battersea. Melanie stretched her legs out onto the red leather seats in the back. She watched the lights of London as the car made its way down the Embankment and over the bridge. Oli had turned the music up high. One hand was on the wheel and the other was steadily moving up Jenny's leg.

Sitting behind them, Melanie didn't understand why she was there. Except that Jenny had asked her to come and the promise of more champagne was always tempting.

The electronic garage door swallowed them up and they piled out into the darkness below. Melanie stumbled on the uneven floor. The place was eerily quiet and their footsteps echoed across the empty space. Jenny giggled loudly in front of her. Strange that there were no other cars. He led them into a lift that, with the turn of a key, opened directly into his penthouse apartment.

A black sofa filled one side of the front room, next to a glass coffee table, with two grey ashtrays and a bottle of champagne. Her eyes were drawn to the lights on the bridge below. Oli pointed over to his dining room. Four lines of cocaine on the table. He had clearly been hoping for visitors.

Jenny swivelled round to look at Melanie. "Wow. This looks like fun."

"Not for me." Melanie backed off. This was way over her head.

"Come on," said Jenny. "Don't tell me you've never done coke before?"

"No. Actually not." Why was she always the boring one?

Oli took their coats and tossed them across a chair. "Don't worry, sweetheart. I'll get you some champagne." He came back with a glass and placed his hand on Jenny's back, while she leaned down to snort the cocaine. With a wide smile, Jenny stood up unsteadily and fell into Oli's ready grip.

Melanie took a long sip of her drink and studied the remaining lines on the table. Should she try it? No. Something was holding her back and she moved to the other side of the room, ready to gather her coat again.

Oli called over. "Don't go yet, darling. No more of this, I promise."

"It's getting late. I really should—"

"No. Here, drink up." He filled her glass again.

She wasn't sure what happened next. Floating mid-air. Oli removing her dress. He was already naked. As was Jenny. Her last thoughts that night were how beautiful her friend was, her skin, her mouth, so soft and luxurious. Three bodies melting, one indistinguishable from the other. She heard a scream, not knowing if it was hers or Jenny's, not caring as she drifted towards unconsciousness.

*

When she woke up hours later, her head was pounding. She was on the living-room sofa. A blanket covered her naked body. Melanie looked around in bewilderment. What had happened? Where was she? The memories of the night before flooded back and she bit her lip with concern. She was sure she'd kissed them both, but had she had sex with Oli? God forbid. She touched herself guiltily, her heart sinking with the confirmation. That was the second time she had cheated on Pierre. And with a complete low-life. Jesus. She had managed to convince herself Lorenzo was a one-off, that it didn't count. But now this changed things. Even if it hadn't been deliberate, it was starting to become a habit. And a dangerous one. And what about Jenny? She'd never thought of her friend like that. Maybe this was like the orgies Jenny always talked about.

Still clutching the blanket, Melanie searched for the others. They were lying intertwined, asleep on the bed. Clearly they had carried on without her. She returned to the living room and reached for her dress. She stretched over the coffee table for her shoes and caught a glimpse of herself in the mirror. The bloodshot eyes and tousled hair belonged to someone else. She moved away and slammed the door behind her. It was already half past five and she had to go home to change.

She was ravenous. They hadn't eaten any dinner last night and she desperately needed something to soak up the champagne. The stale bread on her kitchen counter seemed to taunt her, so she opted for a cigarette, her hand shaking violently while she tried to light it. Staggering into the shower, Melanie turned the water to cold, a trick that usually jolted her back to reality. But her head was bursting and it made no difference. In the mirror her usually glowing skin was sallow and a couple of unwelcome spots had emerged on her chin. Where had those come from? She looked like hell and the make-up made little difference.

Melanie had never felt so sick in her life, but one of her companies had an announcement that day and she had to be in the office by seven at the latest. What had she been thinking? Only an idiot would have gone out the night before. With a heavy heart, she left her flat and waved down a taxi. She couldn't face the Tube today. The driver dropped her off by the corner of her building and she raced through reception to the lift.

Her mobile had run out of batteries overnight and the office phone was ringing when she reached her desk at quarter past seven. "Where the hell have you been?" It was one of the traders downstairs.

"Sorry," she said. "Bad traffic."

"What the hell is your problem? Haven't you seen the news?"

"No." Melanie fumbled with her computer, desperate to turn it on. "What's happened?"

"Jesus, woman. You're the fucking analyst. It's Absolution. Bloody profit warning."

"I'll take a look now and get back to you."

"Make it quick." The phone went quiet.

Shit. Even in her alcohol-ridden state, she could tell the stock was going to drop like a stone. Today, of all days. She'd have to change her recommendation to SELL. Melanie could hardly focus on the print, but somehow pieced together a quick report. Clearing it with the compliance department, she walked downstairs to the trading floor to make the announcement.

Everyone was yelling. The traders were cursing her late arrival and Jonathan's biggest client had a huge position in the stock. Jonathan was furious. "Get over here now," he said. "My client Luke wants to speak to you. How did you get this so wrong?"

She lowered her head. "Sorry. I saw the company quite recently. This news is completely out of the blue."

"Luke better be your first call of the day," said Jonathan. "He bought the stock on your recommendation, and now he's got his face covered in shit. Makes me look moronic too. How could you not know their market was weakening, given all the press out there?"

"Sorry. I'll phone him as soon as I'm back at my desk."

Jonathan glared at her. "Keep me in touch."

"OK." She breathed in and stepped away.

The day was going to be a nightmare. Luke wasn't the only client with a big position. She had put her neck out on this recommendation and it had backfired horribly. To make matters worse, Tony and Alex were both out of the office. No backup at all.

Melanie hurried back to the lift and saw Jenny waving at her. How on earth did she manage to look immaculate, as if nothing had happened? Now was not the time to think about it, so she ignored her friend and kept going. To hell with Jenny anyway. She needed to concentrate on her work and didn't want to dwell on the night before.

Tony called in from Paris, concerned about the profit warning. All she wanted was to go back to bed, but she had to persevere. With no time for lunch, she begged Pamela to buy her a coffee, a bacon sandwich and several chocolate bars from Pret A Manger.

Melanie had no idea how she made it through the day, and she lost count of the number of abusive phone calls and different ways she found to apologise. One bad investment call and the whole prior year's performance was forgotten. Bottom of the research scrapheap. It would take a while to climb back up. Oh, well, it wasn't as if she was the first to go through this shit. She wouldn't be the last either. They would pick on someone else tomorrow.

When the day was over, she returned to her flat and collapsed into an armchair. A few minutes later, her mobile started to ring.

It was Jenny. "You were looking stressed today. Wanted to check you're OK."

"No, I'm not bloody OK. I'm furious. Didn't you see Absolution's profit warning?"

"Yeah, I saw. Sorry about that. Bad luck." Bad luck? Was Jenny completely out of touch?

"And, as you well know, I was hardly in the best shape to deal with it. Thanks to you."

"Thought you did a great job, all things considered."

"In case you didn't get the message, I'm pretty pissed off about yesterday."

"But at least you must have had fun, didn't you?" said Jenny.

"Your bloody boyfriend spiked my drink. What part of that is supposed to be fun?"

"Lighten up," said Jenny.

"You are demented," Melanie shouted. "That's rape, you know."

How could Jenny think it was normal behaviour? Was she that depraved?

"Oh, please, it's nothing compared to what you've done with Pierre."

"Leave Pierre out of this." The mention of his name filled her with guilt.

"Fine, but you can't expect to go back to a guy's house and for nothing to happen."

"Not rape."

"You were just pissed. There was no rape."

"I don't know what planet you're on. That's real abuse."

"I honestly thought you'd like it. I did," said Jenny. "And Oli gave me a massive order today."

"I don't give a shit about that. God, you are self-obsessed. Think about somebody else for a change."

"Mel—"

"Look, I don't want to talk about last night. Let's drop it," said Melanie.

"OK, OK. I get it," said Jenny. "And I'm sorry you're upset. It was supposed to be fun. Doesn't mean anything. Let's have dinner this week. Just us."

"Let's see. I can't focus on this right now." Not only was she disgusted with herself physically, she had come close to ruining her reputation at work. Again. Damned Jenny. It had been a dreadful day and she could only hope it wouldn't have any serious repercussions.

Thankfully, Pierre wasn't in town that week. She hadn't seen him for such a long time and should probably call him, but she couldn't face a conversation; she needed to sleep off her excess. For the first time she was grateful that he didn't live in London.

Thank goodness it was a Friday night. Melanie switched off her phone and plunged into a restless sleep.

That night, Lorenzo's face appeared in her dreams, smiling at her, all the while making love to Jenny. She woke up with a start, sweating and disoriented. Her sheets were drenched and she tore off her sodden T-shirt. Her world was becoming confused and twisted and she was beginning to lose her grip.

She woke late the next morning and turned on her phone. A text from Lorenzo and three messages from Pierre. God, life was complicated. If only she could crawl into a hole and forget them all. She'd deal with Lorenzo later. Rubbing her eyes, she made herself an espresso and called Pierre.

"*Chérie*, what's going on?"

"Sorry, Pierre, it's been crazy here and I needed a big sleep. Had a terrible time at work this week."

"I heard about it," he said. "I've been trying to call you. Didn't you see my email?"

"No," she said. "I've been inundated. Sorry, darling."

"Don't beat yourself up. The market's nuts right now. There are going to be a lot of negative surprises coming up. I can tell you that for sure."

"Thanks. I guess you're right. But I should have seen it coming. I'm feeling a little out of touch with it all."

"As long as you're not out of touch with us? I was beginning to think you had forgotten about me." He laughed. A laugh that was for the first time infused with real concern.

"How could I ever forget you, darling? I miss you so much," Melanie said without hesitation. She loved him and she resolved to become more deserving.

"I miss you too, *chérie*. I have been thinking about you constantly."

"Can you come this week?" He was being so kind. It only intensified her guilt.

"Unfortunately this week is manic here," he said. "The market is playing havoc, as you know."

"Oh, Pierre." Her shoulders sagged with disappointment.

"Don't worry, *chérie*. I'll figure something out. Tell me, what are you wearing?"

Chapter Eighteen

She hadn't anticipated being rewarded for her sins. Her unintention-
ally neglecting him had made Pierre more eager to impress her. Since
Amsterdam, their relationship had calmed down and he had visited
less frequently. But now he must have known that something was
amiss and was clearly desperate to win her back.

The first-class ticket arrived in her inbox on Monday morning
with a message. "Friday night in New York?" Melanie sat back in her
chair and beamed. An entire weekend in New York with Pierre. First
class! It was unbelievable how New York had become such a pivotal
point for so much of her life.

Two minutes later, her phone rang. Lorenzo. She inhaled.
Having ignored his texts over the weekend, she was unsure how to
react. With a shaking hand, she took the call. "Lorenzo, how are
you?"

"Melanie! I'm relieved to get hold of you," he said.

She smiled at the sound of his voice, her previous concerns
evaporating. "Good to hear from you."

"Hope you received my text. I just arrived into Heathrow."

"Of course I got it. Wonderful news." She gulped, not understanding her surge of emotion. Five minutes previously, she had been
focused entirely on Pierre. How was it possible to be this excited
about another man? Particularly after the recent events. What was
the matter with her?

"Are you free for that coffee, or even better, a drink?" he said.

Why couldn't she just say no? There was no need to see him. But
he was impossible to resist. "For you, always."

"Great, darling," he said. "Just tell me when."

She clenched her hands. There was no going back now. "Thursday after work?"

"Terrific. I'm staying at the Lanesborough."

Melanie closed her eyes, hating her own duplicity, but unable to control it. "I'll come straight from the office. See you around six thirty." What the hell was she doing?

"OK. My darling. I can't wait."

Melanie cleared her diary on Thursday to make time for the hairdresser, as well as a much-needed manicure. She slid back to her desk at 2pm and was interrupted seconds later by Pamela. "Hot date tonight?"

"Not tonight." Another lie.

"What's the hair for?" said Pamela.

"Oh, should be a fun weekend," said Melanie, instantly regretting having let her guard down.

Pamela lifted her glasses. "Now, that's news. Who's the lucky guy?"

"Just someone I've been seeing recently."

Pamela inched closer and whispered, "Who?"

"You don't know him," said Melanie.

"Show me a photo then," said Pamela.

Melanie turned her back. "It's none of your business."

But Pamela didn't move. "Is it someone in the office? That's why you're being all secretive."

"I'm not that stupid," said Melanie. Of course it was mad, but at least Pierre worked in a different office. It was a relief that nobody knew.

Pamela placed her hands on her hips. "Who, then?"

Melanie sighed. "I don't want to discuss it. But I promise, if it gets serious, I'll tell you about it. No point until then."

"You're infuriating. It's not exactly MI5 here."

She loved the Lanesborough. Such a classy hotel. Just like him. That divine creature by the bar. He looked up, straight into her eyes. The memories flooded back. Despite all her intentions to behave, she leaned forward to kiss him. The natural thing to do. His hands curled behind her back and he drew her close.

"I missed you, my love," he said. "More than you can imagine."

"Me too." Her guilt must have showed.

"Don't worry. I'm not going to take you upstairs. However much I need to. I know you have a boyfriend."

"Yeah." She turned away. Desperate for him. Praying she was strong enough to resist. "But you know how much I'd love to."

"I know. And one day you'll be free to do as you please. When that day arrives, call me."

She kissed him again. Only a kiss. That didn't count, did it?

He took her hand. "There is no rush, my darling. We are going to know each other for many, many years."

"You think so?"

"I know it."

They sat in that place for hours, talking. And when she returned home that night, her body was exploding. How could she possibly want him that badly? After all that had happened. What kind of person did that make her?

However, it was time to concentrate on Pierre and when Friday afternoon finally arrived, he was waiting for her in the airport lounge. The second man in two days.

Melanie watched him for a few precious seconds before he noticed her. A striking figure, confident and alone at the bar. There could be no doubt that he was expecting company. The champagne was on ice and her glass stood ready.

He jumped up to embrace her, delight spreading across his broad face. "*Chérie*. You are so beautiful."

"Pierre…" It was a relief to see him. Too much guilt. She had to conquer the blackness.

"Here. I've been saving this glass for you," he said.

"My favourite," she said.

"I know, my love. And you know I love getting you a little drunk." God, he was mesmerising. Those eyes full of promises. Promises of lust, of love, of everything that ever mattered. What had she been thinking the day before with Lorenzo? She could have stayed in the lounge looking at him all evening. He ran his fingers through her hair and she leaned into him.

The alcohol had taken hold by the time she reached the aeroplane. Turning left at the door, they entered the small cabin with only a few large seats.

Pierre showed her to her chair. "The only problem with first class," he said, "is the dividing screens between us."

"You're incorrigible." But she loved him all the same, delighted to be with him again. Thrilled by the luxurious cabin.

The plane took off and she closed her eyes. But she could sense his presence, and wondered what he would do next. It was only a matter of time; his hand moved up her leg and he fingered the lace of her underwear. He pulled them lower. "I thought I told you not to wear these."

She shifted in her seat, arched her back and allowed him to continue. His free hand covered her mouth, preventing her from making a sound.

When she opened her eyes again, he was smiling down at her. "Do you think the stewardess saw anything?" asked Melanie.

"Probably." Pierre winked and took a sip of champagne. "She seemed rather jealous."

"You are crazy." She lay back in her bed, now fully relaxed.

A film, dinner and four glasses of champagne later, they prepared for landing at JFK. Circling above the airport, she remembered their first visit. How different it felt now. Back then, she had been a nervous, frightened girl. Now, returning with the same man, she felt confident and on top of the world. New York was an exhilarating city and she planned to enjoy it. This time, work was irrelevant; all she cared about was him.

She remembered Lorenzo with another stab of guilt. Why couldn't she get him out of her mind? She loved Pierre deeply, but it didn't seem to make any difference. Lorenzo made her stomach twist with excitement. But Lorenzo was still in London and she couldn't allow him to ruin her weekend.

Similarly to that first visit the previous year, Pierre reminded her of the landmarks while the taxi wound its way into Manhattan. The same streets, but the view from his arms changed the perspective entirely. Back then, snow had covered the streets. Now the city was sweltering in the early summer heat.

Pierre had booked a suite at the Carlyle Hotel on the Upper East Side, near Central Park. Unlike the previous, trendy hotel they had last stayed in, the Carlyle exuded old-fashioned glamour. Sophisticated. Like him. The bed was enormous and the room was almost the size of her flat in London. His mission to impress had succeeded with style.

On that first night, Pierre unravelled her from the hotel's luxuriously soft, white dressing gown and surprised her with his tenderness. Initially taken aback, she melted gratefully into his embrace. It was pleasing to know he could be gentle too. They were both exhausted from the journey and it felt exquisite. There would be plenty of time for his darker side to emerge.

After brunch on Saturday, they strolled down Fifth Avenue, jostling past tourists and admiring the store windows. He offered to take her shopping, but she preferred to just walk, to be a stranger in this town. They stopped for lunch near Union Square, in one of Pierre's favourite restaurants. Stepping in, the bustle of the city vanished and they were ushered back to a time of faded glory. Crisply dressed waiters politely greeted and escorted them to a discreet table in the corner. Thankfully she was wearing her new black dress. It was an unbelievably elegant place and she was relieved to have listened to Jenny's wardrobe advice.

After they had finished the bottle of Merlot, Pierre rose from the table and motioned for her to join him. She followed him across the crowded room and down the chequered marble staircase, her fingers rippling across the white and black textured wallpaper. She was unprepared when he shoved her into one of the bathroom cubicles at the bottom of the steps. The door clicked behind them as he slid the lock across. Her eyes moved upwards to meet his. Time for him to drop that gentlemanly facade.

His hands skimmed over her hold-ups and discovered her lack of underwear. His voice was hoarse. "Good girl."

She gasped when he pushed her against the wall. Her head knocked against the corner. It hurt, but she had already succumbed to him. He crushed her left breast with his hand, twisting her nipple. There was no romance but, as always, she loved to satiate him.

He stopped. "On your knees."

She obliged, choking, unable to breathe. Finally he tugged her head back with one rough movement. "I'd better get back before they realise what a bad girl you are."

He pulled up his trousers, washed his hands and left the room. Not even a glance back. Locking the door behind him was an unusually hard task. Her hands were shaking uncontrollably. She needed to compose herself. But how? Melanie stared at the wild-haired woman in the mirror. Red marks on her neck and smudged mascara across her face. Why did she keep letting him do this? What part of her loved it so much? It was hard to understand, but at least the abuse was now contained to these brief moments. She had handled it well. By standing her ground, she had enabled the relationship itself to deepen. To some extent, she had regained control and the crazy sex was no longer the driving force between them. Which meant that she could enjoy it more.

Deep breath. One step at a time. She mechanically wiped her face with a wet cloth and began the process of reapplying her make-up. Her powder wasn't thick enough to cover the emerging bruises, but a strategically tied scarf would solve the problem. With no hairbrush, she used her fingers to smooth her tangled mane.

Returning to the table, she watched him sip his espresso, his brooding eyes following her every move. Perhaps her guilty mind imagined it, but she felt the waiter's eyes boring through her back as she inched past.

Pierre looked up at her, his expression half mocking, half teasing. "You are a bad girl."

"That's why you like me, isn't it?" she said, for once a little shy.

"To tell you the truth, I can't live without you. You are the great passion of my life." He placed one hand on her leg and passed her an espresso with the other.

"Is passion enough for you?" she asked.

"Darling, it's everything to me."

"Am I everything to you?"

"You know you are, my love." He took her hand.

Melanie inhaled. "Darling, it's so hard with you living far away. I want to be with you all the time. Can't you move back to London soon?" She immediately hated herself for the question, having sworn that she would never be dependent on a man.

"Of course we will always be together. This passion only happens once in a lifetime. I will visit you as often as I can."

"OK," she said. Not quite the answer she had been hoping for.

The rest of the weekend passed in a blur. Long walks in the park, expensive restaurants and a brief visit to a museum. He seemed calmer after their lunchtime interlude and on Saturday evening, he was gentle and kind again.

In the early hours of the night, Melanie woke to the sound of a passing ambulance. She reached for a glass of water and gazed across at her sleeping man, contemplating their evolving relationship. It was clear that he loved her, although in many ways he remained unpredictable. But perhaps that was one of the attractions.

Every inch of her body ached by the time he put her into a taxi on Sunday night. Pierre had work commitments in New York on Monday and she had to get back to the office. Leaving him after the weekend was such a disappointment.

She sagged with loneliness when the plane took off. The anticlimax was hard to bear.

From Paddington station, Melanie took a taxi straight to the office. She was now a regular at the downstairs locker room, with all her rushed mornings. Fortunately she had managed to sleep for a few hours on the plane. Dragging herself to her desk, she was surprised to see Tony jumping up.

"Where have you been? You're late," said Tony. "I've been calling you all weekend."

It was the only time she had ever switched her phone off for the entire weekend. Typical. "Sorry, Tony, I was away. I sent you a message on Friday that I'd be late in today."

"I didn't see it," said Tony. "There's a potential new deal. Landed on my lap Friday evening."

"Oh shit," she said.

"The bankers are delighted. Business has been drying up recently, and we need to do our best to win it."

"Of course," she said. It was true. The past twelve months had been tricky. With stock prices sliding, it was challenging to make money on anything.

Tony kept talking. "Alex and I have prepared half our pitch and we need your help with some of the numbers. The bankers want something concrete by Wednesday morning and we're going to France next week."

Another deal was the last thing she needed. The thought of having to face Mitch Cooper was quite a blow after such a wonderful weekend. Melanie rubbed her eyes. First class had been incredible, but she was still desperate for a good night's sleep. She'd been counting on a short day in the office, which now seemed impossible.

While she worked on her spreadsheets, her mind drifted back to New York. Memories of Pierre continued to haunt her. The two days together had reminded her of how much she loved him and she needed to tell him. An agonising few hours later, she managed to reach him.

"Pierre, darling. How are you?"

"Good morning, my love. I'm lying in our room. Missing you like hell. Guess what I'm doing right now."

She laughed. "I can imagine. But now is not the time to talk about it. Unlike you, I'm in the office."

"*Chérie*. I want to be lying with you."

"Me too." There was nobody else at the desk, but she looked around, anxious not to be overheard. "Darling, on that note, I have some good news. I'm coming to Paris next week. Any chance you can come back early? I'd love to spend some more time with you."

"I'm sorry, darling, it's just not possible. I've got back-to-back meetings for the next ten days. Going to Ohio tonight, of all places."

She sighed. "Oh, well. Maybe it's for the best. I need to concentrate on this deal."

"*Chérie*, don't worry, I'll make up for it next time."

"I'm sure you will."

It was such a shame, but Pierre and work were not a good combination. She had discovered that a few too many times and, besides, Tony and Mitch would be breathing down her neck.

That week was a nightmare. She hadn't had enough time in New York for jet lag to affect her, but somehow the trip had made her feel unwell. The presentation was a disaster and she couldn't agree with the bankers on the potential valuation. They were pushing for her to be more optimistic with her figures but she didn't back down. It was always the same exhausting battle. The bankers wanted the best price for every deal, but she had to appear to be independent. Otherwise, nobody in the City would ever take her seriously. Particularly in the current environment. She'd be mad to give a rosy scenario.

Long after the other teams had left, she and Alex were toiling away in their corner of the vast room. The city was black and cold by the time she got home each night and daybreak had barely arrived when her alarm sounded. They didn't come close to achieving their Wednesday deadline and she had no idea how they finished the presentation at all that week. Not her finest work, but at least it was done. And she hadn't succumbed to Mitch's demands for a higher valuation.

When Friday night arrived, Melanie almost wept with relief. She had never been so shattered in her life. Collapsing into bed, she passed out, motionless for a full thirteen hours. She woke, feeling drugged, the next morning and remained blissfully in bed until midday. In this mad world of hers, sleep had become the ultimate luxury.

Later that afternoon, she met Jenny for a late lunch. Renewed by her rest, Melanie was freshly excited about her work and her man. Jenny had had a rather more exotic evening the night before and was not shy in sharing her experiences. Her own relationship with Pierre was astonishingly tame compared to Jenny's tales about Oli. Unbelievable that she was still seeing that scumbag, but at least Jenny never suggested a repeat performance of that terrible night.

The lunch continued into the early evening, after which they meandered over to Fulham to meet David for another drink.

When the girls entered the pub, Jenny pulled her close. "Who's the gorgeous man with your brother?"

Melanie recognised him immediately. She hadn't thought about Max for a very long time. She paused. "That's Max."

Jenny raised her eyebrow inquisitively at her friend. "That's Max? Damn, he's hot. What were you thinking by not calling him?"

Melanie sighed. "He's all yours, if you want."

Just as she had with so many men before, Jenny approached Max with an engaging smile, but he looked past her, eyes only for Melanie.

He stood up to greet her. "Long time, Mel. I have missed you."

She gave him a self-conscious peck on the cheek. "Hi, Max." What was he doing here? Damned David. This was the last thing she needed.

David waved for her to sit down. "We're celebrating Max's promotion. Head of early twentieth-century art. He also gave an impressive interview to the *Daily Telegraph* this week. All about German collections. Did you see it?"

Melanie shook her head. "That's great news. Congratulations."

Jenny gave her another sidelong look and Melanie blushed. It was hard to deny what an attractive man Max was, but this was incredibly awkward. And Jenny's inane facial expressions weren't helping.

Max hadn't moved. "You're looking well. How have you been?"

Melanie cleared her throat. "Uh. Fine."

"One of these days, we should have another drink." His piercing blue eyes bored into her.

"Yeah, sure. Why not?" Time passing hadn't lessened her attraction for him. But so much had changed. And she was a different person. There was nothing she could do now.

"Seriously," said Max. "What have you been up to? I hear from David that you're doing extremely well at work."

She tapped her fingers on the table. "Yeah, I've been working a lot. But I managed to visit New York last weekend at least."

"You really do work hard. On the weekends also."

Melanie gave a nervous cough, knowing there was no easy answer. "Um… Well, actually it was with my boyfriend."

"David didn't mention your boyfriend." Max looked away.

"Yeah…David hasn't met him. Maybe that's why."

"Hmm. OK." He took a step back. "Well, it's good to know you've found time to have a relationship."

"What's that supposed to mean?" she said.

"It was a feeble joke, Mel. Look, it's been great seeing you. But I was actually on my way out. Let's catch up another time." He paid his bill and left.

Once Max had disappeared from sight, David turned on her. "Why the hell did you have to bring up that crap about your boyfriend?"

Melanie picked up the drinks menu, in an effort to look indifferent. "Don't know what you're talking about."

"Exactly what I said."

"What else was I supposed to do?" she said. "I wasn't going to lie just to make him feel better."

"Where is this fabulous boyfriend, then? How come we've never met him? For a whole year. He's probably a figment of your imagination, knowing you."

"That's bloody rude. Ask Jenny. I've told you a million times that he lives in Paris. And he's in the US right now."

"Typical of you to find a man who you never see. You're such a workaholic, you've got no time for romance."

"How dare you tell me what to do with my boyfriend? He fits perfectly into my life."

"Isn't that your problem? Listen to yourself. Fitting into your life? You are allowing your job to take over everything. All that money isn't doing you any favours. You're turning into a miserable little cow. Just like I warned you."

"Shut up. You can be such a sanctimonious bastard sometimes." The daytime drinking had shortened her fuse and she rose to leave the pub. What right had her brother to talk to her like that? Did he expect her to jump into Max's arms? She had another man in her life; it was very straightforward.

Her brother followed. "Mel, wait. I'm sorry, I didn't mean for it to come out like that. We should talk about this."

"Leave me alone," she said. "I've had enough of you telling me how to lead my life. Have I ever told you how to behave? Just because you're Mr Perfect doesn't mean that I want to be the same as you." She turned away and didn't look back. Time to go home.

Melanie took a taxi that night, grateful that the driver didn't ask any questions or try the usual small talk. She closed her eyes and waited until the taxi jolted to a stop, indicating their arrival. Twisting the key in the lock, she used her full weight to shove the heavy front door open. Impossibly shattered, even after a long sleep the night before.

At some point she would need to think about the toll her lifestyle was taking. But not this evening. She reached for the radio and turned on her favourite station. For now, a glass of wine and a cigarette would suffice.

Tonight, she didn't bother to sit on the terrace, not caring that the apartment would reek of stale smoke the next day. She sat there for a long time, for what seemed like hours, and listened to the sound of distant thunder. From inside her handbag, she heard the dull vibrations of the mobile phone. Perhaps it was David, calling to apologise. Or perhaps it was Pierre. Either way, there seemed little point in answering. She closed her eyes momentarily – and passed out on the sofa.

Chapter Nineteen

She caught the Eurostar on Sunday night for an early meeting in Paris the next day. Upon entering her carriage, Melanie saw Mitch and groaned; such an irritation to find him on her train. It was hard to understand him – not that she particularly wanted to. One moment he seemed ready to organise her demise and then, the next minute, he was breathing flatteries down her throat.

He waved. "Hi. I asked my secretary to book us seats together."

"Terrific." She gave him a glassy stare. Wanker.

"Thought we could go over your presentation for tomorrow."

Melanie scanned the rest of the carriage. "Where's Tony? I thought he was coming too."

"Think he took an earlier train. Don't know. Sit." Mitch patted the seat next to him. "We've got a lot to chat about."

"That's very kind, but I have a report to finish."

"More important than our meetings tomorrow?" Such a disgusting false smile.

"Obviously not. But I have a day job too. Can't just focus on the corporate work." She smiled back at him. He was odious.

"I hope you're ready. It's going to be a busy couple of days."

"Sure. Don't worry. Tony and I have been hard at work. As you know."

"OK," he said.

"See you later." Melanie turned away and took a seat at the opposite end of the carriage. He wouldn't be able to see that she would be doing nothing at all.

A car was waiting for them in Paris. Mitch turned to speak to the driver in textbook French. Funny how it jarred with his neat East Coast image. But she wasn't about to show that she was impressed. Instead, she pretended to sleep in the taxi, allowing the men to talk.

Through an imperceptible opening of her eyelids, she watched the car pass through Paris and sighed with happiness. Such a beautiful city, the contrast of handsome boulevards and their imposing facades interspersed with cobbled side streets, small shopfronts and three-star hotels.

She hadn't been here for many years. She remembered her trip with David and her parents when she was a child. It was one of her last memories of her father, before he had abandoned them. She hadn't heard from him since. Thinking of those happy times, her mind wandered to David. Over the past year or two, they had drifted apart. But until last night, there had been no arguments, just a gradual separation of lives. How had she allowed it to happen? Fighting was not the answer and she needed to make amends. She just had no idea how. The argument hadn't only been about her work, although she had used that excuse many times. There were other reasons too. David wasn't keen on Jenny, and it was blindingly obvious that he wouldn't approve of her relationship with Pierre. Subconsciously, or actually not that subconsciously, that was why she hadn't introduced them. They were totally different and it would be awkward. David was kind and wholesome, and Pierre… Well, Pierre was unique.

Looking through the rain-blurred window, she wondered where Pierre lived. It was about time she came here for a weekend. Frustrating that he was still in America, but she couldn't afford a repeat of Amsterdam anyway.

Ten short minutes later, they arrived at their destination: a large, impersonal hotel off the Place de L'Opéra. Compared to the Carlyle, it felt dull and corporate. She supposed it was appropriate for a work visit, but she would have preferred something more authentically Parisian. It would have been fabulous to sleep in Pierre's bed. Not that she would have rested. Melanie smiled at the idea of explaining that one to Tony.

Mitch checked in first and waited until she had also received her key. Although he knew where she was sleeping, it was a minor victory that they had been placed on different floors. Less chance of him stalking her.

Finally in her room, she threw her bag onto the green velvet chair and went to investigate. Reasonably large room, yellow bathroom, complete with standard-issue toiletries. Air-conditioned and pristine, but totally claustrophobic. Worst of all, the windows were jammed shut and she couldn't lean outside to smoke her nightly cigarette.

The telephone rang in the corner and she reached across the bed to answer it. She recognised that drawl immediately. "Hi, Melanie. I'm heading down to the bar. Would you like to join me for a drink?"

Exactly the thing she felt least like doing. "How kind of you, Mitch. But I'm a little tired and need to catch up on my sleep."

"You've had a whole weekend to rest," he said. "I'd rather hoped you'd have perked up by now."

"I know. Funny, isn't it? Anyway, I hope you have a lovely evening. See you in the morning."

Melanie waited ten minutes, then took the stairs down and found the back door of the hotel. She lit her cigarette, stepped out into the Parisian night and exhaled. She strolled down the Place Vendôme past the Ritz Hotel, its timeless glamour redolent of the prosperity of previous generations. She moved along to the trendy shops of Rue Saint-Honoré and watched a couple stumble out of the Hotel Costes. What an amazing life. In the space of just over a week she had been to New York, London and Paris. That was something she wouldn't have dreamed of as a child.

No wonder Jenny loved it here. Then again, Jenny only came for pleasure, normally for one of those infamous orgies she was always talking about. Melanie wondered where they were, these dens of iniquity. She wandered the dark streets and felt an urge to find out more. Who were these people? Where did they go? A voice inside her was moving her inexorably in that direction and she had a sudden need to speak to Pierre. The man had opened her eyes to the possibilities and now she was ready to explore further.

She stood back, away from the street lamps, and called him from the shadows . "Hello… Hello?"

"*Chérie*, how are you, darling?" The line crackled.

"You sound far away."

"I am, darling. Minnesota, to be accurate.

"What the hell is in Minnesota?" she said.

"Clients. But, believe me, very few other redeeming qualities."

Minnesota was the last thing on her mind. "I miss you."

"I miss you too, my love," he said. "Where are you?"

"Paris, as I told you."

He paused. "I hate that you're there without me."

"Me too. But I was passing the Ritz and I had a thought."

"How much do you miss me?"

"Stop teasing me. It's so hard to be apart from you. Especially after this weekend. Especially here."

"I want you right now," he said.

"It's very mutual, darling." Her voice turned into a whisper. "Pierre, what do you know about the orgy parties in Paris?"

His laughter was spontaneous. "*Chérie*, you are my angel. We can talk about that when I get back. You will be punished for your filthy thoughts."

"OK, Pierre, goodnight." She inhaled. His response had told her all she needed to know.

That night, they came to her in her dreams. The masked men clambering on top and Pierre watching all the while. She saw him with two other women, dressed in white. Laughing at her. She woke up, burning with desire, and cursed her bad fortune at being alone.

Their Paris office was a block from the hotel, and after a disappointing breakfast, she and Tony crossed the street to meet their French colleagues. No sign of Mitch. Investment bankers kept different hours from everyone else. Paris was a small team; around thirty people, mostly bankers, sales men and analysts. She hadn't analysed any French companies before and the faces were largely unfamiliar. Only Céleste from the training programme all those years ago. Still, it was a relief to see even one friendly face.

Scanning the room, she noticed there were a few empty desks. Which one belonged to Pierre? Perhaps he sat in the glass office in the corner. It was odd that she didn't know if he had an office or a normal desk. She would ask him later.

They were ushered straight to the conference room. She spotted a black espresso machine in the corner. Finally, an office with the right priorities.

Two coffees and an hour later, Mitch appeared with a couple of local bankers. After the appropriate niceties, Melanie handed out the presentations. The big meeting with the corporate client would take place the following day and everyone wanted to ensure it would run smoothly. She was conscious of Mitch's dark presence leaning over her. He rested his left hand on her shoulder while she was finishing her speech. She tried not to shudder.

At the end of the day, Céleste offered to take Melanie to a local bistro for an early dinner. A night by herself would have been preferable, but at least this was more enticing than the prospect of Mitch's company.

In the restaurant, the waiters jostled past the tables and spoke directly to Céleste, ignoring her completely. Given her abysmal language skills, that suited her fine.

Céleste poured the wine. "I've been hearing all about you this year. Sounds like you're doing exceptionally well."

Melanie smiled, delighted by the compliment. "Thanks. I've been lucky, I guess."

"I heard you're very smart. They insisted on having you on this deal."

"Really?" Melanie flushed with pride. Pathetic how it took so little to make her feel special.

"Sure, why not? You know how lucky we are to be pitching for the business. It's our first decent pitch for months and they wanted the best team," said Céleste. "I think it's great they chose you."

"You're too kind." Melanie took a sip, feeling self-conscious at the continuous praise. She coughed and tried to change the topic. "But much more interesting, tell me about you. How's life?"

"I guess I'm the opposite of you," said Céleste. "Haven't been promoted at all. If you ask me, they're a bit sexist here."

"Aren't they everywhere?" said Melanie.

"No, seriously. Look at you. Already a VP. Me, I'm still the most junior on my team. Still, it doesn't matter."

"What do you mean, it doesn't matter?" said Melanie.

Céleste waved her hand across the table, flashing a large diamond ring. The Frenchwoman's face beamed with happiness. "I'm getting married. Thierry proposed a few months ago."

"That's great. Congratulations." Funny how other women had such different priorities. Céleste was incredibly sweet. Had she ever been like that herself? Maybe. Certainly not anymore.

"What about you?" said Céleste.

"What about me?"

"You know. Love life?"

"I'm mostly focusing on work these days. But I do have a fantastic boyfriend. It's still early days though." She wasn't about to go into details.

"How exciting," said Céleste. "It is wonderful to find love. I hope you have much happiness."

Melanie clasped her wine glass. "Thanks."

Céleste gave her a sly look. "Speaking of men, your colleague is so good-looking."

"What colleague?"

"That American one," said Céleste.

Melanie raised her eyebrows. "Mitch?" Not bloody Mitch again. What was wrong with these women?

"Yeah, that one. I remember him from the training programme. He's very handsome, don't you think? I wonder why he's not married already."

"Not sure." Who cared?

"He's quite a catch," said Céleste.

"You think so?" asked Melanie.

"Oh, yes." The girl's face brightened. "He came and had a long chat with me today. And in perfect French. Utterly charming. Don't you agree?"

"Ah, not my sort, to be honest." There was no point in being publicly rude. But seriously, what was it about Mitch? He seemed to accumulate a peculiar fan club. She didn't understand it at all and it was best to move away from the subject. "Tell me more about your colleagues here. Are they friendly? I mean, apart from being sexist?"

"Not too bad. Some of the managers are cool. Henri and Pierre are decent enough."

"I've heard that too," said Melanie. What a golden opportunity to dig up information on her lover. She hadn't thought about it until now. But there was no need for her to pry. Céleste was doing the work for her.

"Pierre's been on particularly good form this year," said Céleste. "When he's happy, that makes all our lives easier."

Melanie tried not to look pleased. "Isn't he normally?"

Céleste laughed. "I take it you've never seen him in a terrible temper?"

"No." Not really. "What kind of temper?"

"My goodness. They are legendary. I remember when I first joined, he threw a chair across the room. Smashed it completely. I believe it was about a deal that fell through or something."

"Gosh. I had no idea he was violent," said Melanie. But she smiled, picturing his dark moods.

"Totally nuts. But he's been OK recently. Haven't heard him yell for ages."

"Wonder why?" said Melanie. "Anything changed?" Did the office know he had a girlfriend?

"Well," said Céleste, "my guess is that he's excited about being a father again. He doesn't talk about it, but his wife told me they've been trying for years for another one."

Melanie never knew the world could come crashing down. Her fingers grasped the wooden table for support, and she barely managed to speak. "Is Pierre married? I didn't know that." Jesus fucking Christ.

"Yes, they are such a beautiful couple." Céleste smiled. "Vanessa is lovely. She has become a great friend of mine. It's a shame that Pierre is not here. We could all have had dinner together."

"Such a shame." Melanie gulped and put both hands down

on her chair, in a frantic attempt to remain upright. How was she going to make it through the rest of the evening? Her meal sat in front of her; an unwelcome obstacle that she somehow needed to eat. She reached for her wine glass in desperation and swallowed the contents. Miraculously, Céleste kept on talking. God knew about what.

Melanie pushed her frites away. "I'm so sorry, but I'm feeling sick all of a sudden."

"Are you OK?" Céleste reached across the table to hold her hand.

"Yeah. Probably too much stress. Not a good thing."

"Poor you. You're definitely working way too hard. Here, have another drink."

"No, no, don't worry. Do you mind if I go back to the hotel now? Sorry to spoil your evening."

"Of course not." Céleste wrinkled her forehead in concern. "I'll get the bill. Feel better."

Melanie kissed her friend and ran. Stumbling past hordes of tourists, she found her way back to the hotel. The small room that she had hated yesterday was now her only refuge in this strange mad city. She collapsed on the floor, sobbing like a small child. She hadn't even cried that way when her mother had died. Melanie tugged her knees into her chest; the feeling of loss was overwhelming.

The damp cold morning arrived as an unwelcome reminder of the night before. Melanie opened the curtains, but it made no difference. The greyness of the Parisian sky was surpassed only by the bleakness in her heart. Bastard. Her reflection in the mirror spoke volumes. Sallow face, swollen eyes. Impossible to conceal. But the tears had stopped at least. Slamming the bathroom door shut, she slumped to the floor and sucked down a cigarette. The steam of the shower would hopefully conceal the smoke, although she didn't care either way. Her mind was on the torturous day ahead. She would have to return to that office and pretend nothing was wrong. The deal would depend on it. And her job probably depended on getting the deal. She longed for her home, her only real sanctuary. She was a stranger in this city, his city. It scarcely mattered that

Pierre wasn't physically in town. Here, in this miserable hotel, his presence was everywhere. He had defiled her body so many times, but this was far more humiliating.

With an effort she couldn't have imagined previously, she dressed and applied her make-up. The result was passable and, although she didn't look alluring, she did feel the tiniest glimmer of hope. Perhaps she would make it after all. Glancing at her watch, she inhaled sharply. Time had felt irrelevant that morning and now she was late for her first meeting. Grabbing her hastily packed bag, she hurried to the check-out counter, where the woman behind the desk carried out her task with exasperating precision.

Finally free, Melanie pushed past an old Japanese couple in the lobby and ran towards the small office round the corner. She straightened her back and raised her head, then rang the office bell, giving an acknowledgement to the receptionist. There was no warmth in her voice, but at least she had managed the gesture. It was a start, but when she saw Mitch summoning her, the facade vanished. He had nothing to do with her situation, but she hated his presence even more than usual. Of all the people to deal with today, why did it have to be him?

Closing her eyes for a long two seconds, Melanie forced herself into composure. Mitch seemed impossibly oblivious to it and, taking a deep breath, she followed him into the conference room. Somehow she needed to channel the fury into something useful. Fuck Pierre. She wouldn't allow him to ruin her career as well. Especially in his home town.

The papers she had compiled meticulously were sitting in a stack on the table. For a moment, she stared at them. So much had happened since she'd last seen them. But she couldn't afford to dwell; the clients were already sitting down. She picked up the paperwork and handed it out.

The morning passed in a blur while she mechanically made her presentations, smiled and shook the hands of those faceless men.

The meeting lasted for hours and after the last man walked out the door, she had nothing left to offer, destroyed and sickened by the energy she had somehow managed to summon.

It was a relief to catch the Eurostar by herself. She switched off her phone and shut her eyes. Two and a half hours of blissful peace. If only she didn't have to wake again.

The next day, everyone congratulated her. Her meetings had gone to plan and the bankers were optimistic they would win the mandate. Not that it made her any happier. Her phone rang incessantly, but she was afraid to answer. Afraid to speak to him. Afraid of her own fury. As she sat staring stupidly at her screen, she noticed a shadow looming behind her. Inwardly groaning at the sight of the American, she glowered at him.

"Melanie, I've been trying to reach you all morning," said Mitch.

She glared at him, cold and empty. She didn't bother to respond. There was no space in her misery to include him.

"I was hoping you could join me for lunch today. We need to work a little harder to find some more deals and I'd love your opinion."

"Sorry, Mitch. I'm busy." She moved her chair away from him. The hostility was somehow lost on him. Why couldn't he piss off and stop pestering her?

He stood there for a while, watching while she began typing a new report. It was clear that he didn't intend to leave, so she turned round. "I'll call you when I get some time."

His smirk disappeared and his expression made his disappointment clear. She shrugged her shoulders and swivelled back to her desk. It hadn't been professional, but at that moment she didn't care, engulfed in her own bitter self-pity.

Her mobile rang again and, in a momentary lapse, she answered it without thinking.

"Melanie, are you there?" Of course it was him. The ground seemed to swallow her. "Talk to me," said Pierre. "What's going on?"

The loathing that had accumulated over the past day was too potent to control. She had no power to stop the words. "Fuck off, you lying, cheating bastard. Don't ever call me again." Tossing the phone to the floor, she gazed down at her feet. The distastefulness of the situation filled her with rage. She hadn't wanted to be diminished by it, but she was defenceless. A stupid, ridiculous girl.

Melanie looked at Pamela, who, for once, was tactfully pretending to focus on something else. It was the smallest of mercies, but thankfully their secretary had no idea who she had been speaking to. At least it wasn't a public humiliation. Compare that to poor Victoria's experience. She should have been kinder to the woman, but it took a wound of your own to realise how painful love could be.

Dragging herself home that night, Melanie re-enacted her affair with Pierre a thousand times. How could she have been fooled for so long? A whole year of complete deception. How had he managed it? How could his wife have been ignorant for all this time? She just wouldn't have believed it was possible.

She thought about the signs she should have noticed. His other life, his home in Paris. He had never invited her there. And she thought about the weekends; he had rarely been around. She thought about all the times he'd phoned her; but it's always easy to make phone calls. And she thought about his wedding ring. She had never noticed any indentation on his finger – but had she ever looked for it? The clues must have been everywhere. It was her own damned fault. For an analyst, she had failed herself utterly.

It took her a full week to speak about it, but finally she went to visit Jenny. The tears came flooding as the door to her friend's apartment opened.

Wordlessly, Jenny clasped her into her arms and, after several silent minutes, softly began to console her. "Darling, they are all tossers. Remember Zack? He was even worse. At least Pierre hasn't been boasting about you to the whole firm, trying to ruin your career at the same time."

"That's true, but God knows what he'll do now that we've broken up. He's very influential. I hope to hell he doesn't take it out on me."

"He won't do that, as long as you don't spill the beans. The last thing he wants is for his wife to find out."

Melanie lowered her head and began to sob.

Jenny moved closer to comfort her friend. "Forget about him. There are so many others out there. You're gorgeous, you're successful. Only twenty-six. You've got so much to offer."

"But I love him. You know that," said Melanie.

"Rubbish. You had great sex with him, so what? You're better off without him anyway. He's a total prick. Move on."

"To what?"

"Loads of guys. Remember Oli? He's always asking after you. He's wild."

"Don't go there."

"Could take your mind off things for a while though—"

"We talked about that already. I can't believe you're still in touch with him. Complete cokehead."

Jenny laughed. "Well, he's quite amusing. Gives me amazing commission. And for the record, he doesn't always take drugs." But she must have seen her friend's irritation – she changed the subject. "You should call your Italian sexpot. He sounded great fun."

Melanie wiped a tear away. "He's probably married too. I mean, he texts me all the time, but nothing more than that. Just like Pierre, playing away from home. Why are they all the same?"

"I don't mean to be nasty, but it's not as if you were faithful to Pierre either." It was a tough comment. Jenny had a point, not that it made it any easier to digest.

"It's hardly the same thing," said Melanie. "I mean, one or two nights is not the same as leading a double life. Besides, I consciously didn't sleep with Lorenzo a second time. Remember? Me and my stupid morals."

"I know. I know. I'm just saying that nobody is perfect. Pierre behaved terribly, but he was obsessed with you. You should try to understand why he did it and move on."

"Me, try to understand him? What are you saying? He led me on for ages. Made me believe we were together. I had no idea he was married."

"You are glum. You'll never pull anyone with that face."

"I don't want to pull anyone," said Melanie. Why did Jenny always think sex was the answer to everything?

"You'll thank me afterwards. What about that fantastic man we met the other night? He's really good-looking and obviously crazy about you."

"Max? You can't be serious," said Melanie.

"Why not? He's hot and definitely not married. You should give him a chance. After all these years, I reckon he deserves it."

"Of course he's handsome, but I was quite bitchy the other night…" Melanie shook her head. "It feels wrong."

"You weren't that bad." Jenny paused. "What's the matter with him anyway? I can't see a problem with it."

"Nothing. But he's in a different world from us. And…"

"What does that mean?" Jenny chuckled. "Not rich enough?"

"That's not remotely what I'm talking about. It's not about money. It's about whether he understands me or not."

"I thought you cared a lot about making money."

"Shut up, I'm not nearly as materialistic as you are," said Melanie. "Besides, he's super-successful at work."

"Give me a break. He may be a hotshot in the art world, but that's not going to bring in the big bucks."

"So?" Melanie stared at her friend. It was true that Jenny only dated wealthy men. But it never occurred to her to do the same. Why should a man's wealth make any difference?

"Nothing. Just go for the sex. No need to get serious."

Melanie smiled. She had to get her mind off Pierre and Jenny was struggling to cheer her up. It was time to make an effort and conquer this stupid depression. Her friend grabbed another bottle of white wine and they continued to discuss Max. That drunken one-night stand had seemed so wild back then…but it now felt rather tame. How things had changed.

"Come on," said Jenny. "Let's give him a call."

"Not now," said Melanie. "I'm not ready."

"That's why you need to call him. It's important never to turn down a good night of fun," said Jenny. "You need to have sex with someone else. You'll see, you'll forget about your Frenchie in no time. What's Max's number?"

"I don't have it," said Melanie.

"Yes, you do." Jenny yanked the handset from Melanie, copied Max's number onto her own phone and called him immediately. Melanie stared helplessly at her friend. She heard the phone buzzing at the other end. She could have stopped it, but she sat immobilised in her chair. What would Max say? She blushed while listening to Jenny's message, but shrugged her shoulders in a ridiculous attempt to appear indifferent.

"OK. That's done. Now, for the next bottle. Red or white?" said Jenny.

The girls curled up on the large blue sofa and devoured another bottle. Since there was nothing to eat in the house, they opted for cigarettes and a Japanese takeaway and talked non-stop about sex. It was always an education listening to Jenny, who seemed to discover a new angle every time. First it was different partners, then it was the orgies in Paris, now it was some peculiar strain of sadomasochism.

At the age of only twenty-five, Jenny appeared to know everything about men and the pursuit of carnal pleasures. Oli was her current fetish and, judging by Jenny's continued interest, he would last a while longer. She always seemed to recycle the same men, although the relationships were rarely exclusive. But she never spoke of love and didn't seem particularly interested in it.

Melanie always felt angelic next to her friend and it was a relief to have such frank conversations. Much easier than talking to David. Imagine that. And David's girlfriend Samantha…forget it. All her friends from childhood, too, had always been so prim and would never understand her darker moods. Jenny simply wanted to be her friend. Men passed through, but thank God for good girlfriends.

Midnight was approaching, but when Melanie stood up to leave, her legs went out from under her. She collapsed on the floor, with bursts of hysterical laughter. She couldn't move and the walls began to dance. She lay down and closed her eyes, spreading her arms to the world. Completely drunk. Her soul was free and she felt the happiest she had been for days. It didn't take much persuasion for her to stay the night in Jenny's spare room.

Morning came and went, and the girls slept until past midday.

Despite her throbbing head, Melanie was still in a positive mood when they strolled over to Westbourne Grove for brunch. Jenny presented her with a Bloody Mary; the best way to eradicate the last vestiges of her hangover. It was a relief to discover life after Pierre and for the first time since Paris, Melanie began to believe things would work out after all.

While they were contemplating pudding, Jenny's phone rang. She beamed at Melanie. "Hi, Max, how are you darling? We were just talking about you."

"No!" Melanie waved in desperation at her friend, who ignored her.

"OK, it's set then. Eight o'clock next Saturday. Do you have her address?" Jenny paused to listen to him. "Great."

Melanie buried her head in the menu, her cheeks burning with embarrassment.

Jenny put her phone down. "You're sorted." A triumphant grin spread across her face.

"You shouldn't have done that." But Melanie was pleased. Perhaps her friend was right. There was no harm in going on a date. It was important to leave the house and forget Pierre for a night. She had already slept with Max once, so a repeat visit didn't really count anyway.

Chapter Twenty

The doorbell rang punctually at eight. It was a mild summer evening and Melanie opted to leave her coat on the rack by the door. She had chosen a flattering but modest wrap dress, accentuating her lithe figure.

Clutching the wooden handrail, she edged down the stairs of her building, taking care not to slip in her new high heels. On the other side of the front door, Max's shadow was silhouetted by the oversized lantern. Such a long time since she'd had a proper date. Wonderful to be courted for a change; where sex was not necessarily the end point of the evening. Dinner with Pierre had always been an afterthought, incidental to his carnal needs.

Max was as attractive as ever. Perhaps even more so. "Hi. How are you?" She hovered by the door.

"So pleased to be here." He kissed her on both cheeks. "I can't believe it's taken me this long to get a proper date, but I'm delighted nonetheless." He took her arm and led her to the taxi waiting on the corner. Max opened the door, allowing her to enter first. Once inside, she was desperate to dispel the awkward silence.

"How's your new job?" she asked. Pathetic question.

"It's fantastic," he said. "I'm travelling more than ever, sourcing some amazing art at the moment for some of our biggest clients. Amazingly enough, the crisis doesn't seem to have affected them at all."

"Cool. Where have you been?" Complete avoidance of intimacy. But what was she supposed to say?

"Just came back from Prague. Incredible city."

"Great." What the hell was she doing here? She looked out of the window. This was a terrible mistake.

The taxi screeched to a halt, throwing her forward.

"Are you OK?" Max gripped her arm.

She nodded. One thing was clear, he was courteous.

"What a relief," he said. "Because we're here. It's a place I've been coming to since I was a child. I hope you like it as much as me."

"It looks lovely." She smiled at him, wanting to give him reassurance.

They followed an old Italian waiter down the narrow stone steps into the dark candle-lit restaurant downstairs. He was telling them about some minor celebrity who had been there the night before and they both nodded politely. The terracotta walls were adorned with framed posters of 1960s film sirens. Their table was discreetly positioned in a dark corner and she sank into the plush red cushions on the sofa.

A bottle of red wine had already been decanted and the waiter poured them each a generous glass. So far, faultless. Time to force thoughts of Pierre aside and concentrate on this beautiful young man. His hair was shorter than before, but still thick and black. Piercing blue eyes were looking intently at her. God, he was handsome. And unexpectedly amusing, with his fascinating stories of foreign art and absurd anecdotes of the nouveau riche clients. Her life of finance and office work was so dreary by comparison. She allowed him to talk, studying him all the while.

By the end of the first course, he had taken her hand and begun to stroke her fingers. A gentle, but masculine hand. Ridiculous that it had taken her so long to get here. Excellent advice from Jenny.

After dinner, they ambled across the road and she didn't resist when he kissed her under the street lamp. "I want you to remember me tonight," he said.

"Was I that bad?" She flushed with embarrassment, recalling her ridiculous one night stand.

He smiled. "I think we were both that bad. You know something funny?"

"What?" she said.

"I haven't touched sangria ever since."

"Me neither." Her lips searched for another kiss. She closed her eyes and forced herself to continue. Her mind was in turmoil. It felt wrong to kiss this man. Her body yearned for Pierre, not him. But Pierre wasn't available and she had to make the best of it. In any other world, Max represented everything a girl could dream of. She had to forget her past.

"Take me home, Max." It had to happen tonight. She might not be brave enough to try again. She would force herself to enjoy the evening with this man. It shouldn't have to be this difficult.

Her heart tugged as she climbed up the steps to his flat. Fifth floor and no lift. His hands were shaking as he fumbled for his keys. She couldn't imagine Pierre being nervous about anything.

It was disconcerting to return to Max's flat after all this time. The same artwork hung on the wall. Something had changed in the drawing room, but it was impossible to pinpoint. Perhaps he had a new sofa or maybe a new coffee table.

He took her hand, led her to his bedroom and unwound her dress. It fell open and he held her waist, with his mouth brushing across her neck. Firm, but not aggressive. She closed her eyes, willing herself to enjoy his touch.

"You're beautiful. My dream," he said.

"Wait," she said.

"Are you OK?" Those blue eyes clouded over. Touchingly anxious.

"Yes, but wait." She took a step back. "My turn." Slowly and deliberately she unbuttoned his shirt, before sweeping it off his shoulders. Broad, strong shoulders. Beautiful man. Next she moved to his trousers, unclipping the single fastening with her fingers. They stood there for a while, absorbing each other, until he drew her close and kissed her hard on the mouth.

It was a relief when his hands moved down to remove her underwear. Falling backwards onto his bed, she beckoned him to follow.

He took time to explore her, kissing her stomach and circling her nipples with his fingers. They grew hard with his touch and she yearned instinctively for him to make love to her. He could have been any man in the world, but her primeval need had conquered her stubborn mind. She pulled him close, begging for him, but he was in no hurry.

He gave her time to touch him back and her fingers moved up and down his torso, as if feeling a man for the first time. After her brutal experiences with Pierre, it was an epiphany. His grip loosened only marginally when afterwards he cradled her in his arms.

She gazed up at him. This was how it felt to be treasured. Peaceful and perfect. She fell asleep in his arms, knowing that he was watching her still.

The daylight woke her early. Opening her eyes, she saw him looking at her from across the bed. Memories of the night before flooded back and she smiled sleepily.

"Good morning, my angel." He leaned over. She stretched, cat-like, her toes skimming against him. He touched her leg under the cover. "How did you sleep?"

"Mmmm." She caressed his face. "That was a lovely evening." Liberating to have come this far. The first big step away from Pierre's tight grasp. Of course, Max had no concept of why she was happy.

"And the best thing is that we both remember it this time," he said.

"I'll remember it always." She held his hand. Such a wonderful man.

He planted a full kiss on her lips. "Darling, I bet you're hungry. Can I get you breakfast?"

"Music to my ears," she said. "Especially if you have good coffee."

"Wait." He passed his fingers across her right cheek and rose from the bed.

She watched him slip into his dressing gown before leaving the room. So easy. So natural. The light was streaming through the thin white curtains, promising a bright morning. An omen. A fresh start, cleansing her soul. A textbook rebound, with absolutely no sense of guilt. No need to explain to anyone and nothing to hide. He had his own interesting life, didn't work at the bank and even David would approve. The aroma of fresh coffee wafted through the door. This man was made in heaven.

He persuaded her to stay, and she borrowed some of his clothes, wrapping his shirt round her slim figure with a belt. "Looks good on you," he said with a smile. He leaned forward and touched her necklace, with an inquisitive look.

"It belonged to my mother," she said, before his question came. It was strange how everyone seemed to think it would have a romantic story.

"It suits you. I'm sure she would be pleased that you wear it." Of course he must have known her mother was dead, and it was a generous thing to say. She liked him a little more for it.

They went for a pizza off the King's Road. The crowds surged around them on the way and the restaurant was hot and noisy. But they didn't notice. His nerves had disappeared and she felt herself warming to his newfound confidence. There was something attractive about strong men and she softened into his embrace.

Sipping his second beer, he stroked her face. "I'm glad the job hasn't hardened you."

"What do you mean?" Where was this going?

"Oh, you know. After David's stories, I had been worried you'd be too tough, but you're as feminine as ever."

She tensed her shoulders. "Thanks." Whatever David had told him, it was inconceivable that Max knew everything. He would be horrified by her past. He was a decent person and she didn't want to defile him too. She shuddered at those memories, but that part of her life was over now. This new man was there to serve a different purpose and he never needed to know.

Her alarm on Monday morning was set for half past four. Even earlier than usual, because she had to get home before heading to work. Wearily climbing out of bed, she gazed at her new lover. The sheets were pulled up past his shoulders and his black curls contrasted with the crisp white pillow. So beautiful, so immaculate. A child compared to Pierre. Stupid comparison. Damn it. It had to stop. Not fair on anyone, least of all herself. How would she ever move on if she kept looking back? Max didn't deserve to be tainted with the same brush. She kissed him on the forehead and left the apartment, easing the door closed behind her.

It took five minutes to find a taxi and she shivered in the early morning breeze. Melanie ignored the driver's caustic comments about her eveningwear. Why did they always feel at liberty to judge their passengers? None of his bloody business. She closed her eyes, giving him no opportunity to continue his puerile conversation.

At home, Melanie made a strong coffee and perched on the balcony for a cigarette. Max didn't smoke and she hadn't had one all weekend. It would be an excellent opportunity to cut down. Disgusting habit, but she sucked a little harder, contemplating her new man. She flicked the discarded butt onto the pavement below and watched it roll to the gutter.

Time to prepare herself for the long day ahead. She grabbed her bag, searching for her phone. She hadn't checked it for a whole day. Hopefully nothing from Tony.

Two messages from Pierre. Would the man ever give up? Irritating that it still mattered.

To hell with him. She was already moving on and her relationship with Max was far healthier and refreshingly straightforward. Exactly what she needed. The weekend had been such fun and she hoped to see more of him.

When Tony arrived at the office later that morning, she greeted him with a smile.

"Good to see you happy," he said.

"What do you mean?" she said. Was it that transparent that her personal life had improved over the weekend?

"You haven't been on best form recently, my dear."

Clearly, it had been that obvious. "I know, sorry. I'll make it up to you."

"Super," he said. "I have some good news for you. My friend at the *FT* wants to write an article on you, after the Extel ratings last month."

Melanie sat up in confusion. "Really, but why?"

"Because we are number three this year and he's plugging you as the one to watch for next year's top position."

"But, I don't understand. It was your name at the top." Why would they want to write about her?

"Stop asking so many questions. I think they want to write about an up-and-coming woman and now you're officially on the radar screen."

"Wow," she said. The publicity would be amazing. Bound to mean better recognition and, of course, better pay. Perhaps it was due to her improved mood, but instinctively she reached over to embrace her boss, who stiffened, with an awkward smile on his face. Funny old man. They never socialised outside work and didn't know much about each other, but he was like the father she'd never had. He had nurtured her career since the beginning and she was enormously fond of him.

Melanie sent Max a text. "Got great news at work. Would love to celebrate with you. Free tonight?"

The response was immediate. "Of course."

At her suggestion, they met in an exclusive Knightsbridge bar. When she arrived, Max was standing outside, talking on the phone. His lean body against the wall. She enjoyed the expression on his face when he saw her.

He hung up immediately. "Hi." An embrace. A slightly formal kiss. "It's good to see you."

"Good to see you too," she said.

"You look incredible," he said. "Haven't been able to get you out of my mind since yesterday. I was very pleased you called."

"Of course I'd call," she said. "What a wonderful weekend."

"Darling. You are my dream," he said. "I'm still amazed you've finally come back to me."

"Me too," said Mel, unsure how to deal with the romantic conversation. She pushed the door open to the bar. "Hope you like it. Haven't been here in ages." One of those amusing nights out with Jenny, where they had been ridiculously drunk.

They entered and took a seat at the counter. The barman handed them both a cocktail menu. An awkward pause as they both studied the list. She'd forgotten how expensive this place was. Probably because Jenny's date had bought all the drinks last time. What an idiot she was to bring Max here.

"Darling, this one is on me," she said.

He cleared his throat. "Don't worry. It's fine by me."

Had she damaged his ego already? "Of course I'll get it. It's my celebration." She flicked through the pages. "I'm going for a Mojito. What about you?"

"I'm not much of a cocktail drinker, but I'll follow your lead," he said. "What are we celebrating anyway?"

Melanie beamed with delight. "The *FT* wants to write about me as the next up-and-coming analyst. They're saying I could get the top spot on Extel. That's one of the major rating agencies."

"Great." A blank look. "What does that mean?"

"I'm really sorry. This must be boring for you."

"No, darling. I'd love to know more about what you do."

What a thoughtful man. "To be highly rated is a major deal for us. Basically means that the investors like my research. But most importantly, I'll make more money at bonus round."

"I see." He frowned. "Is it all about money?"

"Well…" Regretting her stupid comment already. "I mean, that's why people go into finance, isn't it?"

"I don't know. I assumed you enjoy your job."

"Of course I do. I meet tons of people and my research helps them make good investment decisions. It's very rewarding."

"It's about everyone making more and more money?"

"Sort of, I guess."

"Interesting." A perplexed wrinkle between his eyebrows. "I guess I've never thought about life that way. My job is more creative, I suppose. I fall in love every time I find a new painting."

"And that's what makes you fascinating," she said. Jenny was right. Definitely more challenging to date less wealthy men. But for tonight, she would cast that thought aside. She had enough to pay for drinks and the rest didn't matter.

That night they stayed up for hours talking. Without him having to touch her physically, his deep blue eyes spoke a thousand words. Mostly he seemed to want to know her. A unique experience; it had certainly never happened to her before. Not with Robert; he had been a boy, not remotely interested in romance. Not with Pierre; he had been infatuated with her body. And Lorenzo…better not to think about Lorenzo now.

Max was an unusual man. Finally, in the early hours of the morning, she drifted off in his arms.

Something brought her back to consciousness and she peered out of the covers at the clock. She jolted to reality. It was far too late to go to work; she had already missed her morning meeting. No excuse would be good enough and it would be simpler to call in sick. In any event, nothing mattered as much as him.

She gazed at him, sensing that something important had happened that night. He pulled her close, his lips connecting with hers, as if she was the only woman in the world.

"I love you, Melanie."

"I love you too, Max." At that moment, she believed it to be true.

Chapter Twenty-one

The nervous lull of the holiday season ended abruptly in September and Melanie published the industry report she'd compiled over the summer. The economy was crashing and she had decided to put all her stocks onto a SELL recommendation. Although Tony had approved it and they had agreed it was the right decision, she knew it was going to be controversial.

Jonathan's best client, Luke Avery, was furious about one stock in particular. The share price had slumped five per cent on the back of her report. He had called several times that day, demanding that she change her stance. But once the report was out, it couldn't be retracted.

That evening, the office floor was empty when she switched off her computer and hurried down the motionless room towards the lift. It was always a particularly unnerving time of night. Where there was normally such intense activity, the only sign of life was the yellow fluorescent lights flickering unsteadily above her.

This particular day had been more challenging than normal. Being yelled at and questioned had taken its toll, both mentally and physically. In her haste to leave, Melanie had forgotten her umbrella upstairs, and she cursed as she stepped outside into the sleeting rain. But there was no question of going back up. She made a dash for the Tube station, her heels expertly avoiding the cracks in the pavement.

Exiting the station at the other end, she pulled her coat over her head and ran towards her flat. She turned the corner into her street – and gasped in surprise. He was waiting under the portico, looking straight towards her. He must have been standing there for hours. Melanie glared at him, hating herself for the pleasure it gave her to see him again. "What the hell are you doing here?" God, he was attractive.

Pierre grabbed her by the waist. "You gave me no choice. If you won't speak to me on the phone, I had to come see you."

"How dare you." She slapped him hard on the face.

He didn't flinch. "*Chérie*, you know that excites me."

"Stop it, you bastard. I've got someone else now."

"So?" he said.

Melanie trembled, desperate not to show her nerves. "We're finished. Over."

"Whoever he is, he's nothing compared to us."

"He is."

"You can't replace me that easily," said Pierre.

"Pierre, I can't do this." But she knew her hesitation revealed her weakness.

"There is no love greater than ours. No passion like this." He pulled her close again, pressing his lips against her mouth. Despite the hatred, the pent-up desire was impossible to resist. Old memories engulfed her and she kissed him with passion.

Pierre removed the keys from her willing hand and opened the door, as he had done so many times before. As he held her, she felt him unmistakably against her stomach.

In her flat, he pushed her to the floor. "How dare you ignore me? You're mine."

She had always hated the way he spoke to her and this time was no different. Why couldn't he be more romantic? Like Max. But her mind was conquered by something more insistent. She didn't resist when he barely removed his trousers before climbing on top of her.

"You will always be mine, whatever you think." He thrust his fingers in her mouth, forcing her to gag. Complete domination.

She hated him intensely but her body ached for more. His breathing grew harder and his nails began to dig into her buttocks. A light exploded inside her. She had missed him too much. Nothing else mattered. How could she have expected to forget him?

He stopped for a second and she begged for more. But he hadn't finished and his flesh kept beating against hers. Finally, he collapsed, screaming her name loudly.

While he lay there, with his head on her chest, she realised he was sobbing. There was no doubt that he loved her and she too began to cry. Not from sadness, but from the physical joy of his presence.

She clung on to him for those precious seconds, not wanting to face reality. When her mind began to clear, she pulled herself from under his weight.

"Pierre, why are you doing this to me?"

"Is there a choice?" he said. "I love you, darling. You are my passion, my great love."

"But why? Why did you lie to me?"

"*Chérie.*" Those brown eyes pleading with her. "It's not as simple as you think. I love you, that's what matters."

Melanie moved away angrily. "You're such a bastard. I'm not going to fall for your crap anymore. Why didn't you tell me you were married?"

He drew her back. "How could I have told you? You would have never come to me."

"Of course I bloody wouldn't have."

"It would have been a crime to miss out on this. Yes, I'm married. But it's irrelevant. I married a long time ago, to the wrong woman. It should have been you. It can still be you. We can make it work."

"If your marriage is so terrible, how do you explain her pregnancy?" The thought of his child made her ill.

"The child was not planned." He turned his head to the side.

"That's not what Céleste told me."

"Fucking Céleste. She knows nothing."

"That's not what she says."

"She's a naïve little girl who likes to gossip. The child was a mistake. I have been begging Vanessa for an abortion. But she won't."

"Still, you've been sleeping with her all this time."

"Of course I have to sleep with my wife sometimes. That's part of being married, you know. But you are the one I dream of. It's all about you."

"Is that supposed to make me happy? That you dream about me while you fuck your wife?"

"That's exactly how it works. All I want is you."

She felt the ground shifting beneath her. Nothing was as it seemed. She wanted to believe him, but the rot had set in. Too deep to carve away. "Sorry, Pierre. I can't do this. Not like this. You need to leave."

He pulled her towards him. "Doesn't tonight show you everything? Darling, I need you."

Melanie stiffened, refusing to accept his embrace. "It shows me that you want to fuck me. But that's not enough. Go find someone else to sleep with. I'm not your little whore anymore."

"You were never my whore. I love you."

"Is this what you call love?" She spat at him with disgust. "Shoving me to the ground, with no ounce of romance? How dare you come back and do that again?"

"I thought that's what you liked. You never complained before."

"No. It's what you like. Have you ever asked me once what I like?" The moment of passion had faded and she was able to look at him clearly. "You have treated me appallingly and I deserve better."

"I'll give you anything you want," he said. "Anything."

"Are you going to leave your family?"

"I will. For you. Just now, the timing is tricky. But I will."

"Total crap and we both know it. Please go away."

"I can't leave you."

"You will. I swear to you that if you contact me again, I will call your house and tell your children everything." She grabbed his coat and tossed it at the door. "Fuck off."

Pierre made one final attempt to hold her, but she found the strength to push him away.

With both hands, she bolted the door before returning to the window; she needed to look at him one last time. It was gratifying to see his shoulders hunched in despair. She watched until his figure became small in the distance, moving steadily away from her. She knew he loved her, in his own peculiar way, but she had to let go.

Her cigarette glowed sharply red as she sucked deeply, leaning over her balcony, on that wet starless night. The grief she had buried away had exploded into anger and for that she was grateful. He had stripped her bare and there was nothing left to take. The madness inside her had died with his departure that night. It was over and she stood on her balcony staring blankly into her own emptiness. It was time to move on.

She summoned the courage to tell Jenny that weekend, at one of their favourite Mayfair wine bars.

"You did what?" said Jenny. "I can't believe he seduced you again after all that."

Melanie held her head in her hands. "Please don't make fun of me, Jenny. Not now. I feel awful about it. How could I have slept with him after all he's done to me?"

"It is pretty funny though," said Jenny.

Melanie raised her eyes. "Doesn't feel remotely amusing from where I'm sitting."

"You know, if the sex is that good, you could always keep seeing him. I mean, what difference does it make?"

"What on earth are you talking about? He's a bastard. And he's married."

"And?" said Jenny.

"Don't be disgusting, it's not moral."

"You slept with Lorenzo," said Jenny. "Isn't he married?"

"I have no idea about Lorenzo. I never asked him."

"Stop kidding yourself. We all know he's married," said Jenny. "Complete classic."

"What do you mean?" Of course it was obvious, but she hadn't wanted to face the issue.

"Oh, come on. Do you have his home number?"

Melanie shook her head. "No."

"And do you know anything about him? Other than he's good

in bed? Married men have always had affairs. That's the way the world works. Accept it and enjoy the sex."

"What about Max?" said Melanie.

"What about him?"

"He'll be mortified."

"Are you demented?" Jenny was looking at her in amusement. "Where is the upside in telling him anything? All I'm saying is that, however sexy your Frenchie is now, you'll probably get bored of him in the long run. I'll tell you something else, you were never in love with that man."

"I was in love with him."

"That's not love, darling. It's an obsessive masochistic streak you discovered in yourself. Not a bad thing in itself, but don't confuse it for love. Recognise it, enjoy it and use him for sex in the meantime. You might not like him as a person, but physically he clearly does it for you."

"You're deranged. You're telling me to have two relationships at the same time. I'm sure Pierre wouldn't mind that much, but somehow I don't think it would go down well with Max."

Jenny chuckled. "You're even more of an idiot than I thought. Max doesn't need to know."

"Relationships are based on trust," said Melanie, not believing her own words.

"Give me a break. It's not as if you're going to marry either of them, is it?"

"How do you know that?" said Melanie. "Max is quite keen on me."

"Oh, please, he's not the one for you. He's far too nice."

Melanie glared at her friend. "Why shouldn't I have a nice boyfriend?"

"You know what I'm talking about. Don't pretend to be anything other than yourself."

"I don't know what to think anymore," said Melanie. Why couldn't life be more straightforward? "Don't you ever fall in love?"

Jenny shrugged. "No. Reckon it's all over-rated anyway."

"What's over-rated?" said Melanie.

"Love. Marriage. Relationships in general."

"What do you mean?"

"Name one happy couple. One. I challenge you."

Melanie sat back and contemplated the question. It was an interesting point. So many of her male colleagues were having affairs. "I know. Tony."

"Tony?" said Jenny. "You're kidding, right?"

"No," said Melanie. "I'd be amazed if he was playing around. Not the type."

"You never know," said Jenny. "Besides, even if he isn't having an affair, he never goes home. He works like a dog and is always travelling."

"OK. David and Samantha."

"Boring." Jenny opened her mouth wide, pretending to yawn. "Anyway, it's early days for them. Give them a few years and they will have settled into a mundane routine at home where they completely ignore each other. I can picture it now."

"Picture what, exactly?"

"Oh, you know, two or three kids. She'll be a nervous wreck after all that breastfeeding and laundry and by then will have stopped caring what she looks like. Even more than now. He'll be so unbelievably bored by her histrionics that he'll either be down at the pub with his equally dull friends or watching something tedious on the History Channel."

Melanie laughed. "OK, you have a point. Jesus. What's going to happen to us then?"

"Why do you even stress about it? Surely you don't aspire to all that claptrap?"

"What about kids?"

"Who the hell wants kids these days? My take is that they only screw up the best years of your life and then they grow up and hate you. I hate my parents. Why bother?"

"You might want them. One day. When you're in your thirties. Then you'll need to find a man."

"If it gets to that, independent production is the way forward. Who needs a man to interfere and start bossing us around?

Look at both our fathers. Complete arseholes."

"Oh, Jenny. I don't know what to think anymore."

"Hey," said Jenny, changing the subject entirely. "Isn't that Victoria over there?" Their erstwhile colleague was looking as glamorous as ever and clearly had the attention of a couple of men at her table. "Let's go talk to her."

"I don't know," said Melanie. "I'm not in the mood."

"It's what you need. Bit of fun. Bet she's got some good gossip." Jenny was already on the way to the table. Melanie stood up and followed reluctantly.

Victoria raised her eyebrows. "Hi, girls. How are you both?" No sign of resentment.

"Pretty much the same," said Jenny. "We're still at the bank. What about you?"

"Haven't you heard?" Victoria tilted her head.

"Heard what?" said Jenny.

"I thought everyone knew about my new job. Best career move ever."

"Sorry," said Melanie. "I haven't been paying attention." In truth, nobody at the bank discussed Victoria anymore. She had become irrelevant.

Victoria narrowed her eyes. "You have heard of Taton Capital though?"

"Sure," said Melanie. No, she thought, what the hell was Taton Capital?

"I'm their head of sales. Much better hours and pay than the bloody bank. Fund's doing amazingly right now. We've been shorting the market all year. Up twenty per cent."

"That's terrific news. Congratulations." Melanie raised her glass. "Let's drink to that."

Victoria's forced enthusiasm seemed terribly contrived compared to the genuine confidence of the past. But, still, it was good to see that at some level she hadn't been defeated.

They weren't that different. Both of them had allowed powerful men too close. Victoria had been unlucky; her affair was too public, with no escape. And here she was, making her way to the top again. Whether or not her career was flourishing to the degree she was describing was immaterial. The point was that her spirit hadn't been crushed. To an outsider, she would be convincing. Beautiful and fantastic.

While speaking to Victoria, Melanie hadn't noticed Jenny becoming engrossed with one of the men at the table. She sighed, unwilling to participate in Jenny's banter this evening.

"Ladies, I need to go," said Melanie. "Totally shattered." Not so much tired as emotionally drained.

"OK." Jenny barely acknowledged her. She clearly had better things to focus on.

"Great to see you." Victoria handed over her business card. "Let's stay in touch."

"I'd love to do that," said Melanie. And she meant it. Despite their difficult beginning, she felt they could be friends. They had plenty in common. After her recent ordeal, she needed more women like Victoria in her life.

She bade them farewell and made her way into the night. While strolling through the back streets of Piccadilly, she mused on Jenny's words. It was inconceivable for her to go back to Pierre. Poisonous man. How was it possible she'd been so bewitched by him? To hell with Jenny and her madness. She had had the courage to send him away and she refused to weaken again. As long as he didn't reappear and test her fragile resolve.

London in the drizzle. Street lights bravely romantic in this bleakest of weathers. What was there not to love about it? Everyone else hustling past with black umbrellas. But not her. She stopped and lifted her face to greet the moist air. There was something captivating about the city and at that moment, she wanted to share it with someone. Instinctively, she dialled Max's number. She hadn't seen him since Pierre's nocturnal visit, but now she was ready. Max was pure and decent and precisely what she needed.

Max was already home and invited her to stop by. And there he was, waiting downstairs when she arrived. With a smile, he took her hand and led her up the steps.

"Hate your stairs," she said.

"I hope that's not why you've been staying away this week."

"Silly." She gripped his hand. It hadn't occurred to her that he had been worried about her absence. His thoughtfulness always accentuated her own selfishness.

"Still, lovely you're here," he said. "I've missed you."

"I've missed you too." A white lie. But no harm in that.

"Good to hear," he said. "You've been rather quiet recently. Anything to worry about?" He was peering too closely.

She stepped back, knowing that she could never tell him the truth. "Of course not, darling. Work's been a total nightmare. You've seen the stock market?"

He laughed. "Yeah, even I can't get away from the news."

Melanie shook her head. "It's horrific. Not to mention my stupid report."

"What about it? Did something happen?"

She sighed. "I've caused a lot of trouble and some of the investors are angry with me. It's been tricky to deal with and I haven't had a spare moment to myself."

"I don't understand these people that give you hassle."

"It's a strange job, darling."

"Sounds like it," he said. "Still, great that you managed to find the time tonight." He removed her coat and ran his hands through her damp hair. "Let's forget about work for a while, shall we?"

"It's good to see you," she said. It never ceased to amaze her how courteous he was.

"I hope this means you're going to stay all night," he said.

"Of course," said Melanie. "I couldn't possibly resist you."

The candles were glowing in the now-familiar room. Classical music in the background. Max kissed her and began unbuttoning her shirt. "I am going to make love to you all night." He moved his mouth up her neck and led her to his room. On the bed, he tugged off her skirt. "You have such a great body."

"You're the one with the good body," said Melanie. She had never seen another like it. She loved undressing him. A work of art. It didn't matter that he wasn't Pierre. Or did it? She didn't want to think about it right now. She slid backwards in his bed and whispered into his ear. "You can hit me if you want."

"Hmmm?"

She wasn't sure if he had heard her, so she repeated it. "Hit me, please."

He stopped. "What on earth are you talking about? Of course I'm not going to hit you."

Melanie moved away, ashamed. "Sorry, Max. I didn't mean it, just teasing."

"Is that what you want?" he said.

"No, of course not," she said. "Come here." She tried to kiss him but the moment had passed.

Max turned away. She huddled in the bed and pulled the covers over her shoulders, pretending to fall asleep. Why couldn't she enjoy this loving relationship? What part of her needed to be humiliated? Perhaps she had delved too far into the darkness. Perhaps, for her, there was no salvation.

Max didn't fall asleep. She sensed that he was watching her, wondering what had happened. He got up and began to pace the small flat. But she waited. It felt like eternity, but finally he came back and lay down next to her.

Once she heard his rhythmic snoring, Melanie quietly dressed and left.

She walked home that night, in the cold and the dark. It hadn't stopped raining. A night bus slowed down for her, but she didn't catch it; she needed to be alone. She crossed the bridge and stared into the murky water below. She could understand why people jumped. Sometimes life was just too bleak.

After that night, she resolved not to see Max again. Clearly, she wasn't ready for a relationship and it would be wrong to pretend otherwise. Pierre had inflicted more damage than she'd realised and she needed to sort things out by herself. Max was a decent man and it was immoral to use him as a rebound, or as revenge for Pierre. He deserved far better.

In the meantime, she could focus on her work.

*

When the phone rang a few days later, she didn't recognise the woman's voice. "Melanie. How are you?"

"I'm fine," she said. "Sorry, who is this?"

"Céleste, from Paris."

"Hi." Melanie sat up. "Long time. What's up?" Why the hell was Céleste calling? They hadn't spoken since the Paris trip.

Melanie heard the sound of a door click shut on the other end of the phone. Céleste began to whisper. "I'm sorry to disturb you. But I've been worried about you. They don't know I'm calling."

"Who doesn't know? What are you talking about?"

"Pierre. He's been saying some terrible things about you. I'm sorry."

Melanie went cold. How could the bastard have talked? He was even more despicable than she'd thought. "What do you mean?"

"Oh, gosh. So many things. About how his clients hate your big report. You know, dreadful things about your work. That it was a mistake to promote you. That Tony should get you fired. He hasn't stopped talking about it. I don't know what you've done, but he's furious with you."

"He's bitching about my work? My work? Seriously?" said Melanie. What the hell was the man doing?

"Yes. I've never seen him so angry. And I have seen a lot, believe me. I'm sorry to be the one to tell you. But I thought you should know, in case he calls Tony. Pierre is very influential."

Melanie gulped. "Yeah."

"Please don't tell anyone I called. Pierre has been shouting at me a lot recently too. I'll get into such trouble."

"Of course not. Thanks, Céleste. I truly appreciate it."

Melanie hung up the phone and slammed her fist down on the table. Unbelievable son-of-a-bitch. He knew that would hurt her. As if he hadn't done enough already.

Chapter Twenty-two

The financial crisis hadn't abated and it was only a matter of time before all the banks used it as a convenient excuse to cull their labour forces. Not that they generally needed any excuses. Redundancies were a recognised part of City life. The banks always over-hired in the boom years and inevitably over-fired when any downturn arrived. But this time was going to be far more vicious and everyone knew it was coming.

The cull was widely rumoured to be happening on Thursday. Melanie arrived at work earlier than usual that day, having been unable to sleep the night before. She'd spoken to Tony about Pierre's clients, and he had shrugged, apparently indifferent to the Frenchman's views. But Tony was not the one who made the final decisions and it was impossible to know if Pierre had managed to convince the London managers. He'd arranged her promotion, so presumably he could also get her fired. How much influence did he really have? She should have networked harder with the London bosses, instead of complacently relying on her lover. It wasn't as if Mitch would support her either, especially given how rude she'd been to him earlier in the year. What an idiot she had been.

At ten past nine, a phone rang across the hushed room and she saw Alice from Oil and Gas rise from her desk. Alice with the large bottom.

"Poor thing," said Pamela. "She's the first casualty. Such a sweet girl. Works like a dog too. I never understand how they choose."

"What do you mean?" said Melanie.

"That's how it goes. They call people in one by one. The last massive round was a few years before you joined. It was hideous. Reckon we lost about a third of the firm."

"Who calls them in?"

"Management. Watch. She'll be back in less than five minutes and start packing her things. Probably in tears, poor love."

"Seriously? Just like that?"

"Yeah, it's brutal. She won't even get a chance to download her personal stuff off her computer. Some guy in IT presses a button and it all goes into shutdown mode."

"God." Melanie fixed her eyes on the door at the far end of the room. Sure enough, Alice returned. No tears, but her sagging shoulders told the story.

Melanie turned away, not wanting to stare. But she couldn't help notice Alice gathering her possessions and being escorted to the lift. In a flash, career over. Jettisoned by the very company she'd sacrificed her best years for. No farewell party. Nothing.

A phone rang further down the room and a tall man stood up. She'd noticed him before but didn't know his name.

"Alan. In the Pharma team. He only joined last year," said Pamela. "Nice guy."

Melanie buried her face in her screen, pretending to work. But she couldn't. What if they called her? The timing with Pierre could not have been worse. A perfect opportunity for him to get rid of her. The bastard would love it.

The hours passed and she watched as, one by one, people were summoned upstairs. By half past three it seemed to have stopped. People were beginning to talk again. Mostly to see if it had ended. Nobody could tell for sure. Suddenly her phone rang. She froze and Pamela stared at her in horror.

"Don't pick it up," said Pamela.

"I have to," she said.

"Shit," said her friend.

Melanie's hand trembled. "Hello."

"Mel. Hi. It's me, Jenny."

"Oh," she said, momentarily confused. "Jenny. What a relief."

"What do you mean?"

"Thought I was going to get fired."

"Huh?" said Jenny. "Get real, you're the last person they would ditch."

"Don't know about that. I told you about you-know-who."

"Come on. You're the up-and-coming star."

"Thanks," said Melanie. "Anyway, it seems to have stopped for today."

"Yeah, that's the word down here too. We lost three on the desk and quite a few traders. It's been a shit day."

"Who?"

"I'll tell you later. Only one I'm pleased about. But again, not on the phone."

"OK."

"Anyway, that's not why I'm calling. I've got some news for you."

"What?" said Melanie.

"Meet me after work?"

"Yeah, OK, I'll come over." Melanie put down the phone and grinned at Pamela. Whatever it was that Jenny was going to tell her couldn't be that important. Despite Pierre, it seemed she had made it through unscathed.

They met after work in a bar off Notting Hill Gate. Another one of Jenny's favourites. Jenny was already into the first bottle of wine and she poured Melanie a generous glass as she approached the table. "Let's celebrate that we are both still employed and Zack got the sack."

Melanie raised her glass. "It has a certain ring. Justice prevails."

"Isn't it great? So pleased not to set eyes on that two-faced prick again. But, that's not why I called."

"Tell me," said Melanie.

"I've done it," said Jenny.

"Done what exactly?" Melanie leaned in. Clearly another sex story, which would be entertaining as always.

"Slept with him."

"With who?" said Melanie. "It's not the shortest list on the planet."

Jenny laughed. "That might be construed as rather rude, if I didn't know you better. You really don't know?"

"Spit it out. Of course I've got no bloody clue. You're going to kill me with the suspense." Sometimes Jenny could be a bore.

"Mitch, of course."

"What?!" Melanie sat back in disgust. "You must be joking."

"I'm not."

"But…you know he wanted to get me fired."

"You're so paranoid. First Pierre, now Mitch."

"Mitch hates me."

"Don't be ridiculous. He thinks very highly of you. Spent half the evening talking about you. In fact, that's what I wanted to tell you. I think he's obsessed with you."

Melanie glowered at her friend. "What crap."

"It's true. You may have misjudged him."

Melanie shook her head. "I don't think so. And after all I told you about him, how could you sleep with him?"

"He has a cool flat, at least."

"Please don't tell me you screwed him because he's got a large pad? You, of all people, don't need to be impressed by that stuff."

"I don't know. We were having drinks after work. He's so handsome. I thought what the hell. Nothing to lose. I don't work with him."

"I work with him." Melanie moved away, maddened by the conversation.

"That has nothing to do with me. Stop being judgemental. You're the one who went out with your senior for over a year."

"That's mean. You know I'm still not over it. Not to mention what I did to Max." Melanie turned away, tears in her eyes. Poor Max. Why did she always start crying?

"Mel, this was supposed to be amusing," said Jenny. "Don't you want to hear about it?"

"No," said Melanie. "But do I have a choice?"

"Oh, lighten up. I'll tell you. It was hilarious."

Melanie wiped her eyes and sipped her drink, allowing Jenny to continue.

"OK, so he took me to his flat. Massive bachelor pad by the park. Totally perfect, just like him. Not a thing out of place. Bit weird, but I guess he's into all that. Total OCD."

"So?" said Melanie, her interest perking up.

"I was already pretty pissed at the time but, anyway, out comes the champagne. On comes the music. All pretty standard stuff. He's clearly got a seduction checklist. No candles, funnily enough."

"Doesn't surprise me. So how was the sex?"

"Ugghhh, that's the whole thing. Awful."

Melanie choked on her drink. "You're telling me all this to say he's a terrible lover? You're deranged."

"I'm not joking. The whole thing was shit."

"Really?"

"To be honest, I don't think he fancies me that much." Jenny grinned. "I'm pretty sure he'd much rather be with you."

"Disgusting thought," said Melanie.

Chapter Twenty-three

At first she assumed the nausea had been induced by the drinking. The past few weeks had been particularly rough at work and she had compensated with too much wine in the evenings. But the sickness intensified and steadily became more draining. She was hardly able to scrape through each day and her limbs ached with a fatigue that grew more pressing by the minute. If she hadn't been so self-absorbed, she might have realised sooner that her monthly cycles had stopped and that her body was no longer fully her own.

The unwelcome truth dawned on her one morning before work as she patted down her fitted trousers. She was pregnant. And with equal clarity she knew who the father was.

There were never any pharmacies open before she got to work and the time dragged until she could go out for her lunch break. Not wanting to be seen purchasing pregnancy kits, she walked ten minutes to a shop she frequented less.

The man at the counter smiled when she handed over the money. In her paranoia, he seemed to be mocking her. Clearly not married. Such a slut. But she was being ridiculous. They must sell hundreds of these things. What did he care anyway? And why should it matter what he thought? But somehow it did and she hunched her shoulders in shame.

Without stopping at her desk, Melanie went directly to the office bathroom. If she had hoped her fears would be unfounded, the two blue lines on the pregnancy kit shattered any illusions. They beamed strong and bright; there was no mistaking the result. A few other women came and went, but she stayed there, locked away in a cubicle for a full hour, holding her head in her hands. No tears at all. How could she have allowed this to happen? So idiotic. She supposed it hadn't been her fault – he had forced himself on her that night. But it didn't change the facts. Her thoughts rested miserably on the child in her womb; a child with no future.

Finally rising stiffly out of the cubicle, she returned to her desk and told her team she was leaving for the day. Impossible to remain in the office and pretend nothing was wrong. Pamela shrugged. At least nobody questioned her movements anymore.

Arriving at her flat at three o'clock, she lit a cigarette and sucked it down. On one level, it made her feel sick. On another, it was a clear rebellion against her state. An hour later, she called Jenny, who promised to come over straight after work.

For once, Jenny was punctual.

Seeing her friend, Melanie broke down. "Jenny, Jenny, I've totally screwed up."

Without removing her coat, Jenny put her arms round her. "What's happened? Did Pierre come over again?"

"No. Much worse than that."

"Tell me."

"I'm pregnant." And there it was. The dreadful word. At least with Jenny there was no need for pretence.

"I thought you were on the pill," said Jenny.

"I was, but the doctor made me stop a few months ago. Was messing with my hormones. Bloody idiot that I am."

"OK. OK. Who's the father?"

"I can't be sure," she said. Did that make her a complete slut? "Think it's Pierre."

"From that night?" said Jenny. "But that was ages ago."

Melanie wiped her eyes again. "I can't have this baby, Jenny. I can't."

"Of course you can't. Out of the question."

"What a fuck-up. How could I have allowed this to happen?"

To her surprise, Jenny leaned forward and held her hand. "Mel, it's not the end of the world. It happens to tons of women. Welcome to the club."

"What?" said Melanie.

"I had an abortion two years ago. Not very pleasant, but I know a good place."

"You never told me that."

"You never asked. Besides, it's not something I'm massively proud of, as I'm sure you can understand."

"No." This entire experience was truly miserable.

"How far along are you?"

"Don't know. Must be at least six weeks since then."

"What? Was it that long ago?"

"I know, I've been slow at realising."

Jenny laughed. "You're even more of an idiot than I was."

"It's not funny." Why did Jenny make a joke of everything?

"Now, come on. Don't worry about it. I'll sort you out. But you should get a move on. You'll start showing soon."

"Do I look fat?" Melanie instinctively touched her stomach.

"Not at all. But it would be best to get this fixed in the next week or two."

"How the hell do I do that?" Melanie took her friend's hand, desperate for help.

Jenny pulled out her phone and scrolled through her contacts. "There's a great guy. I'll give you his number. He operates in one of those clinics around Harley Street. It won't be cheap, but he's excellent."

"Really? Can this be sorted that easily? What do they do?"

"Don't worry too much about the details. They will deal with everything." Jenny grabbed a bottle of champagne from her bag and started to pour her a glass. "I had no idea what the problem was, but champagne is always a welcome solution. And there's no need to stop drinking."

"Yeah. Good idea." Thank goodness for friends. Where would she be without Jenny? She loved her more than ever at that moment. The cold bubbles felt good on her tongue, despite her body's natural inclination to reject it.

*

Four days later, her appointment confirmed her nine-week pregnancy. Conception from the very passion that had torn her world apart. She had kicked him out, but Pierre had left his mark in so many ways. Cruel, biting irony. She would have to purge him all over again.

Clinically, and with a deep hatred that she could hardly contain, Melanie signed the agreement forms for the abortion. It was impossible to look at the nurse; impossible to compute what she was doing.

The days passed slowly and painfully until the moment she handed herself over to the doctor on Friday morning. She stared at the yellowing patch on the ceiling and heard the snapping of the surgical gloves.

"Open your legs." The doctor's hands pushed her inner thighs. "Wider." His voice was gentle. Completely at odds with what he was doing.

She whispered, barely able to talk. "Is that OK?"

He nodded and she averted her eyes. A large tear rolled silently down her face as the instruments of death moved inside her.

Although it felt like an eternity, the actual procedure didn't take long.

Afterwards, she hobbled out of the clinic and into the lift, the pads between her legs a reminder of her miserable conscience. The steel doors snapped shut and the lift pinged its way down to the ground floor. All she felt was hatred. Mostly for herself. Is this what death felt like? The act of killing had twisted a knife into her own heart. She tried not to focus on the lifeblood that had been sucked from her womb. She tried not to think about the baby and the bewildering nothingness that she had forced it to become. She tried not to think of her blood merging with Pierre's and, most of all, she tried not to think about Pierre.

Her insides ached and the bleeding was still raging, but she went to work as usual on Monday. In this current environment she couldn't be seen to be slacking. Anyway, it was preferable to wallowing in her flat. She'd already spent the weekend by herself and the distraction of the job was a welcome respite.

As she inched to her desk, she wondered if anyone would notice. Amazing that the rest of the world could be impervious to the crushing, bruising ordeal that was threatening to overwhelm her. The fact that nobody seemed to care only served to magnify her own isolation. But on the other hand, she was pathetically grateful for her unobservant colleagues. Even Pamela was uncharacteristically busy.

Max called during her short lunch break that day. She stared at his name flashing up on her phone. She hadn't seen him since that night she had walked out. Apart from one long letter, begging him for space and forgiveness, she had not been in contact. Why was he calling today, of all days? Now, more than ever, she wanted nothing to do with him. She returned to her desk and buried herself in her work, trying to push them all out of her mind.

But work didn't particularly help, because Pierre was always present. Mostly, it wasn't a physical presence, just his name in an email or mentioned in a meeting. But occasionally he would appear in the office, where he would stare at her from across the room. Thankfully he never came to her desk. His furious campaign against her seemed to have abated, but he didn't stop calling. Once a day. Sometimes more. She never answered, hoping he would give up. Would it ever get any easier? She visualised the upcoming birth of his wife's child and forlornly thought of her own dead foetus. She hadn't wanted his baby, but couldn't help imagining how it might have looked. Her own blue eyes and pale skin, or his darker complexion? Although her decision had been rational, it felt wrong to have crushed a life before it had even begun. It should have been allowed to live, this beautiful child of passion. Perhaps she should have given it up for adoption…but how could she have concealed the pregnancy? Complete nightmare. She wanted nothing to do with men ever again.

Chapter Twenty-four

Time didn't heal a damned thing. Each morning, she would wake to the same ringtone on her alarm, slam it on to snooze until she finally dragged herself into the shower. The cold water always forced her into a vague sense of consciousness. God, she despised cold showers. But there was no other way. Sometimes she caught herself touching her stomach, subconsciously connecting with the creation that had been ripped away. She hated herself for remembering and immediately tried to block it from her mind. All desire had evaporated, replaced with an unending void, an emptiness that nothing could fill.

Somehow she retained her capacity for work, but the hours spent at her desk passed in a murky haze. Her reports were written with a mechanical efficiency. She was good at her job and it now required minimal effort. The corporate machine was well oiled and kept moving regardless of her mental state. Every night, she would return to a bottle of wine and packet of cigarettes.

At home, it was always the same. A familiar spasm of dejection when she walked back to her loneliness. When her door clicked behind her, her shoulders sagged; she was alone and didn't need to pretend anymore. Nobody else saw the lifeless flat with its stale smell of old cigarettes. How could they know that she hadn't cooked a single hot meal for herself for over three years? Pathetic though it was, it was her own private sanctuary.

It had been months since the abortion, but she barely spoke outside work, refused to see David and stopped accompanying Jenny out at weekends. Having given her a long reprieve, Jenny finally stormed up to her apartment.

"Let me in, Mel." Loud banging at the door.

Curled up on the sofa, Melanie glared at the door. "Go away," she mouthed.

"I know you're there. Let me in, damn it." Another loud bang.

"I don't feel very well," she said.

"That's been pretty obvious to just about everyone." Jenny shouted from behind the door. "Look, it's only me. Let me in."

Melanie relented and unlocked the door. "OK, you win."

"You look like shit," said Jenny, who had clearly noted the unwashed hair and stained dressing gown.

"Thanks for the pep talk. Have you finished?" Melanie tugged the gown round her waist.

"No," said Jenny. "This has got to stop. Look at yourself. I thought you were tougher than this."

"What if I'm not?" Jenny's reaction to her appearance only highlighted how awful her life had become.

"That's what I'm here for. Remember, I'm your friend." Jenny hugged her. "I've been thinking about you for weeks and I have a solution."

"What can you possibly do?" asked Melanie. "Don't you dare suggest another stupid date."

"Don't worry." Jenny laughed. "No man would look twice at you right now."

Melanie glared at her friend.

"OK," said Jenny. "That was my silly attempt at a joke. I've made a doctor's appointment for you after work tomorrow."

"What kind of doctor?" said Melanie. "I'm not sick."

"You are sick," said Jenny. "And we are going to sort this out together. Trust me. In the meantime, where's the wine?"

Jenny's doctor was on Devonshire Place. A well-known psychiatrist that Jenny's cousin had been seeing for years. After work the next day, the girls waited together, perched on a battered beige sofa opposite two old men. An uninviting, sterile room, complete with a few pictures of artificially photogenic families on the wall. The flickering light in the corner only served to increase Melanie's intense feeling of nausea. What the hell was she doing here?

After twenty minutes, the receptionist called her name and Melanie walked down the corridor to room 8. Jenny stayed behind. A bald middle-aged man opened the door. Blue shirt, white goatee, small black eyes. Dr Stockwell introduced himself, shook her hand and asked her to take a seat.

He glanced at his paperwork. "Melanie. Is this your first time?" She nodded.

"Not a problem. People normally don't know what to expect."

"No." That was an understatement. Not a clue.

"You're here because something is troubling you." He paused. "My job is to help you."

That was fairly obvious. "But how?"

"It won't happen overnight. But generally speaking, the more we talk, the more you will find ways out of your predicament, whatever that might be. Why don't we start with the basics? Tell me anything that comes to mind. Something must have brought you here."

At that moment she realised what it was all about. She could speak, with no shame and no agenda. To someone who, with his bland professionalism, wouldn't judge her. No need to hold back at all. The words flooded out. She spoke about Pierre, about Max and about her infidelity. She spoke about her job and her success, the drinking and the sleepless nights. And, of course, she spoke about the baby. He didn't say much, watching from a respectable distance and taking notes.

Finally, he spoke again. "Melanie. You've been terrific. That's a great start. Clearly there is a lot going on in your life. You've been through a major trauma. All on top of a highly pressurised job. How do you feel about your career right now?"

"What do you mean?" she said.

"Perhaps you might consider taking some time out, for a little while?"

Melanie sat up in her chair. "Out of the question. I'd lose my job. Particularly now."

He nodded. "I understand." He picked up a pen and wrote out a prescription. "Please take these regularly. It's a very low dose and

I'd like to see how you get on. Would you be able to come back next week?"

Melanie took the paper. "Thank you." She wiped a tear from her left eye, not caring that he'd seen. Happy to have found a solution of sorts, she shook his hand and left the room. She handed the prescription to Jenny, who presented it to the pharmacy round the corner.

The first two visits to Dr Stockwell proved to be a great success. Combined with the medication, the conversations helped her enormously. It was cathartic to vent her frustrations and deepest concerns. Without her understanding how he managed, the doctor expertly began to guide her deeper into the past. Her childhood, her mother and finally her father. An old festering wound.

In the third week, she broke down. This strange old doctor had scraped open the surface and the words cascaded out. A lifetime of pain. She had tried not to think about her father for years. He had abandoned them so long ago and she hadn't heard from him since. He could be dead. That was something that hadn't occurred to her before. Would it make any difference? Probably not.

She spoke about the beatings, the women, the alcohol and her mother's bruises. So many times, she had listened from her bed to the arguments, to the slamming of the door. With the silence that inevitably ensued, she would creep to her parents' room and find her mother sobbing by the bed.

One day, he left and never returned. They had waited at the breakfast table and searched for him after school, but somehow, everyone knew it was final. He truly had gone, presumably leaving them for that other woman her parents had always been fighting about.

From that day, his name was never allowed in the house. She and David used to whisper it in their rooms, but never to their mother. They knew the pain it had caused her and were frightened to make her cry again.

As for their mother, she had grown stern and quiet, presumably internalising her pain. She never recovered from the shock. Melanie knew it had killed her, ebbing the lifeblood, as surely as the cancer. She had wanted to die and nobody had been able to help.

For what seemed an eternity, Melanie talked and talked, her chest rising with the effort of containing her emotion. While she sobbed, the man's soft voice began to grate.

"It's wonderful that you are articulating all this," he said.

"What's wonderful about this? Just look. I'm a total wreck."

He stroked his goatee. "It's important to talk."

Melanie snapped, maddened by her own pathetic weakness. Why was she crying in front of this stranger? "Self-obsession is not a quality I admire. I've had enough of this crap. I'm just sorry I had to remember all that shit."

He leaned forward. "Melanie…"

"Look. Thanks for everything. But this doesn't work for me."

"You are doing extremely well. Don't give up now."

But it was too late. Melanie had collected her bag and was heading for the door. She heard the doctor sigh; that resigned, bored sigh of a man who had seen it all before. But she was furious for having partaken and if the man expected her to return, she was equally determined to prove him wrong. Of course her life wasn't perfect, but whose was? At least she was a success at work and everyone respected her. Without the facade, she would fall apart. Damn the sermonising professionals. What could they possibly know anyway?

Still, she was grateful for the pills and the fact that she had at least another month's supply. They certainly helped at the margin. If she was honest with herself, she couldn't have managed without them.

Chapter Twenty-five

The weeks passed and, despite the warnings on her medication, Melanie continued to find solace in cigarettes and alcohol. Although she drew the line at hard drugs, she returned to her drinking binges with Jenny, who was delighted to welcome her friend back. It was a relief to rediscover a sense of normality and one morning, she made an instant decision. Time to call Lorenzo. Someone who wouldn't hurt her and who she wouldn't hurt back. Why hadn't she thought of it earlier?

Hopefully he wouldn't have forgotten her. They'd exchanged a few texts, but she hadn't seen him for a year. Holding her breath, she dialled his number.

He answered on the third ring. "Hello."

"Lorenzo. How are you? It's Melanie."

"Melanie. What a pleasure." A shiver darted down her spine. She had forgotten how intoxicating the man was.

"I was wondering if I could take you up on that very kind offer of yours?" she said. "Hopefully I haven't left it too long."

"Darling, when I said any time, that's exactly what I meant." No hesitation. She loved him for that. And for the fact that he didn't ask questions.

Melanie paused. "Can you come visit some time?"

"Absolutely. What did you have in mind?"

"Come any time. You can stay with me." She surprised herself with the suddenness of her own offer.

He laughed and she pictured him at the other end of the phone. The dark stranger with honeyed eyes and an irresistible kiss. Those were the only details she remembered. But she could never forget the emotions he inspired, or how she had reacted to his touch. Incredible how his voice soothed her soul. He was precisely the tonic she craved.

"How can a man resist?" he said. "Let me arrange some meetings next week."

"Really? So soon? That would be fantastic. Just hearing your voice makes me happy."

"Me too, my darling. I need to make some calls, but it should be fairly straightforward. I am overdue a visit to London. This gives me a wonderful excuse. Perhaps on Thursday and Friday?"

At last, she was regaining control and it felt liberating. It was also a fantastic impetus to organise her apartment, remove the filth and inject freshness back into life.

When he arrived that week, she was ready for him. This man was exquisite. He wasn't trying to dominate her or possess her in any way; it was all for the moment. A complete stranger at one level, but so loving on another. Perfection.

They made love for hours, the young alabaster girl with this most elusive of men. A form of mutual worship. She wanted nothing from him other than his uncomplicated love. The fact that he might have a family somewhere didn't bother her. She didn't want to steal him from any wife or girlfriend. Only a few hours of passion. To him, she was his goddess. She allowed herself to believe it all and it was eternal, just for those sweet moments. Of course it wouldn't last, but it wasn't meant to. Surprisingly simple.

She kissed him on Friday, knowing that he would be flying back to his real life. With complete certainty, she also knew her love for him could be locked away and it would be easy to keep things exactly as they were. It was odd; the less she needed a man emotionally, the more she was willing to provide.

Those two days motivated her to take charge of herself again. She was bored of her own misery and this was an opportunity to snap out of it. Self-pity was pathetic and she needed to be stronger. It had killed her mother, but it wasn't going to get the better of her.

Now she understood why Jenny enjoyed this life. She too was going to pick her men and use them for her own indulgence.

The first target was the most interesting, a challenge that she wasn't sure she could accomplish.

The hotel in Mayfair was perfect. Big enough to be anonymous, expensive enough to attract a certain clientele. A stout old door-man nodded politely and she strode through the front door that Wednesday night. Into the lobby, towards the hotel bathroom for one final check. The image in the mirror pleased her. She had chosen a short black dress for the evening, knowing it was elegant but also extremely alluring. Immaculate make-up. She was ready.

Taking a deep breath, she passed the reception desk, directly to the bar on the other side.

It was disappointingly empty, but there was no turning back. There were three men inside and she had to choose one of them tonight. For her own sanity, she was desperate to see this mission through.

Melanie ordered a glass of wine and sat down in the corner, taking a few minutes to make her choice.

The short, bald one was dismissed. Too fat. For all her new-found courage, she couldn't overlook that basic problem.

The young dark-haired man, or the older blond? The older one would probably be more grateful. Made it easier. She caught his attention from across the room, her chin resting on her hand and one finger slightly between her lips. Her eyes lingered for a few seconds longer than normal. He smiled back. Much simpler than she had expected. The man stood up to approach her.

"Hi. I'm Tom. May I join you for a drink?"

"Certainly. Hannah," she said. She hadn't thought of it before, but offering a different name somehow provided her with an excuse to be another type of woman tonight.

He signalled to the waiter to bring another round and sat down next to her. She observed her companion. Tom was probably in his late thirties and despite the leathery skin was reasonably attractive. A husky, masculine voice. She was pleased she had chosen him.

Melanie glanced down at his hands. A wedding ring. But what the hell. "Is that a problem for you?" She met his gaze.

"Certainly not," he said.

"I am delighted to hear that." She leaned in closer, touching his leg.

His smile broadened. "Any man would make an exception for you."

Liar. His face told a story of a hundred infidelities. But it wouldn't change anything tonight. She had picked him and that was all that mattered. Small talk was not going to be part of the agenda. She lied about her job and where she lived. Draining her glass, she motioned for him to finish his. Her hand slid up his leg, not quite touching the warmth of his crotch. He didn't pull away and she looked at him with all the conviction she could muster. "Tom, I'm done drinking. Shall we leave this place?"

He leaned forward and kissed her. A full, hard kiss. No mistaking the intention. "Of course. I'm staying upstairs. I'd love you to come with me."

Tom threw some money on the table and led her to the lift. Success; she was almost there. Hannah had taken over. With all reservation discarded, she began unbuttoning his shirt. He shoved her against the mirrored wall of the lift, hands moving up her dress.

"How did you know I like it rough?" she said.

"I can always tell." He pushed her harder against the cold metal railing.

"Can you?" She could feel her arms bruising from his grip, but made no effort to stop him.

He lifted his mouth off her neck. "Oh, yes." It was oddly erotic; the prospect of sleeping with a complete stranger within ten minutes of meeting him. The lift stopped on the third floor. Room 312.

Her hands hadn't stopped working and, by the time they entered the room, his shirt was open and falling off his freckled shoulders. He kissed her again. This time in a darkened room. But there was no romance. She pulled away and slapped him on the face.

"Little bitch." No menace in his voice. Not really. "I fight too, you know." He hit her back and grabbed her hair.

"I love it like that," she said.

They fucked with a raw energy that reminded her of Pierre. But she didn't care about this man. Despite the pain, she loved the sense of complete control. Encouraged by her comments, he was rough, violent at times. She watched him all the while; her eyes taking in this strange man, as his unknown body took hers. Like watching someone else. She felt nothing for him, but the act itself was exciting and she allowed herself to enjoy it. She closed her eyes and for a moment imagined that she was lying with her French lover. Tom's voice shattered her illusion: "Baby, baby." Most likely, he'd forgotten her name already. She would forget his soon enough.

Melanie stood up afterwards and took a whisky from the minibar. Pouring the drinks, she sensed that he was watching her and knew he liked what he saw. What man wouldn't? Tom would be back in town in a couple of weeks and asked for her number. Should she see him again? The sex hadn't been bad, but no, she wanted nothing further to do with him. She slipped on her dress, wrote her details incorrectly on the hotel notepad and gave him a final full kiss on the mouth. With her last glance at his naked form, she felt nothing at all.

She still smelled of sex when she got home, the scent of his cologne in her hair. The light blue swelling on her arm reminded her of his hands on her body. His face was already a blur and she knew that soon she wouldn't remember any details at all. A dirty whore who had slept with a stranger for no reason at all. But he had given her pleasure without touching her soul. Exactly what she needed. She smoked a cigarette on her balcony and smiled. She thought about him returning to his wife and kissing his children, pretending his business trip had been the same as all the rest. But that was his problem. Not hers.

Chapter Twenty-six

They were all the same. Melanie knew instinctively which ones to pick. A lingering stare and a deliberate look. The formula was easy and not a single one turned her down. Having never considered herself particularly beautiful, her newfound sexual prowess was intoxicating. She loved the power she had over men and didn't hesitate to use it. Some of them were gentle, some were wild. Some were foreign, some were old. One of them beat her hard with chains and one tied her to the bed for hours. But she didn't mind. It was the price of being a whore.

Whoever these men were, they were featureless and meant nothing. She yielded herself to so many of them. Twenty, thirty. Perhaps more. After the first few, they began to blur into one. She treated them all mechanically and enjoyed the variety that they provided. No man could be her master now. And it was liberating. She never brought them home. Much easier to leave their flats or hotel rooms than to kick them out of hers. In any event, she didn't want to reveal her identity or let them into her life. If at one level she was disgusted with herself, she didn't care. She slept with the men to forget about the past.

At first, she didn't worry if they were married, but soon she began to actively seek them out. They were so easy to seduce. How had she not realised it before? She must have been so naïve. Of course, there were always some who cheated, but it seemed that now she was able to get anyone she wanted. Bastards, all of them. How could women be tricked by the whole institution? Their own fault for being such idiots. Believing their husbands and believing the fairy tale.

She thought about her own father and began to understand him better. As a child she had hated him for leaving and now she hated him even more. He had destroyed her mother and her own childhood. She vowed it would never happen to her.

Now, it was her turn to take revenge on the world. She didn't care about these men or their wives. She didn't care about anything at all. And she never saw the same man twice.

Subconsciously, she must have known she was going too far, because she barely mentioned her outings with Jenny. Even Jenny, who would have certainly encouraged her promiscuity, might not understand.

In shaming herself, she began to discover new depths. It was no longer pretence in a strange game. She was truly becoming a whore, giving herself to any man who wanted her, debasing herself to an unimaginable degree. At some nihilistic level, she needed to see how far she could go. She didn't do it for money, she had enough of that. But what was the difference? Each time she would apply her battle paint. And every time she went to a different bed. In the mornings, she would inspect herself for bruises and the occasional welt. She loved looking at these marks; they reminded her of the creature she had become. The strange thing is that she didn't feel guilty about it. Quite the contrary.

But as one night moved indistinguishably into the next, her character began to change. Although it was impossible for her to realise it, her softness had vanished and she became progressively tougher with her colleagues at work. She began to yell at Alex for the simplest of errors, and she was increasingly dismissive of Pamela's efforts to help her. As the weeks passed, both her secretary and Alex grew more distant.

She rarely saw her brother anymore and, apart from her nightly activities, she barely left the office.

But still, life continued and amazingly Tony never realised how close to the edge she was. He was a good man, and would never grasp the darkness that she suffered. It would never have occurred to him to notice.

Her desk was hidden from passers-by and when she collapsed on it one day with fatigue, nobody noticed.

Perhaps nobody cared.

Chapter Twenty-seven

The morning was dull and grey, just like the ones that had preceded it. There was nothing to suggest it would be different from the other days. She took the same Tube as normal and arrived at her desk at quarter past six. There was no corporate news worthy of mention, so she undertook the usual process of reading through her mass of emails. The phone call at ten o'clock caught her by surprise. Melanie knew immediately that it had been sent to save her.

The man at the other end of the phone worked at a headhunting firm in the City. "Good morning, Melanie, I hope I'm not disturbing you. My name is Dominic Evans from Southfields."

Melanie knew the firm. They had headhunted her former colleagues all those years ago, giving her the first big break.

"Good morning," she said, with a calmness she didn't feel. "How can I help you?"

"Melanie, I'll get straight to the point. I have been asked to approach you about a position in a small corporate finance firm. Their deal flow is starting to pick up again and they need to hire someone quickly."

Melanie looked around. There was nobody at the desk, so she was free to talk. "But I don't work in corporate finance. I'm in research."

"They know that. But they like your research and you have worked on quite a few deals, haven't you?"

"Yes. But it's different."

"Look. They want a female partner and specifically asked for you. Would you be interested in meeting to discuss it further?"

Melanie paused, knowing that this was the start of negotiations and it was vital not to appear overly enthusiastic. "That's very kind of you to call, but this week is a little tough for me."

"Any time that suits you, Melanie," he said. "They are very keen."

"OK. Let me look at my diary." She enjoyed the silence, aware that he was impatient. "Hmmm…" Her diary was mostly empty but she kept him there for a few more seconds. "I suppose I could rearrange an internal meeting on Thursday. Coffee around half past ten. Would that work for you?"

Dominic agreed instantly and, hanging up the phone, she smiled. It was the happiest she had felt in months. Why hadn't she thought of it earlier? Maybe because hardly anyone in the City was hiring. She already knew she would take the job. She cast her eyes around the office, that place that had become a dead cell for such a long time. Yes, she was still earning good money, but she hadn't grown professionally this year and the place depressed her. After the crisis, life as a broker was only going in one direction. It was definitely time to move on. Even better was the fact that Pierre could not follow her there. Those wasted months of nothingness, dragging herself into the office, had to be consigned to the past.

It would be a long three days. She cursed herself for not taking a meeting sooner, but it had been important to play the game. No nocturnal activities for the rest of the week. Although she was only meeting the headhunter, she wanted to look her best and that meant getting some sleep for a change.

They had agreed to meet at the Starbucks near the Bank of England. A safe distance from the office. She identified Dominic instantly. Headhunters were all the same. Clean-cut and over-eager. Easy to spot. Like estate agents. She approached him.

"Dominic?"

He stood up to shake her hand. "Hi, Melanie. Can I get you a coffee?"

"Of course. I'd love a cappuccino please." She watched him walk to the counter. He seemed pleasant and should be straightforward to impress. By now, her reputation in the City was unrivalled in her sector. In any event, they had sought her out and that placed her in a position of strength.

He returned with the coffee and pulled out some papers. "I know you're pushed for time, so I'll get straight to the point."

"Sounds good," said Melanie. She crossed her legs and leaned forward.

"Have you heard of Lewis and Partners?" he said.

"No. Should I have?" Perhaps she should have done a little homework.

"Not particularly, but they've been making a few deals in the industrials space."

"Even now? Our corporate finance team is endlessly complaining about lack of deal flow."

"Yeah, the macro's been tough, but apparently things are starting to pick up again for their firm."

"Good for them. Where do I come in?"

"Basically, there are three partners. All from investment banking. They are searching for someone to help them win clients."

"But I'm not in marketing."

"You have an enormous contact list and are well respected in the sector," said Dominic.

She smiled. Always wonderful to receive compliments. "And you're sure they don't mind that I'm not from a corporate finance background."

"As we discussed on the phone, you seem to have completed many deals. It's enough. They want a woman. Don't ask me why. But they are quite adamant about that."

"Lucky me." Not the first time being a woman had worked to her advantage.

"Believe me, it's quite hard to find someone with the right profile. Basically, you're it."

"That's very flattering." She smiled at him.

"Melanie." He gazed at her with puppy dog eyes. "It's a very lucrative opportunity. The firm really cut back last year, but they are starting to gain traction again and they want to make a big hire. They're prepared to give you a chunk of the equity."

"Definitely sounds quite interesting," she said.

"So you'll meet them?"

"Sure, why not? Nothing to lose." What a coup. She could scarcely believe her luck.

After she left the coffee shop, she found herself wondering why she hadn't thought of leaving the bank sooner. Perhaps it was her loyalty to Tony that had kept her. Or perhaps it was her inner feeling of self-doubt that had prevailed so strongly recently.

The interview was set for the following Wednesday. Tony was travelling and she pretended to have a presentation in the West End. Alex could man the desk. She took the stairs to reception, pushed through the revolving doors and walked a few short blocks across Cheapside. She loved this part of the City and was pleased the new office was in the same area.

As the lift took her up to the top floor, she thought about how far she had travelled since her first interview all those years ago. She had tripped up a few times, professionally and personally, but overall it had been a huge success. She had learnt to manage difficult situations and was more successful than she could ever have dreamed of. Against all odds, she had been promoted rapidly and was earning good money. Apart from Jenny, none of her friends had succeeded in the financial markets. If she could only hold her nerve, this new job could be a fantastic opportunity.

Melanie strode into the room and blinked at the sunlight, which was beaming in from the windows. The three men were waiting and they rose in unison to greet her. Easy to tell that they were admiring her. Always a fine balance to look attractive, yet professional, but today she knew she'd managed. Now it was time to show them she also had brains. She had studied their profiles the week before. The American, Edward, was in his mid-thirties. A kind smile, which boded well. The two Englishmen were older. Clive was probably about fifty, with a small pinched face. Ugly, but sparkling eyes. Terence was marginally younger, but his quiet confidence suggested that he was the leader. Important to focus on him. She knew that the older men had met many years ago in a European investment bank and the trio had a combined fifty years of corporate finance experience between them. She had researched their recent deals over the weekend and was prepared for the interview. Bizarre that they were insistent on hiring a woman, but now was not the time to argue.

"Thanks for coming in Melanie," said Clive. "We are very pleased you could make it."

"My pleasure," she said. "Thanks for inviting me."

"Coffee, tea?" he said.

"Some water would be lovely. Thanks." She poured herself a glass and joined them at the table.

Terence spoke first. "I know you've met with the headhunter. How much has he told you about the job?" She had been right. He was the leader.

"That you're looking for a female partner to help broaden the marketing initiative?"

"That's right. But very specifically, we have heard tremendous things about you. We actually would like an analyst to join the team."

"An analyst?" Melanie frowned. The word analyst was usually a term for juniors in investment banking.

"At a senior level, of course," said Terence quickly. "A slightly different background always adds a dimension, don't you agree?"

"I guess." She nodded, encouraging him to continue.

"We are pushing for more deals across Europe and I know you have covered a lot of the territories."

"Yes." Incredible. They were serving the job on a plate. Almost a reverse interview.

"As I'm sure you're aware, the rewards in this business are considerable. Much more than sellside research. Particularly now."

She smiled. Now they were getting to the point. "What sort of rewards are you referring to?"

"It's very simple, Melanie. We'd offer you equity. But on top of that, your contribution to deal flow will feed directly to a cash bonus. We are strong believers in transparency."

"Very interesting," she said. It was a total gold mine but she had to keep her cool. "I guess the thing that confuses me is why you're hiring in this environment? From our end, there doesn't seem to be much corporate work."

"You're right. It hasn't been an easy year, but things are beginning to pick up. We've got a great niche, with a number of leads that need pushing through."

"That's wonderful," she said.

"Would you be interested?"

"The truth is I hadn't been thinking about a career move. My job is going well at the moment, but I won't deny that this is intriguing."

"We are very keen, Melanie." Terence again.

"I appreciate that," she said. "Can I take a few days to think about it?" Who knew she could pretend to be so passive. Clearly she had become quite practised at lying.

For several days, she purposefully procrastinated. Dominic called many times and, while she was always polite, she managed to give the impression of deep uncertainty. It worked. By the end of the following week, they had added an extra ten per cent to her salary and increased her equity in the firm to five per cent.

Knowing that she couldn't push it any further, Melanie accepted the offer on Friday afternoon. What a coup. She was already outside when she made the phone call and had no desire to return to the office. She took a walk, sat down on the bench facing the cathedral and smoked a cigarette. Rubbing the stub into the ground, she reached for her mobile to call her brother. He picked up on the third ring.

"Hey, stranger," she said.

"Mel! How are you?!" They hadn't spoken for weeks and his delight was evident.

"I'm well, very well, actually. Listen, I can't be bothered to go back to work today. Are you free to go the pub?"

"That doesn't sound like you," he said. "You sure everything is OK?"

"Yes, more than OK. I miss you, that's all." They had shared so much of their lives and now he was the only one she wanted to celebrate with. They hadn't done that for such a long time.

"Sure, let me finish a few things here and I'll come along. The Hereford?" David said.

"Wonderful. See you in half an hour."

Her next call was to Pamela, telling her that she had to go to Mayfair to meet a client. Another lie. But, in any event, there was nothing urgent to attend to and she was happier than she had felt in months.

The Hereford Arms was her brother's favourite pub, with its worn red leather chairs, battered sofas and dusky interiors. An old bronze plaque at the front had a Victorian inscription, but the pub itself had been there for centuries, its dark corners reminiscent of a bygone era.

David was waiting for her by the bar. It was too cold to sit outside and she sacrificed nicotine for the comfort of the sofas. The barman smiled at her. She hadn't been there for a while, and had forgotten what a refuge it was. Many memories had been made here and it was their special place. Perhaps it reminded her of lost innocence. They sat there for hours, drinking their favourite wine, and she huddled into the familiar comfort of his warm arms.

It was particularly delightful not to have Samantha around. She hadn't realised until that moment how much she had missed him. David had always been her rock and she had been flailing around for a long time without him. He was her only family, and she had come horribly close to losing him altogether.

She only had herself to blame. David had tried hard to reach out to her, and she had pushed him away consistently. It had been stupid of her to neglect their bond. Hopefully it wasn't too late to mend, although clearly her brother had moved on to a life without her.

Hours later, David glanced at his watch. Time to go home. It was painful to see him leave. There he was, returning to a loving home. And what did she have? An empty, soulless flat. In her endless quest for more money, was it possible she had lost a grip on reality, on what truly mattered? But time to be positive. It had been a good day. A new job, a new relationship with her brother.

She prayed it would be sufficient to propel her forward.

Chapter Twenty-eight

She couldn't resign for another two months. Bonus time was in January and she would lose it all if she left beforehand. It was annoying enough that she would have to leave so much equity on the table but, at the very least, she wanted to take the cash component.

That left her with the Christmas season to get through, with its associated endless client entertainment. There was nothing wrong with any of it, but her enthusiasm of the previous years had evaporated. Knowing that she was leaving the firm, it was an additional challenge to remain motivated.

Even an evening with her first and favourite client Simon loomed as a chore she'd rather not bother with. But she'd taken him out every Christmas and it would be churlish to deny him dinner this year. Besides, he had supported her heavily since the beginning and she owed him so much. Simon had chosen a small pub off the Strand and was waiting with a bottle of wine. Melanie bent her head to enter through the ancient door, passed the old coat rack and sat down on the brown sofa next to him.

"Hi. Sorry I'm late," she said. She'd never been late for a client before.

"Don't worry about it. I'll pour you a glass. You look like you need it."

"How can you tell?" she said.

Simon pushed the wine glass towards her. "Don't take this the wrong way, but you look like shit. Haven't been yourself for quite a while now."

"Yeah." She turned her face away, not wanting him to witness the unwelcome tears that had welled. It was the kindness she hadn't expected, the gentleness of his gaze that broke her.

"What's up, Mel? We haven't had a catch-up in ages. I've been worried about you." He put his arm round her, turning her face towards him.

There was nothing sexual in that act and she leaned into him, touched by his sweetness. "You're too good to me, Simon." She wiped her eyes. "I don't want this evening to be a total drag. We're supposed to be having fun."

"We always have fun together. I enjoy your company more than you can imagine. You don't have to be happy all the time."

"You mean that?" she said.

"Stop it, Melanie. You're an exceptional woman."

"Thanks," she said. "I guess I'm knackered."

"Perhaps you need to slow down a little," he said.

"Easier said than done." She smiled sadly at him.

"I know. You are a high-octane chick. But promise me you'll get some rest."

"Sure," she said. "Thank goodness it's Christmas."

He didn't probe any further, clearly sensing she didn't want to discuss anything. But when they left the pub afterwards, he embraced her for a precious few extra seconds.

And then, the absolute low point of the entire year. The office party. Having always disliked the experience, she had hoped to avoid it this year. But Tony had insisted on her presence and, unable to tell him of her plans, Melanie was forced to comply. God knows why everyone still carried on with this ridiculous tradition. Invariably filled with inebriated young secretaries, searching for an unsuspecting boss. Or sometimes the other way round.

One of the girls knocked into her on the way to the bar. A high-pitched giggle.

"Look where you're going." Melanie glared at the creature in front of her. A bulging stomach, unflatteringly pressed into a tight red dress. Was there no pride?

"Sorry, darling." Another giggle. The girl was teetering on her open-toe stilettos, clutching a bottle of wine. "Here, you want some too?"

"No, thanks," said Melanie. "I wouldn't have too much more of that if I were you."

"Why not?" A little thin nose peered up at her.

"You really want my opinion?" said Melanie.

"Yeah, I really do."

"Because you'll end up shagging one of those disgusting traders tonight and have it splattered across the firm first thing tomorrow morning." Melanie turned away.

"Stuck-up bitch," said the woman. "Just because you have no idea how to have fun."

Melanie shrugged. The irony was almost funny. She herself was far more promiscuous than all these odious girls. The difference was that nobody at work would ever know it. She, of all people, understood the primeval need to shame oneself. But it was all a question of context and where you chose to let go. Not here, among colleagues and ruddy-faced bosses. Those types of indiscretions would not be easily forgotten on the trading floor.

It was shaping up to be a long night and she took a seat in the corner. She was watching the clock when Mitch approached. A large toothy grin on that hideous tanned face. But something was different tonight. His gait. Mitch, drunk? She rolled her eyes.

"I've been looking for you," he said.

She raised her glass. "Here I am." How boring.

"What a pleasure." He sat down next to her and put a large tanned hand onto her left leg. "Have I ever told you how gorgeous you are?"

"Excuse me?" She moved away from him, hating that inane smile.

But his hand gripped tighter. "You must know how much I like you."

"Stop it," she said.

He moved closer. "You're intriguing. I always thought you were a bit prim, but those stories about Pierre…"

"What stories?" What the hell had Pierre been saying now?

"Don't play coy." He leaned in, his face inches from hers. "I know your little secrets. And I have to say, I wouldn't mind some of it for myself. Such a sexy chick."

Something in her snapped. The pent-up hatred that she had concealed for years burst through. "How dare you talk to me like that?"

"Don't be like that. We have so much in common, you and I."

"You're fucking deluded."

He grabbed her arm. "You're the deluded one. Who do you think saved your job? When lover-boy was pushing to get you sacked? He almost managed. If it weren't for me, you'd be on some scrapheap right about now. Not the best time to be unemployed."

She looked at him in horror, knowing it was true. "I don't believe you."

"You should. Pierre is as loyal as an alley cat. Could have told you that years ago. You need to pick your lovers more carefully. And you should be more grateful to your friends. At this rate, you won't have many left. Little bitch."

She stood up and pushed him away. "Piss off. I want nothing from you."

Running off, she didn't bother to look back. Of course it had been unwise, but she was leaving the firm anyway. Who cared? She had hated that man since the day she'd met him. How could Jenny have slept with him? Thank God she was getting out of this place. Before she left the room, she heard two girls sniggering. Probably about her. Certainly, she would feature in post-mortem gossip the next day, but it didn't matter.

Still fuming, she bounded down the stairs, in search of the exit. She overshot and tripped on a man's hat. In the darkness she could dimly see a couple copulating a few steps below. One great mound heaving onto another. The brief glimpse of the white fleshy buttocks disgusted her and she raced away.

She ran into the night, longing to rid herself of the filth that had become intertwined into her life.

And then, there was Christmas Day itself. She'd always hated it, even as a child. The day her father's shadow had loomed the largest. In her adult life, it only served to highlight her own singleton status.

This year, everything was doubly compounded by David's extraordinary happiness. They had invited her, of course, as they did every year.

This time she accepted, albeit reluctantly, knowing she would be surrounded by smug couples and their pristine relationships. David's friends were unbearably dull, but she had nowhere else to go. And he had promised not to invite Max this year.

At least it was an opportunity to spend time with her brother. Despite all their differences, she would always love him. If she was to maintain their relationship, she had to make an effort with his girlfriend. No doubt there would be endless questions about her private life. Everyone doing their best to help. Why did they all think a man was the answer to everything?

But if she had braced herself to fend off an onslaught, she needn't have worried. On the contrary, her brother's silence on the matter was almost more uncomfortable. It only indicated his conscious effort to avoid the topic. Still, she was grateful. It was always going to be easier to discuss her new job and career prospects; the one area where she had excelled.

But while she heard herself talking, the words rang hollow. What was a new job, compared to the happiness that eluded her? Was it envy she felt, watching couples huddled on the sofa? One had a couple of kids and her brother had his new dog. No doubt there would be a baby soon. Of course she was happy for him, but the contrast with her own life was disconcerting.

Chapter Twenty-nine

With the festive season behind her, she counted down the days until her January bonus was safely tucked into her bank account. Finally, she was able to approach her boss, one of the few people she was genuinely sad to leave. On the day she picked to confront him, he was uncharacteristically late and she anxiously tapped her fingers until he arrived at half past ten.

"Tony, please can I have a word with you?" It was hard to meet his eyes. Tony had been her mentor and she would not have succeeded without him.

He looked up, ignorant to what was coming next. "OK, give me a minute."

"Please can we go into the office?" she said.

Absent-mindedly he collected his coffee and followed her into the conference room. She closed the door behind him. He took a step backwards, clearly startled. It was the first time she had summoned him into the room like that.

Unsure how to begin, Melanie mumbled a few words. "Tony, you know how much I have loved working with you…"

"Melanie?" The situation had dawned. "Don't tell me you're leaving?"

She nodded. She hadn't prepared herself for this feeling of guilt or the sadness on his face. It was worse than infidelity. "I'm sorry, Tony. I owe you so much and it seems horribly ungrateful, but it's time for me to move on."

"But weren't you happy with your bonus? I personally lobbied for the increase. You know it wasn't the easiest time to get a bonus."

"Yes. The bonus was fantastic. I can't thank you enough."

"And you were promoted. You're a director. Two days ago."

"I know, I know. I'm being a total scumbag, but I've been offered the opportunity of a lifetime. I just can't turn it down."

"Can I do anything to change your mind?"

Melanie frowned. "Sorry, Tony. I wanted to tell you first."

"At least tell me where you're going?"

"Lewis and Partners. It's a small investment banking boutique."

"Who?" he said. Clearly he had assumed she would be moving to a direct competitor. That would have been more normal. "But you're not a banker."

"I know, and I've thought it through. There are enough synergies and the opportunity is fantastic."

"Why would you give up the research? You're Extel-rated now. Might even make the top spot this year."

"Of course you're right, but I need a change."

"Nothing I can do?" he said.

She shook her head. "But I'd love it if we could stay friends. Would mean so much to me."

"OK." He moved away to open the door.

She watched him return to his desk, his shoulders hunched with disappointment. It was over and there was nothing further to discuss. So formal, so strange. He had been like a father to her and she was casting him aside.

The next step was much easier. Hand her formal resignation letter to HR and pack up her bags. There wasn't much to take. She had prepared for this day and, over the months, had been emptying her personal contents from the building. Once her resignation was accepted, she would be required to leave the premises immediately. Promising to stay in touch, she kissed Pamela and Alex and left.

Melanie handed her security card to reception and pushed through that revolving door for the last time. A simple act that she had done so many times, but today it was final.

She tripped as the sun blazed into her eyes, blinding her momentarily. She turned right, down the little lane that had been there for centuries, past the chemist and the coffee shop. A young man in a blue pinstriped suit ran past, jostling her. He was obviously in a hurry to be somewhere. Everyone had a destination, except for her. Frightening but so liberating.

As a result of non-compete clauses, she would not be able to start her new job for three months. It was called gardening leave in the City but, without a garden, it was almost always used as a wonderful opportunity to travel. She had considered travelling throughout Europe, perhaps with a prolonged stay in Spain, but Jenny had also offered her father's villa in the Caribbean. At this time of year, that was far more appealing.

She flicked open her mobile. "I've done it, Jenny!"

"About time," said Jenny. "You've been going on about it for long enough."

"I know. But it's done now. Hey, I was thinking about your dad's villa…"

"What about it?" said Jenny.

"You know you mentioned that it's empty?"

"It's free. Bit of a shithole, don't get too excited. But yours if you want to borrow it."

"You sure your dad won't mind?"

"He won't even notice. Don't think he's been there for years. God knows why he hasn't sold it. But I'll email him. Honestly he won't give a damn."

"Please let me know what I owe you, Jenny".

"Don't worry about it. Never a bad thing to have someone check on the place. I might even join you."

"That would be amazing," said Melanie. "Really, you're a star. It's exactly what I need right now."

And indeed it was. The winter had been particularly bleak and she desperately needed to forget her concerns for a while.

Kicking off her shoes that night, she poured a large glass of wine and began to imagine the tropical breezes and white sandy beaches. Before Jenny would be able to change her mind, Melanie opened her laptop and booked the first flight available.

The next week was spent in a manic shopping spree, searching for appropriate clothing and finalising all her household bills.

She forgot to call her brother until she reached the airport, and she left a short message on his answer machine.

Chapter Thirty

The journey to the Caribbean was hot and sweaty, but her worries evaporated the minute the propeller plane touched down at the tiny airport. Stepping off the plane, a wall of hot air hit her and she surveyed this small outpost. Two customs officials chatted amiably by three small flags. One of them stamped her passport and waved her through.

A man named Buster was waiting for her with a small rusty car and a bottle of water. A large smile creased his face into a thousand lines; delight at having a visitor. He had worked for Jenny's family for twenty years and had been told to look after her.

Buster drove her to the other end of the five-mile island and showed her around the beach house. Jenny hadn't exaggerated. Gloriously basic. Two bedrooms, with bleached-wood furniture. A couple of fans and a few decaying hammocks. No air conditioning and no hot water. A small unappealing pool sat in front of the house and there was a crude stony path leading down to the beach. Paradise had come.

On the whole, there wasn't much to do. Unsurprisingly, Jenny never joined her. Work commitments had forced her to stay behind. Or perhaps she couldn't face the rustic lifestyle. But Melanie didn't mind; it felt wholesome to be alone for once.

She paced the same beaches endlessly and read all the novels she'd forgotten about. A lovers' paradise, with nobody to share it with. Just the way she wanted it. She spent hours by the pier, at the bottom of the garden, staring out to sea. With one foot in front of the other and her long legs stretched out, she let her hair fly into the wind. Her thoughts dived into the translucent seas, pushing her sins away with the tide. At times, the skies would blacken and, for the briefest periods, the showers came. But it was warm and inviting and she wouldn't run from it. The bohemian existence washed away all traces of city elegance. With nobody to impress, her make-up bag remained untouched in her suitcase and, as fresh freckles surfaced across her nose, her roots grew long and dark. Her newly healthy glow reflected a vigour that she hadn't felt for months.

Occasionally she would make her way down the winding, pot-holed road to the tiny town, taking a seat at the beach-side bar. The old barman would nod at her, all the while humming along to the local radio. She smoked thoughtfully, watching young couples sipping rum punch through colourful straws and the old men playing backgammon in the corner. They didn't trouble her, presumably sensing that the stranger wasn't looking for company. Melanie never stayed long; it was fun to gain a glimpse of the evening life and then slip away before it became a part of her.

At first the days passed slowly, as she moulded into her new surroundings and the Caribbean rhythm. But soon her body began to unravel from its urban tensions, the days blurred and the weeks raced by.

With only a week left, she woke up one morning to the sound of birds. Panic in her heart. It had taken her a while to adapt, and now it was almost time to leave. As the hours began to speed by, she allowed herself to concentrate on her life back home and particularly to think about Max. Having taken the time to calm down, and to consider the situation rationally, she wondered whether she could make the relationship work. Perhaps she had been wrong to cast him aside. Once she settled into her new job, she would definitely call him, to make amends. All in due course. Her suffering had bruised them both and she needed to find the right moment.

But at least she was calm again. Her new doctor had prescribed her two months' worth of medication but she had barely touched the pills. The crashing waves and hot beating sun had sufficed.

The only news from the outside world had been David's engagement to Samantha. They would be getting married in the summer.

No great surprise. As far as she was concerned, they had been practically married for years. It could have been worse. Samantha was dull, but nice enough. Melanie vaguely wondered whether she would one day find a suitable husband, but dismissed the idea. A man was not the answer right now.

On the final day, as the little plane left the remote tarmac, she was sorry to be heading back home. It had been wonderful to forget the world for such an extended period. But she had signed a contract and had a job to do. There was no option.

Circling over London, Melanie held a glass of wine in her hands. She drained it before the stewardess could remove it. Scouring the grey contours of the city, she wondered bleakly why she had returned. Perhaps it was the alcohol, disgusting though it was, but it occurred to her that the lives of other people were so mundane. Not that hers was any better.

What was it all for? God knows she had made some strange choices. Endless hours in grey offices with equally grey men. A life without daylight. She had prostituted her body, but had she also been prostituting her soul for her career? To make enough money to go out at the weekend, get drunk, find a man to sleep with and return to the office on Monday morning. All for money, to be independent. But until this moment, she had never questioned it. Thinking of the individuals she had jettisoned over the years, she wondered how she had become so uncompromising. Was it her career choice that had hardened her? Or perhaps it was a result of her relationship with Pierre. Or perhaps she had brought it upon herself.

Melanie cast her mind back to the gentle barman on the island. He seemed far happier than most of her co-workers. They were all sucked into this seemingly mindless quest for nothing at all. Why did she want all that bloody money anyway? Maybe David was right. Perhaps she was too extreme. She'd always thought all the others were losers. Until now. Time on the beach had showed her a different, calmer life. And she found herself wondering what was better.

*

Turning the key to her flat, she shivered involuntarily. Musty and cold. Apart from the cleaner, nobody had been inside and, like an old friend that had been abandoned, it smelled sad and lonely. Looking around, it no longer reminded her of her mother. Instead, she saw the dirty memories. The floor where that strange man had raped her, the place that Max had kissed her, the sofa where Pierre had taken her. And the bed. The bed told a million stories of them all. It was too much to bear and she closed her eyes in despair.

There was only a week left before her new job and she used it for a therapeutic spring clean. She threw away old photos and books that Pierre had given her. In the tattered red box in the kitchen drawer, she discovered those two business cards from that first interview. Victoria and Pierre. Melanie rubbed her head ruefully. Pierre had seemed friendly at the time and she had been far more been apprehensive about the woman. It was cruel how life could mock.

With her green cigarette lighter, Melanie lit the corners of the cards and watched as the small ring of fire gradually took hold and engulfed them. She flicked the ashes into the sink and ran the cold water. Stupidly symbolic, but it had felt cathartic to burn his name. However, the fact that she still hated him was frustrating. Would she ever get over him?

Going through her cupboard, she began to separate her work clothes and decided to keep the designer suit from her first trip to New York. Pride was not strong enough. In any event, Pierre had given it to her before the relationship had started. She found Max's shirt in the cupboard and decided to keep it too. If he allowed her, she'd like to meet him again. One day.

Chapter Thirty-one

At twenty-eight, Melanie was far younger than the other three partners at Lewis and, apart from two secretaries, the only female at the firm. Catapulted in at the top. Expectations were terrifyingly high. But she was used to operating in a man's world and it didn't faze her. It was fantastic to have a fresh start and be able to make her own deals. Rule number one: no office romance. It helped that none of the partners were remotely attractive.

In her first week, they asked her to go to Madrid. A new deal was kicking off and they needed someone to relocate for at least a month. Of course nobody else was free. Married people never seemed to have the time for anything. Nonetheless, it was an exciting prospect to take on her own deal, working with the management team of a small Spanish engineering company. The firm was fifty per cent owned by a private equity group, which was hoping to sell its stake to a large American conglomerate. The company's finances were in a mess and it was her job to liaise with the Spanish finance director and accountants, before the big presentation in the US.

Apart from an amusing interlude with Rafa, an unusually tall Spaniard staying in the same apartment block, Melanie worked solidly for weeks. She spoke daily to her colleagues in London and together they produced their presentation and valuation for the sale. She spent only one night back in London before heading out to America.

David had left her several messages and she called him on her way to the airport. He picked up on the first ring but let her speak first.

"Hi, David. It's me. How are you?"

"Mel, you've been a nightmare to get hold of." Clearly he was pissed off.

"Yeah, sorry. I've been busy."

"Back to your old ways then," he said.

"That's unfair. You know I've just started a new job. I have to get it right."

"At least have dinner with me this week. We've got a lot to catch up on. There's something I need to talk to you about."

"What?" she said.

"Not on the phone."

Melanie glanced at her watch. "I'm on the way to the US, so sadly I can't make dinner."

He hissed with fury. "When are you back?"

She sighed. "I don't know. Depends on the deal."

"You and your bloody deals." Now he was shouting at her.

"Stop it, David. I can't handle your sermonising." Here they were, back to square one. With a plane to catch, it was the last thing she could handle.

"Suit yourself Mel. Just hope you'll be back in time for the wedding."

"Of course I'll be there." Jesus. She'd forgotten about the wedding. No wonder he was stressed. Next month. Where had the time gone? "I am sorry. I know you've got a lot on your plate. I promise to make it up to you afterwards."

"Sure. Whatever you say." He didn't sound convinced. "Have a good trip."

The phone went dead. Not the best way to end the conversation, but there was no time to dwell. The deal was waiting.

She slept all the way to Atlanta. Exhausted, but confident. She was caught off guard, however, by the man who faced her in the room the next day. They'd emailed and spoken on numerous occasions, but she shivered when she saw him. Carbon copy of Mitch. What was it about all these immaculate-looking Americans, with their sparkling white teeth? She tried not to hate him on sight, but the thought of Mitch gave her renewed energy to win the deal. It became very personal.

"Good morning," said Lookalike, with that familiar fake smile. "Thanks for coming all the way to see us. Hope you had a good trip."

"Yes, thanks." She shook his hand and looked him directly in the eyes. "It was fine. Good to meet you."

He offered her a glass of water. She accepted, and took a seat at the boardroom table. As she delved for her presentation, the Spanish finance director by her side remained silent, hands shaking beneath the table. She hadn't expected him to be this nervous. Clearly she would have to do the work.

She turned her attention to the American. "Thanks for seeing us today. I know we've spoken many times, but I'm pleased to have the opportunity to run through the memorandum in person."

"Great," said Lookalike. He opened the presentation and flicked to the back. He paused. "There are a lot of discrepancies in these numbers."

The man obviously had no times for niceties. "How do you mean?" she said.

He pointed at the page. "These forecasts are ridiculously optimistic. The market is saturated in Spain as we all know. Not to mention that the whole country appears to be going to hell right now. How exactly are you going to manage an eight per cent annual revenue growth over the next ten years?"

Melanie tapped her pen on the table. "Our competition has gone into administration and we are taking market share very easily."

"That's not what I've heard," he said.

"It's already happening. Just last week we won a new contract. Hasn't been made public yet, but that one deal will boost earnings significantly. In fact these projections are extremely conservative."

Lookalike shrugged. "We all know that you need us to buy the company. Otherwise, it will be heading the same way as the rest. Down the plughole. Our board believes it would be better to wait and buy it from the administrators."

"That's entirely wrong," she said. "Despite the macro situation, the business is very robust."

"Even if that's the case, which I very much doubt, we would have to factor country risk into the valuation. Which will be considerable."

"We do agree that country risk is high at the moment, but—"

"This is not a straightforward situation," he said, interrupting her. "We're going to have to take an in-depth look at all your assumptions." The onslaught was relentless. Much harder than she had anticipated.

"As I said, these numbers are very conservative." She looked to the Spaniard for some assistance. "Franco, why don't you explain a little more about the competitors?" Not helpful that he was acting like a moron. He coughed, shuffled in his chair and finally started talking.

Listening to the Spaniard, Melanie sat back and wondered where to go next. She had been expecting to discuss valuation metrics today, not to be stuck on these basics. Complete nightmare. Maybe that's what corporate finance was all about. In research, she'd never been exposed to these sorts of meetings. Perhaps she should have invited one of her colleagues to help. But that would have been an admission of failure.

After forty minutes, Lookalike stood up. "I'm terribly sorry, but I have to leave for a lunch meeting."

Melanie looked up in horror. Was it over? After all this? "But we haven't had the chance to finish the presentation yet."

"Come back tomorrow," he said. There was no further discussion. A long arm held the glass door open for her to pass.

"We will. Thanks." She nodded, hating him.

After they left the building, the Spaniard touched her shoulder. "You said this would be easy. He didn't seem at all interested."

"Of course he's interested." Even though she didn't feel it, she had to project confidence. Otherwise they were dead. "He's playing hard to get. To pay less. He needs this deal more than you do."

The Spaniard smiled wryly. "Don't know about that. He's right about the Spanish economy."

"Relax." She put an arm round him. "We'll pull it off. But it may take time." Time was what she didn't want to spend in this hellhole of a city. Summer had barely started and Atlanta was already a fucking furnace.

*

Thankfully, she was right. As she had suspected, or at least prayed for, it had all been a game. He was an excellent poker player, but after a long week of discussions Lookalike caved in. Not the price they had hoped for. Not even close; the bastard had been too good. But a conditional offer had been agreed.

There would be many more negotiations until closing, but she was proud to be able to deliver this small result to her team back home.

Chapter Thirty-two

Back in London on Saturday morning, Melanie slept for most of the weekend, and spent the following week answering Lookalike's emails and organising her other office paperwork. She had been abroad for almost two months and hadn't had time to settle in. Not to mention the fact that David's wedding was on the following Friday.

She had tried not to think about it. Samantha had called her many times for advice but she hadn't helped. Blamed her job as usual, but the truth was she didn't like the idea of losing her brother. The wedding made it official. She had been steadily pushing him away for a few years and now another woman – that woman – would be more important to him. It was tough to digest.

On top of that, weddings invariably highlighted her own single status. This one was particularly painful. She didn't have a date for the party and David had allowed her to invite Jenny instead. It was thoughtful of him, particularly given his negative views on her friend.

The wedding would be held in an old church in Chelsea, with a small reception in Knightsbridge. Fingering the embossed invitation that morning, she felt a small pang of guilt. Samantha's family had no money. The day must have cost her brother a fortune. He hadn't asked for charity, but she should have offered. She was earning a multiple of David's salary and it wouldn't have made any difference to her financially. The richer she was becoming, the meaner she got. She should have been more generous. What had stopped her? Was it the fact that she didn't want to share everything she had worked so hard for? Or was it that, despite all her success, she was essentially jealous of his happiness? Perhaps it was time to grow up.

Getting ready for the day, she slipped on her blue Pucci dress and began to think about Max. So much time had passed and so many other men had passed through. How would it feel to see him again? Would he still be interested? More to the point, could he forgive her appalling behaviour? It was time to find out. She had been too proud to ask her brother, but there was no need; she was sure Max would be there.

On David's side of the church, she watched his friends pour in. Looking for Max, Melanie was unprepared for the beautiful brunette by his side. How had that happened? She'd blinked and he'd found someone else. Except she hadn't blinked; she'd been sleeping for months, years even. How long had it been? Of course he was blameless, but the shock was rude. She tried not to stare as Max held his girlfriend's hand during the service and she pretended not to care when, later that evening, they danced in front of the band.

She hated that he didn't notice her, that she had become invisible to him. At that moment, she wanted him intensely. Why had she never desired him that way before? So messed up. With only herself to blame, the pain was unbearable. As she sat there, drinking yet another glass of second-rate white wine, Jenny pulled her aside.

"Get over it," said Jenny.

"But she's so pretty. How can I ever compete with that?" The brunette was gorgeous. And so young.

"She's not as pretty as you. But it's not the point. You don't want him anyway."

"I do. I really do," said Melanie. God, the wine was filthy. She should have helped her brother with the budget. How could she have been so selfish as to overlook it?

"Only because he's taken," said Jenny.

"Look at him. He's perfect." Gazing at Max from across the room, Melanie couldn't understand why she had left him.

"I guarantee you would not be interested if he were single. How many times did he call you after you dumped him? How many times did you call him back?"

"Fuck you." What did Jenny know anyway?

"Fuck you too." Jenny chuckled. "Come on, there are a couple of single men at the bar. Not that hot, but I'm sure they'll get better with a few more drinks."

"I'm not interested," said Melanie. But she followed. Not that she spoke to anyone. Only ten o'clock. She'd have to wait a little longer. Sister of the groom couldn't be the first to leave.

Alcohol was the only sensible solution. She ordered a gin and tonic. At least they couldn't screw that up. As she perused the crowd, an old man approached. She wasn't in the mood for small talk and turned her back, pretending not to have seen him. To her irritation, he moved to the other side, his slow-sunken eyes fixed with intent.

"Hello, Melanie," he said.

She sighed inwardly. No escape from yet another tedious conversation. "Hello," she said without enthusiasm.

"Melanie, I've been trying to find a moment to speak to you all day. I can't believe how beautiful you are."

A little taken aback, she studied him more closely. Tall, with the distinctive appearance of a man who had once been very handsome. His hair, although entirely grey, was full and thick. Strangely familiar. The day had been exhausting, filled with meaningless encounters, and she was struggling to make a connection. Under old fleshy eyelids, bright blue eyes reminded her of someone, but she was unprepared for what came next.

"Don't you remember me?"

She shook her head, bored by the conversation. "No, sorry."

"It's me, your father."

Melanie recoiled. "No." She knew immediately that it was true. The same man from her childhood. Much older, skin mottled by time. But definitely him. She gripped her chair in a desperate attempt to steady herself. What was he doing here? What right did he have, after all these years? Why had David invited him? Staring at this most hated of men, she felt nothing but revulsion. He had left when she was a small child who had been desperate for his return. But she had spent most of her life trying to forget him and there was nothing of that child left in her. Trying to conceal her shock, she turned away from him.

"Please go away." She lunged for her drink and waved her hand drunkenly in his direction. "I want nothing to do with you."

"Melanie. I've missed you."

He attempted to put his arm round her, but she shrugged him off. "Bullshit."

"I know I've been a terrible father, but I'd love the chance to make it up to you."

"You stopped being my father the day you deserted us." Melanie jumped from her stool and ran to the door. Grabbing her coat at the exit, she stepped out into the night and enveloped herself in the urban seclusion.

At that moment, she didn't care that she had abandoned her brother on his wedding day. He probably wouldn't notice anyway. Damn him. How could he have invited that monster? She hurried past the glittering shops in Knightsbridge and on to South Kensington, where she boarded a night bus. Pressing her nose against the dirty window, she watched the crowds below and was grateful for the anonymity of this large city.

It was impossible to digest the events of that short day. How could it be that all this had happened on her twin's wedding day? David's happiness couldn't have been more removed from her own desperation.

On one single day, she'd lost both David and Max, and her father's sudden reappearance provided an additional reminder of a tortured childhood. Another man who had abandoned her many years ago. Sobbing in equal abundance of hatred and remorse, she hobbled down her street, oblivious to the stares from passers-by and to the little girl who was pointing at her. All she needed was to reach that blue door and submerge herself into the sanctuary of her apartment. Once inside, without thinking, she made her way to the drinks cabinet.

The next morning appeared in a murky haze as she dipped in and out of consciousness. She knew vaguely that she was on the sofa and when she opened her eyes, the light was pouring in from the open window. Her throat was parched and a small hammer was insistently beating in her head.

She moved her legs to stand up, but was dizzy with the effort and sat back down. Bile began to rise in her throat, but she didn't have the energy to get to the kitchen. Her chest shook and she vomited violently on the floor. Disgusting, but she felt marginally better. Ignoring the mess, she lay back down and tried to reflect on the night before. Dimly, she recalled running into the flat, drinking the remainder of the whisky and smoking the rest of her Marlboro Lights. She hadn't felt this wretched for years.

She must have dozed off because when she opened her eyes again, the light seemed different. Her phone was ringing, but she ignored it. Stepping around the pool of stale vomit, she tiptoed to the kitchen cupboard, looking for something to eat. Managing a cracker, she felt ill again and ran to the bathroom, retching out the remains of the previous night's excess. She huddled up in tears and passed out on the bathroom floor. Her mobile didn't disturb her until well into the afternoon.

The hot shower scalded her naked body in punishment. She relished the pain, somehow trying to reconnect herself to the real world. Her holiday had allowed her to become delusional. She had managed to restore the facade, but the rot had set in too deep. Who would want her now? Scarcely surprising that Max had moved on.

Crawling to the fridge, she searched again for food. As usual, there was nothing and even the milk had gone sour. But after not eating for an entire day, she was ravenous. She threw on a tracksuit and went to her local twenty-four-hour supermarket. Pre-cooked chicken and a packet of cigarettes. No wine. She couldn't stomach alcohol today.

The woman at the checkout counter reeled visibly in her presence and Melanie reddened with a self-consciousness that she hadn't felt for a while. She glanced at her reflection in the door as she left and was shaken by the sight. She couldn't carry on this way. The woman staring back at her was teetering on the edge of the abyss and she had to fight it this time.

Limping home with her supplies, she vowed to be stronger. Her apartment reeked of stale cigarettes and forgotten ashtrays. The cleaner hadn't turned up that week; dirty clothes overflowed from the basket and the dishes were piling up in the kitchen. How could she have sunk to these same depths again? She couldn't afford to do it this time. She had a new career and still needed to prove herself. Rubbing her head, she took an aspirin and washed it down with a Diet Coke.

Chapter Thirty-three

After that weekend, she chose not to think about her private life. There was nothing to go home for and it was far easier to throw herself into her job. At any opportunity, she volunteered to travel and, when in London, she stayed late at the office every night. There were always meetings to attend and the potential client list was limitless. At work and abroad, she knew she was impressive. Nobody knew her personally, which made it easier. It kept her out of harm and her mind off her vacant personal life.

The firm had gained traction since she had joined and the M&A market had picked up significantly. Private equity firms were now calling on a daily basis to discuss deals and she had more work than she could cope with.

The four partners began to look into hiring a couple of new associates to manage the increased workload and they agreed that she could contact her old colleague Alex. A long time had passed since her departure, so she was able to call him without violating her non-compete clauses.

They arranged to meet for drinks after work one Tuesday. When Alex pushed open the door she sat up in surprise. The boy had matured handsomely.

"Hey, stranger." He bent over to kiss her on the cheek.

"Wow. Alex, you're looking well." The transformation was astonishing.

"Was thinking the same about you," he said. "Can I get you a drink?"

"Thanks. Any dry white would be lovely." She crossed her legs and smoothed down her skirt. Jesus Christ. Were they flirting? How could she hire someone as handsome as this?

He came back with a bottle. "Tell me. How's the new job?"

"If you want the truth, I'm working like a dog. But it's fantastic." Melanie played with her hair and kept staring at him. "What about you?"

"Great." He smiled at her. "Actually, I was promoted this year."

"That's fabulous." Not good news. A promotion meant he'd be harder to recruit.

"Yeah. VP already. Made much easier by your leaving. Not that I don't miss you, of course."

"Of course. Congratulations." Melanie raised her glass to him.

He took a deep drink. "Thanks."

She shuffled in her chair. "What's the gossip? I've been out of touch. How's everyone?"

"Gosh, where to start? Your old client Simon is pissed off with you."

"Why?" she said. But she knew why.

"Says you never call him now that you don't need his commission."

"I know, I've been overloaded. You're right. I need to get in touch." Dear old Simon. He'd been a loyal friend, and instrumental in improving her reputation within the investment community. How was it possible that she had neglected him, and never returned his phone calls? There was certainly no ill will; she simply had to make more of an effort. Funny thing about this life. She was always leaving the best people behind. "What about the rest? At the bank, I mean."

"Pretty much as you left it. Pam's still there, and Tony is working like hell. Never goes home to his family. Nothing's changed. I just finished a deal with him, which was fun."

"Sounds good. What deal?"

"French one. With your old boyfriend."

She went cold. "What boyfriend?"

"Mitch. Who did you think I meant?" He laughed.

She sighed with relief. "I don't know. How is the old bastard?"

"Same as ever. He's quite funny, actually, in an American kind of way." Alex paused. "But the one that was talking about you the other day was Pierre."

Melanie froze. Pierre. How did Alex know about him? "Oh," she said quietly. "How is he?"

"Fine. I guess. Don't know what you saw in him though. He's a wanker, if you ask me."

She gulped. "What are you talking about?"

"Mel. I'm not an idiot."

"I'm not saying you are."

"You obviously think so," he said. "But seriously, you know what office gossip is like. Don't worry about it."

Melanie blinked. "Does everyone know?"

"I guess. He was hardly shy in sharing information."

"Seriously? What's he been saying?"

"Let's not get into that." Alex put his arm round her.

Melanie turned away to stop the tears. Not a day passed that she didn't think of that man. Mostly she managed to hate him. But hatred was such a complex emotion. Why did it still hurt? "I was bloody stupid. Had no idea he was married."

"Don't beat yourself up. It's finished now. You've left the firm. Nobody cares."

"Yeah. Maybe you're right." How humiliating.

"Anyway, I'm sure you've moved on. Any new boyfriend?"

"No. That's a long story. I seem to be pretty shit at keeping a man."

"Tell me about it. My girlfriend dumped me last week. Told me I never spend enough time with her."

"Something about this profession. Do you think we are destined to be single?" she said.

"Can I tell you a secret?" He was staring at her now.

She had an inkling of what was coming next. "Do you think it's a good idea?"

"No. But now that you're no longer my colleague, I think I can."

"Do you want to be my colleague again?" she said, trying to move away from the subject.

"I'd love that. But there's something I'd love much more." He leaned into her. No. Not him, too?

He kissed her on the mouth. Her lips parted, but she moved backwards. "This isn't a good idea, Alex."

"Why the hell not? I've wanted you since the day we met."

She hesitated, realising her attraction to him, but not willing to accept it. "No, please don't." But it was too late. He was holding her, kissing her and she responded. She had no idea why. Perhaps it was loneliness.

Again, Melanie forced herself to stop. "I can't do this, Alex. Not with you. You're my friend."

"That's exactly why you should. You've always said you end up with the wrong sort of man. Here's your chance to get the right sort. I'd actually treat you well."

"I don't know anymore what I want. But not this. I can't do this with you."

"So why did you invite me here tonight?" he said.

"Can't we have a civilised drink together? Like old times."

"We could. I figured it could be more. We always got on well."

"I know it sounds mad, but I was going to offer you a job." She laughed. "I guess that's out of the question now."

"Seriously, Mel. I'd go crazy sitting across from you again. Watching you waste yourself on all those idiots." He stood up. "Look, I'm sorry if I misunderstood."

"It's OK," she said. But it wasn't and they both knew it.

"I'd better go," he said.

"Oh, Alex, I'm sorry."

"Don't be. I understand." He kissed her on the right cheek and left, without looking back.

Chapter Thirty-four

Twenty-nine candles on a cake. The past few years had flown by, but at least it wasn't the big one. No need to panic. She smiled across the table at her brother. She hadn't spent a birthday with him for years and she owed him that small token. After the last guest departed that night, she poured out the end of the champagne and sipped it on the sofa. David waited until Samantha left the room and came to sit down next to her.

"Mel, there's something I've been wanting to talk about…"

"What?" she said.

He cleared his throat. "I'm terrified of pissing you off and I don't quite know where to start."

"Spit it out." She drained the glass.

"OK. I'll get straight to the point. I've arranged a blind date for you."

"Don't be ridiculous." She glared at him. "Why on earth would I need a blind date?"

"You haven't been yourself for a very long time. I know your work is important, but please give it a chance."

She sighed. This was the type of conversation she had been trying to avoid.

David must have known she was annoyed, but he carried on. "He's perfect for you. I promise you'll thank me afterwards."

"It's very thoughtful of you, but I can manage very well by myself."

"Who are you kidding? You haven't had a boyfriend in ages. It's not normal."

"Please don't start lecturing me again. I'm fine. And for the record, I have had boyfriends."

"I don't mean one-night stands." His quiet voice spoke volumes.

Melanie lowered her head. How indescribably humiliating. Until now, she had assumed her double life had been hidden away. How had he found out? But it was impossible that he knew everything. She hadn't told a soul, not even Jenny. "I'm not sure what you're talking about."

He was looking at her intently, although not unkindly. "I am not judging you. All I'm saying is that you'll thank me for this. Please go. For me. Well, for you, actually."

"Fine," she said. "But just this once. And I'm only doing it to get you off my case."

David laughed at her and she pushed him away. Exasperating for her impeccable brother to find her weak spot, especially on their birthday. He should have picked a better time to talk about it, although she had to admit that he hadn't had the opportunity lately.

The date was set for ten days later, a typically busy day, with her phone ringing endlessly all morning. At lunchtime she begged the new junior to cover for her and ran to the salon. A blow-dry and manicure always made the world seem better. Although the date was bound to be a disaster, she should at least make an effort.

Despite her best intentions to spend time getting ready that night, she stayed at her desk late, finishing a presentation with Clive. By the time she arrived home, she only had twenty minutes to prepare herself. That same small black dress. She'd worn it so many times, with so many men, but it always did the trick. She could finish the make-up in the taxi.

The car dropped her off in front of the restaurant and she pushed through the large glass doors. The maître d' greeted her and took her coat. Who was the date? The man at the bar eyed her appreciatively but she dismissed him. Bald and old. At least fifty. David wouldn't be that cruel.

Walking round the corner to her table, she caught her breath in surprise. She had forgotten how alluring he was. "Max." He was so striking.

A tentative smile as he stood up. "Hello, darling."

"This is a surprise," she said. "I thought…"

"I know," he said. "But I swear I'm not going to let you run away again."

"Oh, Max." She had spent so long pushing him away that she hadn't realised how strongly she cared for this man. Tears welled in her eyes and she embraced him.

"Sorry I missed your birthday," he said. "But I can't bear small talk. Desperate to see you privately."

The waiter poured them each a glass of champagne and Max tilted his drink towards hers. His hand was trembling. Clearly, he wasn't as confident as he was pretending. "I haven't stopped thinking about you since the wedding."

"But…but you were with someone else."

"Yes. I was." He smiled sadly. "I did it to piss you off, actually. I have plenty of pride too."

"But you seemed happy with her."

"Amber is a fantastic girl, and I tried hard to make it work with her. But it's very simple. She's not you. I've been beating myself up about it ever since."

"It's not your fault. We both know I behaved appallingly." She looked down at the table, unsure how to proceed. "Please forgive me."

Max took her hand and stroked it. The most natural thing in the world. "Darling, let's agree that you've had a tricky time and possibly you acted irrationally. But there is nothing to forgive."

How could he be this saintly after the way she'd treated him? "No really, you didn't deserve it. But I'm better now. I promise."

"That's what I've been hoping. That you might be ready to try again."

No hesitation. "I'm ready."

"Good." His hands were gripping hers more tightly. "We've been here before, but we're both older now. Wiser too, I hope."

"Yeah. But I've been through a lot of shit."

"I know and I've spent a long time thinking about it. It's taken me a while to reach this point also. I know you have demons. We all do. But I assure you, I can handle it."

"I don't know if you should even go there. I'm messed up." Melanie raised her head, begging him not to agree.

He fingered her hair and touched the nape of her neck. "Mel. Whatever it is that's troubling you, let it go. It's over now."

She sighed. "Is it as simple as that?"

"You know what I think?" He paused and took a deep breath. "Everything we've been through. All the experiences, mistakes. The hurt. It's all a rehearsal for this moment. I've known it for such a long time."

"Do you mean that? After the way I treated you?"

"Would you stop worrying about the past? I've agonised also, but let's move on."

"I'm scared. That's all." She turned away, forcing herself to fight the tears that threatened to destroy her evening. Not to mention the mascara.

"Princess, I'm a little scared right now too. But you're such a gift to me. I've known that from the moment we met. It's just been hard to convince you." With those words, it was impossible not to melt. He kissed her and she leaned into the familiar fullness of his mouth. She inhaled the scent of his skin, a salty freshness reminiscent of her long beach walks. He continued to play with her hair. "You are more lovely than you realise."

She smiled gratefully at his kindness, wondering how much he understood about her. Inconceivable that he had grasped the depths of her despair, but it seemed possible that he was willing to forgive her.

"We have a lot of catching up to do," he said.

It was nearly midnight by the time they reached his house. Tonight, the stairs didn't bother her. She remembered the beautiful stone fireplace in his drawing room and noticed a new painting on the wall. He took her coat from her shoulders and kissed her deeply. The kiss lasted until he carried her to the bedroom and removed her clothes. She exhaled and her body gave in to the relief at finding him once more.

She woke up before him and gazed sideways at his handsome face. He had changed; the years had added a new maturity. Even better looking, if that was possible. A beautiful man, with a seemingly stubborn love of one woman. She didn't understand how it had come to pass, but she knew it was rare. She certainly didn't deserve it.

His blue eyes opened slowly. "Mel. Finally you're back."

"Of course I'm here, my love," she said.

"Last night," he said. "Last night was beyond anything."

"It was amazing." And it had been beautiful. To be worshipped like that. "Unbelievable. It was, you are."

"Darling, the only thing that is unbelievable is that you have apparently never been loved before. Certainly not the way I love you."

"Oh, Max." The tears had come now. Why did it hurt to be loved? Was it the fact that he was right? That until this point, she'd only allowed herself to be abused and she'd never let her guard down with a man. Not really.

He clasped his hands round her fingers. "You know I am going to marry you," he said.

"Darling, let's not rush." Melanie kissed him to silence his words, immediately hating his neediness, but hating herself more for her own negativity.

"I'm in no rush. But I've never said that to anyone before. And I mean it. You are the woman for me."

"You are the man for me." Marriage was far from her thoughts. But she was desperate for it to work. This man was meant for her and she didn't want to mess it up again.

That next Monday, when she walked to work, her footsteps seemed lighter. Everything seemed brighter. She greeted the new receptionist and took the lift upstairs.

Passing her colleague, Melanie called out to him. "Hi, Clive. How are you?"

He glanced up. "You're in a good mood. What's changed?"

"Aren't I always?" she said.

"Not exactly, my dear." He laughed. She knew it was true. She'd been incredibly grumpy recently. Not rude. But definitely grumpy.

"I guess life has turned a corner."

"Cool." He picked up his phone to call a client. Not the type to delve. These men kept to themselves. Unlike at Silverton, there was zero gossip in the firm.

Sitting at her desk, she looked out over St Paul's Cathedral and decided it was time to move on to the next stage. Max had been sent to her, miraculously, for one more chance.

She called him. "Hi, darling. It's me. Was thinking of you."

"Hey, you at work already?" he said.

"What do you mean already? It's nine o'clock."

He laughed. "You know, you have a very different concept of work from the rest of the human race."

"Nine is late compared to my last job."

"I haven't left home yet."

She chuckled. "You and your damned art world." Max and David were the ones on a different planet. But perhaps it wasn't so bad after all.

On her way to the Tube that night, she called Jenny. "Hey, guess what?

"Tell me," said Jenny.

"I'm back with Max."

Jenny chuckled down the phone. "You're kidding."

"No, why should I be kidding?"

"You already dumped him once. Normally that's a sign that you're not right for each other."

Melanie groaned. Perhaps it had been a bad idea to tell her friend. "That was a long time ago. I'm a different person now."

"I give it two weeks," said Jenny.

"That's unbelievably mean."

"Harsh but fair. I'll bet dinner that you're bored by then."

"I'm simply not playing that game. Why can't you be happy for me?"

Jenny laughed. "OK, darling. Have fun. Call me when the honeymoon is over."

Melanie hung up, without responding. Jenny could be a bitch. Why shouldn't she have a stab at happiness? With this fantastic man who clearly adored her. Why not?

*

To prove her point, she didn't call Jenny for two weeks. After a fortnight she sent a message. "Still going strong."

Jenny texted back. "Cool." That was it.

Without her friend interfering, Melanie switched her entire free attention to Max and the impact of his positive energy was incredible. With her renewed zest for life, the days became easier and work was a pleasure. There was still the drive to push through deals but her softness was coming back.

The man was a revelation. The opposite of Pierre, not to mention all those other men. He wasn't after her body. On the contrary, he seemed to love her body because it was part of her. She would watch him gazing at her. There was such loveliness in that face. And because he was not part of her working world, she could truly leave the office stress behind when she was with him. Jenny might not agree, but she couldn't have asked for a better man.

Chapter Thirty-five

As she was preparing to leave work one winter evening, her receptionist called up to her. "Your father is waiting for you in the downstairs lobby."

"Tell him I'm busy." Melanie hung up. How dare he come back into her life? Not now, when everything was perfect. She wanted nothing to do with him.

Her phone rang again. "I'm sorry," said the girl. "I couldn't stop him. It's just me at the desk."

"What do you mean?" said Melanie, raising her voice.

The girl sounded hysterical. "He's on the way up. What do you want me to do?"

Melanie took a deep breath. "Nothing, I'll sort it out." She couldn't call security. She'd have to deal with the brute herself. She waited for a few minutes, knowing he would be there soon. When he appeared, she pressed her nails into her hand and stood up. "What the fuck are you doing here?"

"Melanie, that's not the way to greet your old man." He smiled but his legendary charm was meaningless to her. The scars were too deep.

Melanie blocked his path, with her hands on her hips. "You can't barge into my office, you know."

"Apparently I just did." He surveyed his surroundings, seemingly unfazed by her hostility. "You're doing rather well for yourself. Fantastic office."

She scowled, hating the bastard. What was he doing here?

"I heard you're a partner," he said. "I've been reading about you on the Internet. Congratulations."

Melanie didn't move. "Why did you come here?"

"Perhaps we can go for a drink and talk about things?" he said.

"Sorry. I'm late and have to go meet a friend. Next time, please call and make an appointment."

"I've tried quite a few times, as you know."

It was true. But she'd ignored him. Hoping he'd disappear, forever this time. "You should have got the message," she said. "Now please, can you leave?"

"Sure, darling. I'll accompany you to the Tube station." The man was unbelievable. How could he be impervious to her fury?

Clive looked up from across the room. She couldn't tell if he was annoyed at the disruption, or concerned. He had one of his unreadable expressions. In any event, this was not the place for an open argument.

It was clearly going to be impossible to shake her father off in the middle of her office, so she agreed to his request. The sooner she could get rid of him the better.

She hurried to the station, but with her high heels, it was easy for him to keep up. "You know, Melanie, family is important. Try to be a little understanding."

"Why should I be understanding? You lost that right a long time ago. When you deserted us for that stupid woman."

"We split up years ago."

"It makes no difference now. I don't see why you think I'd care."

"What if I told you that I'm in real trouble? I need your help." He grabbed her wrist. She twisted her foot as he forced her to stop.

She spat at him with fury. "What right do you have to come here and beg? You, of all people."

"I'm your father. You owe it to me."

"I owe you nothing. Do you have any idea of the pain you caused us? You're despicable. I resent I even carry your genes."

For the first time, he appeared startled. "That's unkind."

"So what? I had thought you couldn't go any lower in my estimation, but you've just proved me wrong. You will get nothing from me. Ever. Fuck off back to the hovel you came from and never contact me again."

Melanie pulled away from his clammy, gnarled clasp and hurried to the Tube. She didn't look back. The pain was deep and very real. His presence and that cloying cologne dredged back the memories that she had spent a lifetime suppressing. Wounds that had been inflicted all those years ago rose to the surface. An irrepressible urge to scream. She wept with hatred and with sorrow. She wept for herself and for her mother; her vapid helpless mother who had been defeated by her husband's cruelty. She hated him and hated the reminder of how unloved he had made them all feel.

Finally in her living room, she let out a sigh of relief and wiped her swollen eyes. Her life had moved on from him so long ago and she didn't need him. It was upsetting that he had made her cry, but now that it was out of her system, she felt better. The man was irrelevant. She had to make him irrelevant.

Rather than her usual solution of diving into a packet of cigarettes, she called Max and vented her frustration down the phone.

"What a bastard," said Max. "Would you like me to come over?"

"There's no need, darling. I'll be fine."

"Of course you're fine, but I'm coming. Now. I'll bring pizza."

"I can't resist pizza."

He chuckled. "What a relief I've finally found the way to your heart."

"That's for sure. And I can't tell you how much I appreciate it."

Melanie put the phone down and smiled at the thought of her boyfriend. Thank God she had done something right. There was no need to dwell on the past; it was all about the future. It didn't matter that she looked dreadful.

Thoughts of her father evaporated the minute Max arrived. Her best friend. Her salvation. There was no denying that everything was better when he was around. They lay comfortably on the sofa watching television, his hand absent-mindedly stroking her arm. It was the most natural thing in the world and she sighed with happiness.

The demons had been put to rest. She had been pushed once more to the limits of darkness but, somehow, she had found her way back. Thanks to him.

*

One day, several months after their father had appeared in her office, Melanie broached the subject with her brother. It had been festering for too long; she needed to close that chapter and David was the only person who could help her.

When she began speaking, David hunched his shoulders. "I'm sorry," he said. "The last thing I wanted was for him to upset you."

"I'm not angry. Please don't get me wrong." Melanie paused. "I just want to know why you brought him back into our lives. After all this time."

David gulped. "I don't know. He contacted me a while ago and I thought it was appropriate to invite him to the wedding. He is our father, after all."

"You should have told me," she said.

"I tried to, if you remember," he said.

Melanie wrinkled her nose. "When?"

"So many times. Remember when you were on your way to the US, or who knows where?"

"Yeah." She hadn't had the time to see anyone back then.

"It's not an easy conversation to have on the phone."

"Still, you should have."

"I know, and I'm sorry," said David. "I had no idea he was after money."

She sighed. "In a way, it's been positive. When we were kids, I spent so many years hoping to see him again. But I have to say, it felt good to yell at him, and get it all off my chest. We never expressed any of that when we were little and I'm relieved to move on. I don't need him at all anymore."

David put his arm round her. "We all have different ways of dealing with things. I'm glad you've put it behind you."

"What about you?" she asked. David hadn't spoken of this for years. Not even when their mother had died. For the first time, she wondered how it had affected him.

"It's a funny one," he said. "On one hand, I sort of feel the same as you. But on the other, I actually want to keep a dialogue open."

"Seriously?" Melanie frowned.

"Yes. He's certainly not after my money." David smiled. "And I should let him know he'll be a grandfather soon."

"What? Already?" Melanie sat up, shocked. "I mean, congratulations, of course."

"You could act a little happier," said David.

"Of course, I'm delighted. That's great news." She paused. "Wow."

"I'm sure you'll be a great aunt."

"We both know I'll be totally crap. But I'll try." Her laugh sounded hollow even to herself. She clasped her stomach, remembering her own vacant womb. It was disconcerting how the emptiness persisted.

Chapter Thirty-six

Over the months that followed, her friendship with Jenny was the one constant reminder of her past, as well as being the most divisive feature in her relationship with Max. Jenny had also recently moved jobs, enjoying a multiple of her previous salary in an American bank based in Canary Wharf.

To begin with, Melanie had openly told Max when she was meeting her friend, but it didn't take long for the deception to start. Max clearly disapproved of the friendship and lying became easier than having an argument. The odd fabricated business dinner became more frequent and the girls began to spend many evenings together, similar to their single days. Although the one-night stands were no longer tempting, the lure of the dark nightclubs and meeting strangers was too enticing to deny. Melanie's ability to compartmentalise became useful once more. She convinced herself it was harmless. As harmless as the odd secret cigarette and additional bottle of wine that she no longer allowed herself at home.

Not that Jenny was much help. On one of their many evenings together, her friend confronted her. "How's that dull boyfriend of yours? Found himself a decent job yet?"

"Don't be horrible. He's got a fantastic job."

"Get real," said Jenny, finishing her second drink. "What the hell are you still doing with him? He's never going to amount to anything."

"Don't be such a fucking snob. He's damned successful in his field. He won an award the other day."

"Still earning about twenty grand, I bet," said Jenny.

"He earns much more than that and, for the record, his job is very prestigious. Is money all that matters to you?"

Jenny laughed. "You are funny. You always told me that's what you were after too."

"For myself. I never said I was looking to find a man with money."

"I don't understand you sometimes," said Jenny. "There you are, working your arse off, letting him sponge off you. Why the hell do you put up with that?"

"That's unkind. He does not sponge off me."

"I'm not being unkind," said Jenny.

"So what are you being? Not particularly nice, that's for sure."

"I'm your friend. And this is precisely what friends are for. To tell you things nobody else dares."

Melanie took a sip of her drink. She didn't like to admit it, but at one level Jenny had a point. She'd started paying for most of their dinners. Not to mention last month's weekend in Edinburgh. But plenty of couples had unequal salaries and it infuriated her that Jenny was constantly trying to pick her relationship apart. "I don't know many people that would put up with your nasty comments. Are you jealous that I'm happy?"

Jenny shook her head. "Not remotely. You couldn't pay me to be stuck in a boring relationship like that."

"Why do you feel the need to be such a bitch? You're lucky I love you so much."

"You're lucky I love you. I mean seriously, when's the last time you looked in the mirror?" Jenny poked her in the stomach. "You're becoming frumpy. Few extra pounds here."

Melanie sucked in her belly. "I'm smoking a lot less. That's all."

"Whatever you're doing, it doesn't suit you."

"I'm happy," said Melanie. "Doesn't that count for anything?"

"You aren't kidding anyone," said Jenny. "If you're so happy, why do you have to lie to see me?"

"Why do you think? Because Max doesn't think much of your values. Maybe you're the total weirdo. Stop judging me by your own warped standards. Why shouldn't I settle down?"

"By all means, settle down. But not with him."

"Stop it," said Melanie.

"No, I'm not going to. This is important and you know it. Tell me honestly, when's the last time you had great sex with him?"

"What the hell has that got to do with anything?" This time Jenny had gone too far. Mostly because she'd hit a sore point. Her life with Max had settled into a mundane routine. But wasn't that how relationships were supposed to evolve?

"See. I was right." Jenny laughed and waved over to the barman for two more vodka tonics. "Let's get drunk and forget about men for a while. Or maybe let's get you laid with someone sexier."

"I've moved on from one-night stands. Maybe you should focus on doing the same." But she was desperate to change the subject. "Speaking of which, tell me about the men at your office."

"Talk about dreary," said Jenny. She'd taken the bait. What a relief.

"No talent in the whole office?" said Melanie. "There must be thousands of them there. Don't believe that for a minute."

"Obviously there are loads of men. Huge bloody place. Floors and floors of people. But everyone is so uptight these days. Don't know if it's the bank or I'm getting old."

"I can't believe nobody is chasing you. You, of all people," said Melanie.

"That's the point. They are all shit scared. So damned PC these days." Jenny reached for her glass. "I was amazed last week. One of the traders was reported for wolf-whistling an intern. Can you imagine?"

"Pathetic." Melanie shook her head, remembering Zack and all his colleagues on the trading floor.

"I mean, where's the spirit? These young girls are so serious. Why can't they relax and enjoy the attention?"

"I guess sleeping with any co-workers is out of the question. Poor old you." Melanie laughed sarcastically at her friend.

"Oh, sod off." Jenny grinned. "Doesn't mean I can't carry on out of work."

"Even if you're getting on a bit," said Melanie.

"At least I'm not getting fat and boring," said Jenny.

Ignoring the latest insult, Melanie observed her friend thoughtfully. Working for a large American bank was clearly going to be more corporate. The smaller banks had always been far more relaxed. But a new dynamic was now pervasive throughout the City. Especially after the recent crisis. The City's character was constantly evolving and, without realising it, the financial market had changed its attitude to women. At least superficially.

Her younger self, with a need to prove that she would succeed with just her brains, would have embraced the concept. But something had died in this sterile new world. She thought about her own job. She hadn't even realised it until this point, but there was absolutely no sexual undercurrent anywhere. With anyone in the firm. It was all about work. Then again, that's what it should be. Shouldn't it?

What she hadn't told Jenny was that she had been house-hunting for weeks and had recently exchanged on a house near Lancaster Gate. As much as she loved her small flat, it would be wonderful to have something on the Central Line, so that she could commute to work in less than half an hour. And there was a strong possibility that Max would move in with her. She knew her friend would ridicule her newfound stability and she was anxious not to mess it up. It was important to focus on the positive forces in her life and, at some point, she would need to cut Jenny loose.

Her first major argument with Max was two weeks after that drink with Jenny, and most likely induced by her friend's comments. The day she completed on the house.

Melanie turned the key and entered. Buying a place hadn't been an easy decision; her biggest commitment to date. Funny how she had always rebelled against the idea of ownership. But here she was. Finally. As she was peering through the paned-glass windows in the kitchen, with their long view down the narrow cobbled mews, she heard a knock on the door. Irritated at having her moment disturbed, Melanie waited a few seconds before answering.

Max was standing, handsome as ever, in his chinos. "This is amazing." He wrapped his arms round her waist and kissed her on the top of her head.

How fraternal. "Hi, Max."

He stood there, not letting go. That same smile that normally

charmed her. "I've brought some wine. Let's celebrate."

She laughed, still annoyed at the interruption. "I haven't got any glasses or a corkscrew."

"Don't worry," he said. "It's a screw top and we can drink straight from the bottle."

She took a swig, passed him the wine and sat down on the floor next to him. "I don't want this to come out the wrong way, and I know whatever I say won't sound right."

Max put the bottle down. "What?"

"Um…do you mind if I spend the night by myself?"

"I thought we were going to camp out."

"I know, but I want to be alone in my flat tonight."

"Darling, what's the matter?" he said. "Bad day at work?"

"No. Not at all."

"So?" He peered at her again.

She coughed nervously. "It's just that I've worked really hard to get here and I wanted to have a little time to enjoy it by myself."

His eyes narrowed. "Because I didn't help you with the mortgage."

"It's not about that."

"What's it about, then?" he said.

"Well…"

"I knew it." Max stood up and glared down at her. "What is it with you and money? It's not all about who earns more. We are a couple now."

"We're not married." She turned away, hating herself for sounding like Jenny. But knowing it didn't make her stop.

"Melanie, this is unlike you. What's got into you?" His face took on a pained expression that she'd never seen before.

"Please don't take it the wrong way," she said.

"What other way is there?"

"It's hard to explain," she said.

"Mel. You're being a bitch and I'm only going to say this once."

"What?" She stared at him. He'd never called her a bitch before. It was the truth, of course. But odd how it hurt much more, coming from him.

"Just because I love you doesn't mean you have the right to walk all over me. You can be tough at work, but not with me. I won't hang around if this bullshit continues."

She looked away, stunned by his anger and unsure how to respond. Of course she felt awful and it would have been appropriate to apologise, but something stopped her. She heard the door close, but didn't turn round to see him leave. At that moment, she didn't remotely understand why she had acted that way. Only that she wanted to be alone.

Melanie reached into her bag and pulled out a cigarette. The first one at her new home. Despite the gnawing feeling of unease, the nicotine felt blissful.

The following day, she began the process of taking deliveries and unpacking. Buying the house had been brave, but she was pleased she'd done it. Such a major improvement on that small flat she'd lived in for years. Unbelievable how much London property cost. Three million pounds. The house was lovely, but hardly palatial. It had taken her six years to put together the deposit, and she was supposed to be one of the successful ones. God knows how other people could afford to live in this city.

Melanie walked back to the kitchen to pour a coffee and noticed her phone ringing softly from her bag. She picked it up, instantly recognising the American number.

"Lorenzo. Long time." It really had been a long time.

"How are you, my darling?" he said.

"Great," said Melanie. "Actually fantastic. First day in my new house."

"How exciting," he said. "I'd love to come see it."

"Oh," she said, flustered. "Are you in London?"

"Arrived this morning," he said. "Would it be OK if I stopped by?"

"Lorenzo." She paused. "As much as I'd love to, I can't see you anymore. You know I've got someone else now."

He laughed. "I'm aware of that. But don't worry. It's just a drink. I promise I won't lay a finger on you, if you don't want. It would be so wonderful to see you."

"My place is a mess. I haven't unpacked yet." She stumbled over her words.

"I'm sure you know that I'm not interested in your house. Don't worry about a thing. I'll bring dinner."

Of course it wasn't right to meet him, but it didn't have to end in sex. She should be able to see him without taking it any further. Hurriedly, she ran a shower and started to prepare herself. He would arrive within the hour.

With her hair still dripping and no trace of make-up, the doorbell rang. God, that was quick. There he was, at the door, with a bottle of champagne in one hand and a box of sushi in the other. Tossing them onto the nearest crate, he pulled her close in one smooth motion. She tried to push him away, but there was never any real chance of resisting. The choice was made and, for that brief moment, Max was forgotten. The guilty truth was that she wanted him as much as ever, this dark stranger who gave her nothing but pleasure. Magnificent, this foreign man. Uncomplicated and flawless.

They drank the whole bottle, but the sushi lay forgotten as they moved into the bedroom. His lips touched her ears. "I love you, Melanie."

She looked into his eyes, surprised. It was the first time he had ever said something like that. "Really? I mean, we don't know each other. Do we?"

"Darling, I told you a long time ago that we would know each other for years. I meant it then. I mean it now."

"But we live so far apart. We have our own lives."

He stroked her stomach. "It's complicated. Definitely. But our love is not complicated at all. When you opened that door, I couldn't believe how beautiful you were. The lover I have always dreamed of and more."

"Oh, Lorenzo."

"Don't cry, my love." He wiped the tear from her cheek. "We have much to celebrate."

"Don't you care that I have a boyfriend?" Shouldn't *she* care she had a boyfriend?

"I don't think about it. Unless it's a problem for you?"

"I don't know anymore what to think," she said. Except that her mind was in turmoil. As much as she was enjoying the attention, her stomach knotted with anxiety.

"Don't overanalyse, my sweet. We were meant for each other. Whatever the circumstances. And I will never hurt you."

"No, you don't hurt me." But it did hurt. Inexplicably. She kissed him to silence the words.

In the morning, he kissed her and left. Closing the door, she lit a cigarette and collapsed on the ground in tears. What had she just done? Why had she allowed that to happen? She didn't love that man. Didn't want to love that man. It was just sex. Incredible though it was, it was all meaningless. Pleasuring her body was fucking with her head.

Max, Max. How could she have done that to him? How could she have done that to herself?

With Lorenzo's departure, she desperately tried to refocus on her boyfriend. Not that she deserved him. How could she claim to love Max and cheat on him so readily? The ease with which she had succumbed to infidelity troubled her even more than the crushing guilt. She was good at lying, she knew that, but why was she was so easily dictated to by the needs of her body? Utterly weak and vile. Worse than all those men she had previously despised.

After she had sent him several text messages and pleading phone calls, Max finally came to visit a week later.

The doorbell rang at eight. She took a deep breath and, with a pounding heart, opened the door. He stood quietly outside, hands in his pockets. She smiled at him, suppressing her overwhelming remorse. "Darling, come in."

He held the door with his right hand, but didn't lean forward to kiss her. Something different about him today.

"I'm sorry about the other day," she said. His lack of warmth was unnerving.

"Me too," he said.

"No, seriously," she said. "I was out of order. It was…"

Max hadn't moved. "Don't explain. I don't want to hear."

"I need to talk about it." She took his hand and led him to the sofa. "Silly of me, but I was excited about the house. Just wanted to have it to myself for a couple of days. But that's done."

"I don't want to stress you out," he said. "If you need space, that's fine."

"No, that's not it. You're perfect. Really, you are." And he truly was. The incident with Lorenzo only served to highlight her own selfishness and stupidity. Given the mistakes she'd already made in the past, how could she have been such an idiot? The man who stood in front of her was the one she wanted. Why had it taken such a long time to accept it? If only she could erase Lorenzo from history and wipe the slate clean.

Melanie reached over to the coffee table and pulled a key from the ceramic pot. "Here, this is for you."

He didn't move. "I don't want your keys."

Her heart sank. "Why not? I thought—"

"Mel, I've been thinking." He gestured around the flat. "And I'm not ready for this."

"But, it's our new life together." This wasn't like him. This time she had truly screwed it up. Now that she was certain of what she needed, why did this have to happen?

"I came here tonight for one very simple reason," he said.

"What?" Was Max breaking up with her? She'd been utterly duplicitous, but that didn't make it any easier.

"To tell you that although I'm madly in love with you, you can't treat me like one of your business deals that you kick around. The other day was a real wake-up call for me."

Melanie gulped. "That's ridiculous."

"No, it isn't. You know what I mean. And I've been giving it a great deal of thought."

"What?" Melanie hunched her shoulders, despising herself more by the second.

"Ever since the beginning. Since that very first night. I've been here for you and I can't help but feel that you still take me completely for granted. I tried hard to understand. For years. But I'm sick of it now."

"How can you say that? I love you."

His eyes clouded over. "I'm not sure you know what the word means. And until you do, I can't keep investing in us. It's killing me."

"Don't do this, Max. I need you." And for the first time, she meant every word.

He embraced her. "It hurts like hell. This love I have for you. But, in itself, it's not enough. I need some space right now to be by myself."

Her body sagged further. "Don't break up with me. I promise I won't mess it up anymore."

"I'm not breaking up with you, although I probably should. Even your brother tells me I should walk away."

"David?" How dare David do that? Her own brother?

"The truth is I'm not sure you know how to have a relationship."

"But we've been together for almost a year. Has that meant nothing?"

"Be honest with yourself. For once, take a hard look in the mirror and tell me what you see. Who are you?"

"I'm not sure what you mean by that." Did he know about Lorenzo? Surely not possible.

"What I believe is that your career has fucked you up. God knows what you've been through, but I'd say your priorities are now totally misguided."

"How can you say that?"

"Tell me. What comes first every time? Me or your work? Me or money? What is your life really about?"

"That's an absurd thing to say. It's not just me. You're always on the road also." But of course he was right. She had cancelled on him so many times. And he'd never complained. Until now.

"You know I'm right. And you also know that you can't stop. I don't want to play second fiddle to your career anymore."

"Can we talk about this at least?"

"That's what we're doing."

"Sounds like you've already made up your mind." She moved

away from him, shaking with despair. Not wanting him to see her tears. But he pulled her back and kissed her on the mouth.

"I know it's not easy," he said. "But you have to grow up. And more importantly, you need to think about what you truly want from life."

She nodded. "I swear I will do better. I want so much for us to work. I'm sorry if I hurt you. I never meant to do that."

"OK, Mel. That's a start. But I'm pissed off with you right now. And I don't want to see you for a while." He stood up.

"Max…" She looked up at him. Pleading for him not to leave.

"I'm going away for a few weeks, which is no bad thing. Don't call me, because I don't want to hear from you. I'll be in touch when I get back."

And with that, he was gone.

Chapter Thirty-seven

It had been a long week. Tuesday's day trip to Geneva had always looked optimistic. With a tight timetable, she'd missed the last flight home and had been forced to stay in an airless three-star airport hotel. A cancelled meeting the next morning had led to her working through the night. Although this job was generally more fulfilling, the hours were excruciatingly long. Far worse than research. It just didn't stop. And the negotiations could be endless. Why couldn't people make decisions? One particularly tiresome deal had just closed and they were asking her to start something else. Sometimes she wondered where her energy came from.

Thankfully, Friday had arrived and she had something different to look forward to. Her small black suitcase sat neatly under the table, largely unpacked from her trip the week before. But she wasn't travelling for work. A romantic weekend in Rome. With Max. She hadn't seen him since that day, but they'd spoken a few times and officially they were still together. He'd called on her birthday with the invitation. Of course she'd accepted, delighted at the opportunity to make amends.

Melanie had just begun to type an email to a client when her phone rang. It was Jenny. "Hey. I've got an invitation to that party I was telling you about."

"What party?"

"You know, that VIP one I've been trying to get for weeks. Please come with me. It's going to be incredible."

"Sorry, Jenny, I can't tonight."

"You haven't been out with me for ages."

"I just can't."

"Don't tell me, you're back together with Mr Boring. Let me guess. Pizza in front of the TV?"

"You are venomous. I've already told you. We are going to Rome tonight."

"God, you're dull," said Jenny.

"What's dull about Rome? More exciting than the inside of some stupid nightclub."

"It's not a nightclub. Anyway, you're an idiot to go. You know he's going to propose, don't you? How pedestrian. Whatever you do, don't accept."

"What are you talking about?" said Melanie. "He's taking me for my birthday. My thirtieth, remember?"

"Be careful," said Jenny. "Now you're thirty, he'll be thinking you're desperate to settle down."

"Don't be ridiculous. There is no way he's going to."

"So tell me, why else would he arrange the most perfect weekend trip? Not like him to stick his hands in his pockets."

"That comment says more about you than him. Go find your millionaire lover if that's what you want. I'm sick of you being such a bitch."

"Suit yourself. But this party is going to be amazing. Full of Hollywood."

"I don't give a damn about that. Those women only make me feel ugly."

"You're just jealous," said Jenny.

"I hope you have a great time. But I need to go now." This wasn't the time to gossip and there was so much to do at work.

"OK. Call me on Monday. And remember to say no."

Melanie hung up and shook her head. Sometimes Jenny's conversations could be mindless. And cruel. But while she kept working, her mind wandered. Would he propose? No, of course he wouldn't. Not after the way she'd treated him. Max was right. She had to grow up. If she wanted to make the relationship work, the damned lies had to stop. Empowering at first, but they had taken over her life, one destructive step at a time. Impossible to separate herself from that poisonous web she had intricately bound.

How had she become so adept at being someone else? Someone she didn't remotely respect. And why had it taken her so long to understand the pressure it inflicted? Perhaps the night with Lorenzo had occurred for a reason; compelling a naked look at her soul and forcing a radical change. Looking out of the window, Melanie inhaled with an ironic sense of relief. It was time to let go of her double life. No more Lorenzo. None of that shit. With her newfound sense of perspective, her future with Max was obvious.

Clive walked over to her desk and broke her train of thought. "Melanie, I'm sorry to ask you, but I need a favour right now."

Melanie grinned, relieved by the distraction. Clive was so disorganised. "What is it this time?"

"I'm supposed to interview someone. Apparently he's quite good, but I forgot about my client meeting."

"Not today. You know I'm scrambling to get out of the office early."

He must have seen her pained expression and began to plead further. "I know, I'm truly sorry. But my client has just flown in from New York and I have to go see him. I can't get out of it."

"Jesus, Clive. I don't believe you only just found out."

"I know, I know." Now he was begging. "A screw-up in my diary. Totally embarrassing. Promise it won't happen again."

"Yeah, right." Story of her life, covering for everyone. Why was she always left to pick up the pieces?

"Please can you take the interview? Please?"

"Fine. But who are we interviewing?" It had been such a busy week and she hadn't heard about any new recruits.

"Don't know."

"Oh, that's helpful," she said. This place was chaotic.

Clive scratched his head. "Terry saw him last week and wants a second opinion."

"Is that all you know?" How exasperating. "A few facts would be helpful. You know, so I don't look like a complete moron."

"Don't worry," said Clive. "I'll get my secretary to give you the details. Terry said he's got great experience, but has been out of the market for a few months. Probably a good time to snap him up as a junior partner."

"I haven't heard anything about hiring more junior partners."

Clive shrugged. "I guess we don't have to. See what you think. Trust your opinion. He's in reception. Thanks, darling."

"What? Now?" she said. Clive scuttled out the door. Oh, well, Clive was covering for her this weekend, so she couldn't complain. Still, she wasn't in the mood for an interview. There was so much to finish before leaving the office, and she couldn't afford the time. She didn't want to be late for Max. Typical of Clive to spring this on her at the last minute.

Melanie picked up the CV from Clive's secretary and headed towards the meeting room. Her mind was still on the weekend ahead. She smiled at the thought of seeing Max again. Thrilled at the chance to make things right. The fact that he had invited her away was a fantastic sign and she was confident it would go well.

Entering the room, she poured herself a large filter coffee and sat down to leaf through the papers in her hand.

His name beamed up from the top sheet and she jolted backwards. Pierre, coming to interview at her firm. How could he appear again like this? Especially now, at the exact moment she was turning her life around. She cursed Clive again and held her head in her hands. This was going to be hell. Taking a deep breath, she straightened her skirt and checked her make-up. It was the smallest of mercies, but at least she had made a special effort to look good today.

Melanie was still sitting when he entered the room. It was important to seem indifferent, but nothing could have been further from the truth. Her hands were shaking. Despite all the torment he'd put her through, or perhaps because of it, she had never managed to forget him. The man had impacted her life indelibly; she'd given him everything and he'd made a fool of her. The memories haunted her still. Had he planned this meeting? Poisonous bastard. Melanie stood up to greet him, unsure how to begin. An awkward pause.

"Welcome to Lewis and Partners." Melanie produced a crisp

white business card. So far, so formal. Those rugged features hadn't changed. Apart from a few additional grey strands, he was the same.

Pierre fingered the edges of the card. "Hello, Melanie. How lovely to see you." No emotion on his face either. Incredibly hard to read.

"Please take a seat." She pointed to the chair. "It's been a while."

"You look wonderful," he said.

She stared at him, attempting to understand her feelings. "Thank you. I was surprised to see your application. Why don't you tell me what attracts you to our firm?"

He frowned. "I think you know my background. Not very different from yours."

"Except that you've been out of the market for a while now, so effectively I'd be your boss." She tapped her nails on the table and looked directly into the familiar brown eyes, disgusted by the passion they used to inspire. "How would you feel about that?"

"Melanie. I know we didn't part on good terms. But that was a long time ago." He lowered his head. "I was emotional and stupid. And I'm truly sorry if I hurt you."

"That's history. I've moved on." And for the first time those words rang true. Years of suffering evaporated with that small sentence. Hard to believe this man used to wield such power over her. Impossible to grasp the degree to which he had once controlled her. But she was no longer that same young girl and the dynamic between them had changed irreparably. Now she was in control and he meant nothing.

"There's not a day that passes that I don't think of you," he said. "I needed to see you again."

She raised her eyebrows. "Don't go there…"

He reached across the table to take her hand. "It might interest you to know that I'm divorced now."

Melanie didn't flinch. Hatred was morphing into indifference. "Why should that interest me? You're here for a job interview."

"It's not the job I'm after."

Melanie stood up, her eyes fixed on his. "In that case, this meeting is over."

He moved forward and clasped her arm. "Melanie, wait…"

Shrugging him off, she walked to the door and gave him a final satisfying stare. "I'm sure you can find your own way out. I have a plane to catch. Goodbye, Pierre."

Lightning Source UK Ltd.
Milton Keynes UK
UKOW01f1830160516

274361UK00001B/1/P